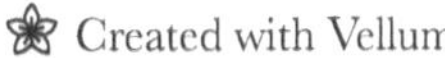 Created with Vellum

A GRIMOIRE FOR GAMBLERS

A Trove Arbitrations Novel

AMANDA CREIGLOW

Waldron Lake Books

ONE

A Train Wreck

Every grief is its own. I tighten my grip on the hammer, look up at the padlock affixed to the attic hatch, and shiver.

Cold permeates the house. The furnace must have broken again and let the chill of the early March morning seep in through the cracks. My dad was a terrible landlord. Granted, it's hard to be a good landlord from inside a mental institution, like my father was for the last eight years of his life. I guess I should blame the property managers. Bit rude to blame a dead man, anyway.

I'm stalling. I've put this off all week. It's time to do it.

The coffee hasn't kicked in yet, so it takes me a second of staring up at the lock I can't reach in order to put together what's wrong and what I should do about it. I'm average height for a woman, so that doesn't get me close enough to the ceiling to use the hammer on the lock until I drag a chair over from the dining room.

Lock in hand, head close to the textured plaster ceiling, I hesitate. My natural compulsion against destruction stops me, but this is my house now, and I'm allowed to break it if

I want. It's one of the few benefits of my dad's passing, and the judge deeming his original instructions—that the place should be burned to the ground upon his death—unenforceable and nonbinding from a legal standpoint. Hard to claim you're writing a will while of sound body and mind when you check yourself into an inpatient psychiatric facility the very next day.

I move the lock to the side, line up the hammer, and hit down hard on the body of the lock between the arms. The first three tries don't do it. By the fourth, I'm frustrated and annoyed, and apparently my frustration is enough that the lock gives up the ghost. I maneuver the now-compliant little device out of place. Then I gracefully—if I do say so myself—pull the attic hatch down with me as I dismount the chair.

When I do, the squealing of the moving hatch, and the slightly sweet, musty smell of the attic drag me back. Way back. Back to eight years ago when nothing was broken.

My father was always working on one train set or another when I was young. I spent hours up there with him. He'd passed his scattered mind on to me, and I think he wanted to pass his salve for it on to me, too.

"Focus on the details," I can still hear him say, ringing down from the attic above me. "Breathe, and focus." The things he'd always say as he let me assemble a little tree to go next to the track or alter a stock train to make it just so.

In the week and a half since his death, most of which I've spent alone in this house, I've been unable to shake the feeling that he's still up here. I find my eyes wandering up to the ceiling, now and then, as if I could see through it to where he stands spending time with his trains. When waves of wishing I could see him come, I feel foolish—like I should just go up to the attic and see him if I miss him so much. Feeling foolish—like he's still here even though I know he isn't—is preferable to the alternative, so I've been leaning into it, avoiding proving my grief-stricken magical thinking wrong. Even when you know a comforting lie is a lie, it still works. At least, it's been working for me. For certain values of working.

This is an act of closure. Pulling down the sliding ladder on the hatch is an act of closure. Climbing the rungs and emerging in a heartbreakingly familiar way into the dusty, worn-in space of the attic is an act of closure.

And god fucking dammit, closure hurts. The undeniable physical pain it causes deep in my chest doubles me over, forcing me to breathe deeply to pass through it. It's enough to make me miss all the time I've spent feeling numb this past week.

After what feels like hours, I rub my eyes—even though they're dry for now—and straighten. The space is almost entirely as I remember it. It's tall enough that I can stand up in most of it, even if I have to tuck my head between rafters toward the edges. A bare bulb hangs down in the center of the space, but the only light right now comes from the three dusty windows: one on each gable end and one on the dormer that extends out over the porch. They let in a diffused pinkish glow that makes me feel like I'm in an artsy movie with too-careful framing and not enough plot. Something like what my longtime boyfriend, Faisal, would make me watch.

It's beautiful. I stop and recognize that. God, this room hurts, but at least it's beautiful. And so quiet, and peaceful, and solitary.

Until a whirr from the large diorama train set in the middle of the floor shatters the moment. I stare at it, dumbfounded. The set was the last one my father worked on before he walked into a mental institution and insisted they commit him and place him on perpetual suicide watch. It's a half-finished recreation of a portion of Springfield set on the same large square table Dad always used as a base for his projects. That itself always seemed weird to me—Dad usually liked to invent worlds for his train sets, not copy the real one. But the strangeness of that thought is overshadowed by the movement of the train.

He left it plugged in all this time? He went through all the trouble of installing a padlock hasp, locking it up and throwing away the key, but left the train set running? My eyes track over to the outlet on the wall he usually used to power his train sets, but I see nothing plugged in there.

I don't remember him changing much toward the end. I remember him being a little more distracted, a little more consumed by his hobbies. But I had just graduated high school and didn't spend a lot of time thinking about my dad. Even if I had, I probably would have just called it adjusting to the idea of an empty nest. But it's still hard to imagine him suddenly deciding he needed to hardwire a train set, let alone learning the skills to do it.

I step toward it, thinking I'll investigate. But a wave of emotion hits me as I approach the little train, chugging along. It feels like him. I feel warm and whole for the first time in a week and a half—maybe the first time in eight years.

I hesitate when I see something that doesn't belong. There's a large locket on the end of the diorama, holding down a sheet of paper adorned with a few handwritten lines. I creep toward it like it's a live snake that might strike at me. I leave the locket in place and slide the paper out from under it, barely breathing. It's my father's handwriting—I think—but without its usual care or elegance. Maybe scrawled quickly.

STOP. It reads. *STAY OUT. IF YOU WON'T, AT LEAST WEAR THIS.*

Now the tears come. It's hard to grieve a man when it feels like a part of him died long ago, when he was overtaken by a mental illness none of us knew he had and every psychologist that saw him called something different. But it feels like an insult—like an attack—that his mental illness got to him even up here. That it infected this place, his sanctuary. It's wrong. It's unjust. It's unfair.

The little train comes around close to me, and without really thinking I reach out and flick it over. It rolls a couple times before coming to a stop, and I choke back a sob and an apology.

The sudden vibration of my phone in my pajama pants pocket jolts me out of the moment. I want to be annoyed, but I'm grateful for the interruption, and even more grateful when I see the words *Faisal – Swiss SIM* on the screen.

"Hey hotshot," I say, my voice cracking a little from the tears and the early hour.

There's a slight hesitation before he answers. "Hey Beth," he says, softness in his voice. I'd told him my plans; I tell him everything.

I breathe in and out slowly, not sure how to broach the subject we're both thinking about.

He broaches it for me. "Are you up in the attic?"

I lean on the edge of the train set, letting it hold some of my suddenly-too-heavy weight.

"Yeah," I say, my voice uncomfortably thin. And then I sweep all that up and put on a breezier tone, telling him things he already knows in order to build in a little distance. "Told myself I'd do it by the time I went back to work, and today's the day, so…"

I think the shift in subject will bring us back onto safer ground, but he doesn't take the bait. He almost never does unless it's clear I need him to. And I love him for it.

"What's it like to be back up there?"

I stare at the rolled-over train, taking it in—the once-bright colors on its body, the little valley at the bottom it's landed in, the tall, strong tree it's up against.

"Weird," I say, followed by a deep, rushing exhalation. "He left the last train set he was working on running. For eight years! He knew he was leaving it. Who *does* that?"

A practiced exchange passes between us in a moment, all unspoken. We've done it enough times, with each of us in either role, that we don't need to say it out loud.

People suffering from mental illness.

Crazy fucking people.

Yeah, people suffering from mental illness.

We met in a support group for people with family members in the nuthouse. Faisal gets it.

"Beth," he says, the gentleness in his voice just about overpowered by a Swiss German PA announcement in the background.

"Yeah," I say. "I know."

I stretch up, stifling a yawn and reaching my hand up to rest on the seventies' style paneling on the sloped ceiling. I can just about touch it from here. For all my activity this morning, it feels like I'm just now waking up.

"What's Zurich like?" I ask, like a brand-new person. Or like a normal person.

"Oh, you know, Swiss."

The comfort of familiarity wraps around me like a warm blanket. I respond almost in singsong, my usual reply. "And what's *that* like?"

This time I'm sure I can hear the smile in his voice at the familiar exchange. He was hesitant to go, but it would have felt wrong for him to stay—would have felt like we're letting this upset our lives more than it had to. Things already felt too disruptive with moving into the house on such short notice.

"Exactly like you'd think."

There's a long pause while I zone out and trace the pattern of some specks of dust floating in the dawn light coming through the closest window.

"Do you want me to come rushing back home with a dozen roses and some Swiss chocolate?" he asks in a tone that's half joking and half concerned.

"And get *fired?*" I say with mock horror.

"They'll never fire me," he says, returning my playful tone. "They worship me as a god."

Faisal's master's thesis involved finding experimental new nanotech uses for a particle-counting machine—which is apparently a thing. After he finished, the company that makes the machine hired him. He spends the bulk of his working life traveling to research labs and universities, helping them learn to use the device properly. He calls himself a walking manual at parties, trying to downplay it when people tell him how exciting it must be to meet so many scientists in his field all around the world.

"As well they should." I drop my voice to a husky, over-done sexy whisper. "And they don't even know why."

He laughs, and the rich, contagious flavor of it reaches me even over the thin connection from an ocean and a continent away.

"You're gonna make me blush around all these fine, upstanding businesspeople."

"Don't be silly, I know you. You're blushing already."

We smile together, apart.

"No," I say, after a blissful, melancholy moment. "I'm fine. I've got this."

I'm getting him off the phone, and I didn't even

mention the locket or the note. I don't want to. I'm not sure why.

"You bet your ass you do," he says.

"Nah, I'll bet yours instead. It's better."

That laugh again. "Agree to disagree."

We exchange *I love you*s, and he tells me he'll text me from the hotel when he's checked in before the line goes dead. He's pulled me out of the weird, dark space I'd been sitting in, and I'm grateful for that. I can't live there. But without thinking, I pick up the locket and drape the twine loop around my neck. I don't have it in me to look in it just yet, but feeling it around my neck is a comfort. I'll take it.

I take a breath and let it out slowly with building determination.

Right, then. That's enough of that. For today, anyway. For now.

TWO

A Coincidence

God, it's good to be back in a routine. Bereavement leave makes sense, and I'm sure I needed it, but there's something to be said for the healing power of feeling like a person again—just getting into clothes and leaving the house.

Granted, I don't have a routine for going to work from this location. I've only been in it for less than a week. My dad's been dead for less than two, so it all moved pretty quick. But I grew up in this house, and it was luckily between tenants, so I jumped at the chance and the distraction.

As I drive into work, I notice tiny things on my commute that have changed. Some construction is a bit further along. Some storefronts have changed their displays. Springfield isn't tiny, but it isn't a big town either, and the journey from my house to the parking garage next to city hall only takes me past three drive-through coffee places.

As always, I pick Jolt-a-Go-Go, which has easily the

worst name, but just as easily the best coffee. I'll fight anyone who claims differently. I don't know what they do with their milk, but I'm pretty sure it's magic. Or illegal. Or both. Even if I weren't relieved to be getting back into the grind and giving myself something new to distract myself with, heading into town would be worth it for a cup from Jolt-a-Go-Go.

The first few sips of the coffee pull me in with the healing glow of familiarity. I park in the parking lot that the little cluster of municipal buildings share and head through the nicely manicured garden space in front of city hall with my ambrosia in one hand and my laptop bag in the other.

The guard manning the security desk at the far end of the lobby smiles with a little too much positivity on his end, making me feel a bit self-conscious about returning to work. I'm just smiling back when a blur of motion in front of me stops me short, nearly spilling a bit of my coffee on my favorite work blouse.

"Hey!" I say, stifling the reflex to apologize. I expect the figure in front of me to apologize instead, but he doesn't.

He's big. At least a foot taller than me and wider than he should be. He's got heavy features that are twisted up in concern and too much dark hair that seems more like it sprouted than grew. He's wearing layers and layers of faded, worn clothing, but he doesn't smell. Like, at all. Of anything.

He looks like he should smell, like he should be dirty somehow. But he's just unkempt, and the Manilla folder in his hands is crisp and new, like he just bought it and has been treating it very carefully. He holds it out to me, not acknowledging the coffee.

"This is yours," he says with a booming voice that echoes back from all the shiny, hard surfaces of the lobby. I feel like he's holding back, trying to speak to me gently, but just from the sheer volume of sound, that can't be a correct guess.

The security guard has started moving toward us, and I catch his eye and shake my head almost imperceptibly. I think for a moment he won't get it, but he must, because he stops and stands by, watching closely but not moving. The strange man's quiet, restrained intensity and abrupt manner is off-putting, but off-putting people vote, too. And he looks more uncomfortable and out of place than dangerous. I put on my wide, designated public relations smile.

"Can I help you?"

I don't, however, accept the offered folder. This isn't the first time this has happened. We have an intake address for the office, both for physical mail and for email. But now and then people look on the website, identify me as a friendly face with an intentionally vague job title, and send me things directly instead. I'm probably going to have to accept the folder anyway, but I at least have to make a token try at refusing it so that I can tell the admin staff officially attached to our generalized inboxes that I did.

"You're Elizabeth Baker? You work for the mayor?"

He remembers my name off the top of his head. Probably won't be any getting out of this one.

"I am. But if there's anything you need to get to her, you should probably—"

With patient but firm strength, he presses the folder into my chest. I can sense, more than see, the security guard tensing.

"This is yours," he says again.

His voice, like last time, booms, but I can tell he's still trying to keep it gentle. I take half a step back both on instinct and so I can accept the folder with some semblance of grace. As I do, my laptop bag, resting on the floor against my legs, tips over. My smile falters for a moment, but the man in front of me replaces it with his own, too big even for his wide face and with far too many gleaming teeth.

Then, as if remembering something, he fixes the coffee in my hand with an odd look I can't quite identify. Desire, maybe?

"Best coffee in town," I offer weakly. I usually feel more in control of these situations. Maybe it's the grieving daughter of it all putting me on unsteady ground without my consent.

He shrugs, noncommittal.

I should give him my coffee.

What? No. Where did that even come from?

But, then again, it's still an uncomfortably chilly time of year, and I would put good money on it that this man does not sleep inside.

Maybe four days after Dad died, my older sister Olivia sent me a link to a YouTube video about the grieving process. The video was mostly filled with the kinds of things that I know Olivia would find helpful, because they're steps and charts and road maps. She's good at that kind of thing.

But there was one opinion the video presented as fact that stuck with me: Grief turns some people cold, and some people kind, and you have the power to choose which way you go. You choose with your actions.

As much as I don't want to let a too-certain-for-its-own-good YouTube video dictate my life, I know it'll bother me all day if I don't at least offer.

"Would you like this?"

As I say it, I realize how dumb it sounds. I should offer him money to go get his own. I've drunk some of this one!

My offer is more rude than it is kind. But the big man doesn't seem to mind. He scoops up my coffee cup with a hand more like a force of nature than a human hand, and takes a long, deep drink.

I don't know if this man is a devoted follower of our lord and savior Jolt-a-Go-Go, but he does seem able to sufficiently appreciate it, at least.

He gives one final decisive nod, and then he's three steps away in half a breath, and I'm left standing in the lobby with the security guard.

I smile at him, and he returns it, again with a little too much enthusiasm.

"Morning, Miss Elizabeth," he says, breaking the spell of my unexpected encounter with the big man. "Welcome back."

"Morning, Doug," I say, shoving the folder under my arm so I can head to the security station and put whatever that was behind me.

What a weird day already. Pretty sure days didn't use to start this way before I went on leave. I certainly don't blame concerned citizens for getting a little intense about their pet projects. If nothing else, it shows they care. And we need people who care about things.

But still.

I try to put it behind me, but what greets me as I walk through the halls and toward the section of the building reserved for the mayor and her staff isn't much better. The people I see that I know are a little too friendly. A little too accommodating. I hear "welcome back" a few too many times, and every time I do, it feels painfully obvious to me that everyone knows why I wasn't here last week.

But when I get to my desk, I regain some of the positive momentum I had started building on my commute. I can do this.

I get my laptop plugged in and set up. It's got updates to run and it was bought on a government budget, so it'll be a bit before I can even start downloading what I'm sure will be a tidal wave of emails. I brought my laptop home with me the day before I found out about Dad, with the idea that I'd get some work done at home that night. That… did not go as planned.

In my peripheral vision, I spy no fewer than three co-workers sneaking glances and hovering, deciding if they should be the first to come over to me. I do my best to look busy and unwelcoming. I'll have to deal with all that sympathy eventually, but I just need a second.

I read the few cards on my desk in the meantime, mostly to look occupied. I pick at the plate of chocolate chip cookies in plastic wrap that accompanies one of them, and I fervently wish Linda in accounting every bit of the good karma she surely deserves as I idly eat one.

I glance at the laptop. Still loading, but I'm out of cards. I need something else to occupy myself before the sympathetic hordes descend.

My eyes drift to the folder.

I wasn't going to look at it immediately. I have actual work to do, I'm sure, once the computer remembers how to computer. But hey, I guess there's nothing wrong with satisfying my curiosity first.

I'm not sure what I expect. Probably a conspiracy theory I'll have to lay aside and hope the man doesn't follow up on. He didn't seem like the type to forget about it, but one lives in hope. My final guess as I open up the folder is that it's about something in the water supply. It's always about something in the water supply.

But the first thing that greets me is a newspaper clipping with a picture of a man, probably late thirties, with a kind, open face and a little girl hanging around his neck and staring up at him with an adoring smile.

The realization hits me like a gut punch—it's an obituary. *He passed away… he is survived by…* He looks so young. I scan the words, looking for the age, and see that I guessed right. Thirty-seven. Nine years older than me. The obituary is a little longer than usual. It's glowing in an almost frantic way, and some grim portion of the back of my mind notes that we didn't seek an obituary for Dad, and no newspaper felt compelled to write one.

It doesn't say how he died. No mention of a long "battle" with one illness or another. It feels defiant in that way, to be honest.

I turn over the article and steady myself. It's a 5x7 photo of the same man. Only this time, he's not smiling. His eyes are open, and behind him, pavement gives way to overgrown grass.

Blood smothers his neck.

Barely breathing, I pick out the wounds. The many, many deep vertical and slightly angled cuts. There are six of them. No—seven. His bloody right hand lays across his chest, clutching one of those multi-tools that dads like to carry, its tiny blade extended.

Who the fuck commits suicide like that? It's not painless. It doesn't even look planned, really. Why would you not use a razor? Why would you cut yourself *there*? Why would you do it outside? It feels more like self-destruction than suicide.

I turn over the photo with all the terrified care of an archeologist dealing with an ancient text and see another behind it. It's a closeup of the weapon. I shudder and go to turn it over, but my eyes gravitate toward a few lines of crisp but odd-looking handwriting on the back of the photograph. It reminds me of the letters I got from a

German pen pal I had back in high school: cobalt-blue ink, precise too-round swoops, a big flag hanging off the one, and a crossbar through the seven.

Lakeview Elementary.

12:07 p.m. March 20th.

Three days after Dad died. I put it together on reflex, setting aside the idle curiosity of how long it'll be until I don't count dates off that way.

But an *elementary school*? I flip back to the obituary and look more closely at the photo that accompanies it. I know Lakeview Elementary. I went there, once upon a time. And I recognize the background in the picture.

I flip forward, putting it together. He killed himself on the playground of his daughter's school. My dad died on a Saturday, so March twentieth was a Tuesday. School was in session. Children saw. Maybe *his* child saw.

My eyes widen. I expect to find a forensics report next. A private citizen shouldn't have one, but then again, a private citizen shouldn't have these photos, either. I shouldn't be looking at this. I should be turning it over to the sheriff's department, along with a detailed description of the man who gave it to me.

Instead, morbid curiosity forces me onward. I see a photo of another woman, her body wrapped around the wires of an electric fence with a horrifying zeal. Her face isn't visible, but her body looks lean in the way old people get sometimes.

I recognize the background of this photo, too. There aren't that many electric fences in town. This one is at the zoo, between two other fences around the bear enclosure. I try to think of how someone could get there. They couldn't fall. It would be hard to force someone into it. You'd have to climb. You'd have to really want to.

I pick this photo up and look at the back, expecting and finding that same neat handwriting.

Fred Wilmore Memorial Zoo.

12:07 p.m. March 23rd.

I blink. Again—three days. I don't know much about the usual rate of suicides in town, but that can't be right, can it? Especially for such public acts...

And at the same time. At the *exact* same time.

I put the picture down, my hands trembling. There's another obituary behind it. Another woman, this one young—younger than me. Her hair is long and blonde and straight, her features delicate. I don't read the obituary in detail. I look for the date of death.

March 26th.

The trembling in my hands intensifies. Slowly, I lay the photo face down on top of the others. I have to will my eyes to look at the next photo in this macabre album, because I'm not sure I'm ready to face it.

"Heya, Lizzie!"

I jump, my shoulders hunching defensively. Angela is there, smiling and holding a plate of cookies. Her eyes search down toward my desk. I reach my palm out across the obituary to hide it from view—hopefully without calling attention to it. But her eyes stop on Linda's cookies, her face twisting in disappointment.

"Oh, you've already got cookies."

I smile. "Don't mind more!" My voice is strained under the effort of holding back a scream. I'm split in half by the sharp disconnect between Angela's bright casual air and the creeping horror of what I just saw.

I take the plate from her, hoping that will head off the sympathy I know is coming. It's meant well, but it's hard to hear, anyway. Especially right now.

"Well," Angela says brightly, "I just wanted to welcome

you back. We all do. And we're all so, so sorry about your father."

I wave a hand, as much to dispel the inappropriate, incongruous anger I feel at her words as the other, sadder feelings.

"Thanks," I say, contradicting my own motion. Angela seems to get the hint.

"Anyhooooo, she wants to see you," she says.

My eyes flick to my screen, still loading.

"I know, hitting the ground running, right?" Angela continues. "But I'm sure it's about the train thing. You picked quite a day to come back!"

The bottom drops out of my stomach. A new, undefined terror shoves aside the horror. My face smiles despite that.

"The train thing?" I echo.

She blinks at me.

"Oh, you haven't heard? I thought everyone had heard. Train derailment. Real freak accident. Nobody's talking about anything else. I heard they think it flipped over *three times*."

My pulse races. I look at my screen again, willing it to load so I can google this. I need to see the pictures. I need to see the differences.

No joy.

"Better get in there!" Angela says, brightly. "Oh, and it's good to have you back. I said that, right?"

I barely feel my legs as I stand on them, pulled toward the mayor's corner office along with a small stream of people I recognize.

I'm not usually afraid that I've got my father's illness in me. Not *usually*. That's more the kind of thing Faisal worries about for himself, and I've spent so much time convincing him that those reassurances have rubbed off on me. But I've also done enough reading to know that extreme emotional stress can sometimes trigger underlying mental issues.

Stress like a death in the family. Would that be enough?

I shake my head to gather my thoughts and breathe deeply as I make sure the folder on my desk is closed. It's a coincidence, that's all. I'm not breaking with reality or anything else. Coincidences happen. And where would the lines of my break with reality even be? Nothing fits cleanly. It's just been a weird morning.

But then, if this *is* me losing it, I wouldn't be able to tell the difference, would I? If breaks with reality weren't convincing from the inside, no one would fall for them.

I file into the office. Three of my workers stand at attention there already—a writer, our liaison with emergency services, and a media consultant. We have a surprisingly robust public relations staff for the mayor's office in a small town. There are those who have commented that it's because our boss, Sharon, has higher political aims. Those rumors are right, but of course we never confirm them.

The mayor, Sharon, is in her late forties. She had a career as a university professor before she went into politics, which is how I met her. Faisal likes to say that I hitched my wagon to her star, but that's not really it. It's more like she gave me the idea of getting a wagon in the first place.

I'd been pretty cynical about the world in general since my father lost his mind—something I find I share with a lot of people who have had one personal tragedy or another —and Sharon had the impressive ability to cut through that cynicism and make me believe that the problems in the world might be fixable. And that she was going to be the fixer.

Does the amount of loyalty I have toward her make me

feel a little uneasy? Maybe. I tend not to think that being a follower of anyone is a good call. But Sharon keeps proving my faith in her justified. And when I look around at the other people she attracts, I tend to like them. Being in good company is always reassuring.

Plus, she's crazy smart. Her policy stances are solid, and she adapts them to new evidence and considers new arguments with an open mind and a sharp, intense analysis that still surprises me when I see it, even after years of working with her.

"Elizabeth, welcome back," she says in a precise, businesslike tone once we're all assembled. "We're all very sorry for your loss."

She means it, I know, but in a way that she's not going to give it time right now in this discussion. And she doesn't sound like she means it. Performatively caring she is not. Which has been a recurring challenge for us to work around in the world of local politics. She blows right by and on to the task at hand.

"So, what do we know about this?"

Ryan, our liaison with various emergency departments, starts talking about the details. I don't hear him. My eyes are fixed on the muted television screen in the corner of Sharon's office, playing the news.

It's the same fucking train. The same hill. The same old tree and graceful curve of the fallen cars. Only now there's blood, and people milling around, and…

Ryan has stopped talking. I can feel eyes on me. I struggle to pull my gaze away from the screen.

I can't buy a coincidence this big. That same queasy terror I got when Angela first said the word "train" grows. My mind is betraying me. I'm losing it. I've lost it. I have to staunch the bleeding. I need to relieve stress and schedule an appointment with… who? Someone. What do you do when you're losing your mind and don't want to? I should have come up with an emergency plan to implement at the first warning sign. Faisal has one. Olivia might even have one. I should have made one.

I clear my throat.

"I apologize," I say, the words only breaking a little bit. I try to sound calm and professional, and I think I mostly succeed. "I think I've come back to work too early. I need a little bit more time."

The words don't sound like me, and everyone in the room knows me well enough to notice. Sharon's incisive gaze settles on me. I feel analyzed. Not unkindly, but still.

She knows my father's history. She looks at me and performs a risk-loss analysis. Her eyes flick momentarily to the screen, and it's as though she knows why it's affecting me, even though there's no way she could.

"Of course. Take the time you need. Check in next week and let us know how you're doing."

And then she turns from me to one of the staff writers and starts talking again. I suddenly feel invisible the way you only can when something important is happening and you're not a part of it.

I keep my breaths and my steps measured as I head out the door. I hear my name spoken in a few voices that I recognize, but don't bother to match to names. I ignore them. I have to get out of here. I have to get home. I have to look at the train that can't be as I remember it.

I should go back to my desk and gather my things. That would be the responsible thing to do, especially considering the contents of the Manila folder on my desk. But I don't know for sure that I can make it there and get out of the building without someone seeing the look on my face. And I don't need anyone seeing the look on my face.

I feel like running all the way back to the car, but I

restrain myself. I walk instead, as fast as I can without drawing notice. And just like that, my momentum reentering the world falters. Sometimes I thought Faisal had been afraid I would fail to relaunch, but it's worse than that. I blew up on the launchpad.

THREE

An Intruder

All the way home, I think about the attic. I think that I'm going to run up there as soon as I get home and make sure. But instead, I slump down on the couch as soon as I've shut the door behind me. I sink my head into my hands as I fall into the cushions.

No. This isn't supposed to happen.

I should tell Faisal. Call and talk to him. In one of his bouts of paranoia, when he thought that he'd end up like his aunt, he'd done some research on local psychologists. Maybe that would be useful.

But I don't want to worry him, don't want to admit to anyone other than myself what's happening. I'm seeing things and hearing things, and I don't even know for sure what's real.

What are the hallucinations? That strange big man in the lobby—was he real? He didn't seem right. If he wasn't real, what was the security guard reacting to? Had I hallucinated the reaction, too?

Was I just remembering the trains wrong? The real

one, or the fake one? Where are the lines? I still can't see the lines.

I'm smart. I'm grounded. I'd prepared for the possibility that things might go off the tracks in my head—really, that pun, now?— in an oblique, non-specific way, but I don't feel prepared or in control now.

Footsteps on the porch interrupt my panic spiral. I stand, trying to get my breathing under control. If this is a real person, I need to seem stable to them. If I have any chance of heading this off and keeping this private so it doesn't derail my career—really, again?—then I need to seem normal in this interaction. Or, at least normal-ish. Most people get grief. I'll get a margin of grace for the grief.

I wait for the knock on the door, but there isn't one. Instead, the door swings open, and a man steps into my house.

Man is an insufficient word. Male model? Sex god? I've been told that focusing on your physical body and grounding yourself in physical sensations is one way to try and get your mental and emotional reactions under control. If that's the case, this guy is just what the doctor ordered.

He's just a little above average height. His impeccably tailored charcoal suit doesn't do justice to his swimmer's build, but it also doesn't hide enough to keep me from noticing and reacting. His sandy-blonde hair, a bit lighter than mine, could use a haircut. It gives him an attractive just-out-of-bed look that some men carefully craft. It's genuine on him, though—I feel immediately certain of that, for reasons I can't quite put a finger on.

I don't usually notice the color of people's eyes, but the flashing green of his is hard to ignore. His strikingly handsome features bear a bright, manic smile.

"Right," he says, looking me up and down and sizing me up in an instant. He steps around me toward the kitchen. "Sit down."

His voice is deep and rich and dripping with the kind of power that sends women willingly off cliffs they see coming. As he says the words, his left hand moves in a weird, precise gesture—his fingers twisting up in an unnatural way and then releasing. And then he's past me, not looking back over his shoulder as he finishes the sentence.

"Good girl."

And just like that, his distracting attractiveness is null and void. Convenient, really.

"Excuse me?" I say, my voice lower than usual, the sharp edge laced with the feeling of loss of control that I'd been feeling before he came in. Might as well put it to use.

He stops in his tracks and turns.

"You're not sitting," he says, his voice still gorgeous but no longer disabling.

"Nooooooo," I say, like speaking to a struggling child. "That's right. I'm not."

For a fleeting second, he looks scared. Panicked. But he recovers quickly.

"Sit down," he says again, command in his voice. He contorts his fingers in the same way he did before and studies me.

I raise my eyebrows and feel no compulsion to follow directions.

After a second, he lets out a breath.

"Huh," he says, like someone who had just seen a perplexing work of art. "That's interesting."

He isn't really here, a thought screams at me from the back of my head. *If anything's a hallucination, he is. You don't have to be afraid of him.*

And that's true. Probably. But until I can be sure, I

figure I better act like it's all real. Safer to believe it is and find out I was wrong than the other way around.

I reach for my phone in my pocket, pulling it out like a weapon.

"What's interesting is that you're trespassing."

That hits him with another flash of panic—but again, quickly covered.

"You know," he says casually, "I've never been a fan of the police. Law enforcement, I mean. Not the band. Love the band."

"We have a sheriff's department," I say offhandedly, caught off guard by the light, friendly tone in his voice.

"Oh really? What's the difference?"

If I hadn't been holding down a mounting sense of terror, I'd have thought the curiosity in his voice sounded genuine.

I don't feel like explaining it right now, so I raise the phone, and his face goes hard. He mutters something under his breath and the front door slams off to my right.

"No," he says, the word etched in ice. Then he turns and puts back on his light demeanor. "Okay! Magic— magic, magic, magic. Where's the magic hiding..."

I look at my phone as he wanders off through the house. I usually get five bars in here, but now there's no signal. I take two steps and try to open the door. It isn't locked, but it doesn't budge. Not like something's holding it, more like it's a fake door on a set that was never made to open.

My heart rate, already high from losing my mind and imagining an intruder in my house, skyrockets. I try the window beside the front door, but it's the same, even after I double check that I've unlatched it.

Okay, back door. I just about run to it, though before I

get there I'm already coldly certain what I'll find. The same. The window over the sink! The same.

It's crazy. This isn't how the world works, and I shouldn't accept it. I swallow that down and remind myself I'm ignoring that. That's later. We'll sort that out later.

I look at my phone again. I'm still connected to the Wi-Fi. Maybe iMessage would work? Can you text 911? I refresh the page I had up in Chrome as a test, but it fails.

Without fully considering it, I pull a knife from the knife block. He won't let me out? Fine, but he won't like being stuck in here with me.

I don't think about how useless I would be in a fight. I've never been in one. I'm never going to be in one. We're purely in deterrent territory here.

"Hey." The intruder's deep, cheerful voice comes from the hallway. "Did you know there's a dining chair over here?"

Faisal's right—I really should start putting things away after I'm done using them.

As I walk to the hallway, chef's knife in hand, I hear the familiar creak of the attic hatch coming down and the quick sound of footsteps climbing the ladder. I won't catch him in time to stop him from getting up there, but I realize in a flash that I won't have to.

Six long strides and I reach the lock I'd forced open with the hammer a thousand years ago this morning. I scoop it up from the floor in a fluid motion, dropping the knife. Then I throw all my anxious strength into sliding the ladder up.

I can't look graceful as I jump up on the dining chair, force the hatch back up into place in the ceiling, and slide the lock back through the hasp. I don't lock it, but that doesn't matter. From that side, he's trapped.

I've… got him?

I climb down off the chair, breathing heavily, and pick up the knife I dropped. I sit down hard in the chair, heart still going crazy. Footsteps keep going over my head, as though he hasn't even noticed I've trapped him.

"Oh!" I hear a cry of delighted surprise, the sound muffled by the ceiling between us. "A voodoo train! That's new."

There's quiet for a minute or two, and I focus on my breathing. I don't know what the fuck is going on, but whatever it is, I'll be better off facing it with a clear head.

"Okay," the intruder says, when I'm just starting to get myself back under control. "I've broken that enchantment, so no more incidents like the one this morning. Your little voodoo train is just a normal train again. But I'd like to talk to whoever enchanted it. When will they be home?"

My jaw clenches involuntarily. I don't answer.

"Hello?" he says. "Can you hear me?"

I search around for something to say, but I don't find it fast enough apparently, because the next thing I know, the intruder's voice is right next to me—seemingly coming from a space about a foot away from my head.

"Do you mind letting me out of here? It's a bit dusty."

I wave my hand through where the voice sounds like it's coming from, but there's nothing but air. I listen more closely and hear the shift of the intruder's weight up there.

Ventriloquy through walls. To quote a stranger who doesn't exist: *That's new.*

"No," I say, not particularly loudly. "I don't think I will."

My suspicion is correct—he hears me. I know because I hear him sit down hard above me and a sigh comes from the same place his voice did.

"All right, I don't know how much the wizard in your life has told you, but picking a fight with another wizard on his behalf is not a good plan. Wizard pissing contests usually go badly for all involved. And *really* badly for those not involved."

"Wizard," I say, with no feeling in my voice whatsoever.

"Oh, they haven't told you?" the intruder says. "Seems rude. But they did protect you, so let's forgive them. It's a good protection spell, too. Can't say I'm not impressed. Say, who is it?"

Now that I'm out of immediate danger, I feel numb.

"Undo whatever you did to the cell service," I say, instead of answering his question.

The chuckle coming from the space in front of me is dry as the Sahara.

"So you can call in the police and keep me busy wiping memories for the next week? No thanks."

I roll my eyes, and maybe he can see me, too, because he corrects himself quickly.

"Oh, right, the *sheriff's office.*"

I should be most upset that he broke into my home and started breaking reality, but if I'm honest with myself, I'm more annoyed with his tone right now. My words come hot and harsh when I reply.

"If you could get out of that hatch, you'd have done it already. Pretty sure if you want to get out of the windows up there, you're going to have to undo what you did to the house. You might want to think through your alternatives, bub."

I'm not at all sure of that, but I'm hopeful. Hopeful is *like* sure, if you squint and turn your head to one side.

But also, what am I doing? Who says "bub"?

"You'll let me down eventually," he says.

I shrug.

"Maybe I won't," I answer. "Maybe I'll give you the

choice of dropping the trap or dying of thirst. I've got nothing to do. I can sit here."

There's a long pause, and I keep my face impassive, just in case.

"You're not going to kill me," the man says.

Maybe he can't see me—you'd think if he could see the knife in my hand, he wouldn't be so sure.

"I'm pretty sure you're not real. Try me."

Another exasperated sigh.

"Really? You're one of *those*? Of all the reactions people have to finding out about magic, this one has to be one of my *least* favorite. It just reeks of a lack of self-confidence."

"I'm confident one of us is trapped in an attic, and it isn't me."

"Oh, please. You trapped me, but I trapped you first. Don't get all high and mighty."

I laugh, breaking the tension. "Okay, it's a standoff. I'm in a standoff with a figment of my imagination."

"If I'm not real," the voice muses, almost wistfully, "I can't hurt you. So you might as well let me go."

I shrug. "Or you *are* real, and reality is broken. And if that's true, I feel safer with you up there."

There's a long silence. I think about leaning my chair back to rest against the wall behind me, but that seems like a bad thing to do while holding a knife. Finally, the man speaks again.

"Okay, I guess we wait for the wizard to get home and try to get in the door, then. Not the best way to meet him, but he really should have come said 'hi' when he moved into town. This is as much his fault as mine."

I ignore the gender assumption and lie. "No one's coming home. I live alone."

Faisal won't be home for a week. It's true enough for the intruder's purposes.

"Oh, the voodoo train in the attic was just there when you moved in? Nice try. I might even buy it if you didn't have the protection spell on you."

I don't respond. I'm holding the cards. Plus, he's in my head. Probably.

He breaks first. "All right, let's start over. I'm Max. What's your name?"

He's a picture of perfect manners, and I respond to that politeness involuntarily.

"I'm Elizabeth."

"Nice to meet you, Elizabeth. Whose train set is this?"

Oh, hell. Why not? "My father's."

The intruder hesitates. When he speaks again, his voice is gentle. "I'm sorry I have to be the one to tell you this, but he isn't your father."

I glare daggers at him through the attic hatch. When I don't respond after a long moment, he continues with a hopeful tone in his voice.

"Or… maybe you already knew you were adopted?"

"I'm not adopted," I say. "He *is* my father."

I should say *was*, but I don't. That still feels like personal information. Max doesn't need to know.

"If this is his train set, he enchanted it. Ergo, he has magic. Ergo, he would have passed it on to any natural-born children he had. You don't have any. I don't see it on you, and you'd know if you did. You'd see mine on me. I'm sorry, I really am, but he's not your dad. And he knows it."

I stare at the wall. It's not true. I know that. I have too many of my father's failings to have gotten them from anywhere else. I try and figure out what his assumptions tell me. The intruder must be interpreting my silence as emotional turmoil, because when he continues, his voice is bright. Consoling.

"But that doesn't mean he doesn't love you. I mean, he protected you. That's something."

My hand goes to the locket tucked away under my shirt, and I pull it out. And now I'm sure he can't see me because he goes on talking.

"He probably did it when you were asleep, which is why you didn't notice. All the protection spells I've heard of are pretty noticeable to apply. And they don't last that long, so it's not like he did them when you were too young to remember or ask questions…"

While he talks, I open the locket. Instead of a picture inside, there are gears in perpetual motion—like a watch without a face or hands.

Which can't be right. This thing is too light to have all that clockwork inside of it. And shift the object as I might, I can't see anywhere that a battery might be hiding to keep it moving. Plus, the gears are silent even when I hold the locket up close to my ear.

"He *will* be back here, though." I tune back in to hear the intruder's words. "A wizard doesn't just leave magical items lying around. So I'll wait. Want to play twenty questions? I spy with my little eye?"

He says it lightly, but with determination. I see no other option.

"He's dead," I say. The words hurt.

"Oh," he says, full of gentle surprise. "I'm sorry."

I don't respond. Eventually, he continues. There's still pity in his voice, which makes it softer. I've gotten used to hearing that particular kind of softness over the last week.

"That makes things simpler. I don't see any other magic around, so nothing more to do. The protection spell on you will fade. When it has, I'll be back to clean up."

"Clean up?" I say, the words dull in the suddenly stale air around me.

"Your memories," he supplies, like it's not a horrible thing to say. "It'll be weird to know all this until then, but don't worry. When I'm done, it'll be gone, and everything will be fine. There's no reason you need to know he wasn't your father. I'll take that, too."

He says it like he's promising to do me a favor. I don't know how to correct a misunderstanding so profound. So instead, I say nothing.

Eventually, I hear steps over my head leading to the closest window. I can just make out the sound of the old, resistant frame squeaking open. A mass of swinging legs and arms falls to the ground. I wonder if he's hurt, but I can't muster any genuine concern for him. It's relief for myself, not for him, that I feel as I see him get up and walk away.

FOUR

A Discovery

When the intruder is gone, I move mechanically. I pull my phone out of my pocket and verify that the signal has been restored. I go back to the kitchen and replace the chef's knife in the knife block. Then I take it back out and rinse it off. It had briefly been on the floor in the hallway, after all.

I think carefully about each action as I do it, using the simple, straightforward chain of actions to try and ground myself.

It's crazy to think that what just happened was real. It's foolish and risky to assume it wasn't and stubbornly act in defiance. I don't know if it's a skill or a sign of instability that I can hold the two opposing concepts in my mind at the same time and shrug off the cognitive dissonance.

I've got to go back up into the attic, as much as I don't want to. Not to verify that the train looks the way it did on the news—I feel certain that either it does, or my mind will convince me it does. If I'm making this up, my hallucinations have been consistent thus far. No reason to doubt that they'll continue to be so.

But I need to make sure the wizard isn't still up there. Yes, yes, I saw him leave. But I've been seeing a lot of things lately.

Plus, there's something bothering me about the attic. Something that was wrong about it this morning that I can't put my finger on, other than the movement of the train in the absence of electricity. Maybe it'll be the "magic" or whatever. Maybe when I get up there, it'll feel normal, and I'll be able to discount it and move on. Yes, move on, and just keep this necklace on indefinitely to keep the evil wizard from destroying the integrity of my memory.

Jesus, that *does* sound insane.

I get back up into the attic with practiced ease. This morning, it felt like I was restarting old machinery that had laid dormant for years, but now everything's back up and running. The muscle memory of the many times I joined my father in the attic to watch him working on his projects comes back into place. The only thing out of the ordinary is the weight in my chest as I do so.

The attic is precisely the same as I remember from this morning, only a little brighter from the progression of the day outside the windows and with more disturbed dust. I sneeze and look at the footprints that lead to the wizard's escape window. He left it open, and the chilly spring breeze feels good in the stuffy space, with all the heat from the house below filling it. I don't close the window.

Almost perfunctorily, I look at the train I flicked this morning. It looks exactly as I remember it, even when I get up close and examine it. I am careful not to touch it. I don't even breathe on it too hard. Sure, the wizard said it's just a train now. It's no longer "enchanted." Still, *not* gonna risk it.

I don't question that my dad would have linked a train

so it follows the motion of a real train if he had the ability. That seems like exactly the kind of thing he would do. I can just about picture his face as the train started moving. But I don't believe he'd do it knowing that *his* train could also affect the real world. Especially not with the instructions he gave in his will. My father was a lot of things, but careless about the possibility of harming others was never one of them.

My hands shake again. I must be nervous, and just too mixed up to be able to feel it properly. I pull out my phone and search for a news report of the crash to compare the images to the train. It isn't until I read the words "no casualties" and feel a rush of relief so strong I nearly fall to the ground that I realize where the anxiety came from.

For the second time in one day, I brace myself against the table to stay upright. Then I lower myself as gently as I can to the ground, giving in. With that question answered, the one I couldn't even bring myself to ask, everything else feels more manageable. My thoughts begin to clear.

I have to move forward like both things are true: I've lost my mind, and also I haven't. That means figuring out what's going on, but doing it in such a way that my life won't be disrupted too badly. Eventually, it'll become clear, one way or another. At the very least, Faisal will come back, and I can't hide this from him.

Faisal. The thought of him feels like a physical dagger in me. All his worry, all my reassurances—and somehow, *I'm* the one who ends up with the problem.

That's not relevant right now. I push the thought of him aside and try to figure out what to do next. I'm drawing a blank, and it takes a full few seconds to realize that I'm staring straight at what was bothering me about this room.

Sometimes, I used to sit underneath the table when my

dad worked on trains. I'd bring up pillows and blankets and treat it like a fort, well after the age when that was a normal thing to do. Dad always encouraged it.

But there's no accessible "underneath" for the table that the current train set sits on. A thick, black velvet cover hangs down around it.

Why? Dad did a lot of things, but they all had reasons in his mind. To him. I can't see one for the fabric in front of me. He never cared about how "professional" his workspace looked.

Which means he didn't put it there to look professional; he put it there to conceal.

I turn on the flashlight on my phone and lift the bottom of the fabric, using the light to peer underneath. I find exactly what I expect to. Score one point for the insanity explanation.

There is a box under the middle of the table, as far from any of the edges as it can get. It's awkward reaching it, and even more awkward pulling it out, heavy as it is. It's one of those black sheet-metal cabinets, the kind you'd find in an office with terrible coffee and too much middle management for its own good. It's not a safe, but it has a lockable door. I have to grab it by the silver handle to get it to move, and it's heavy enough that I'm afraid I'll bend or break something in the process.

When I have it out from under the table, I drag it into a puddle of light from the window the wizard used to escape. Moving around has stirred up more dust. The exterior of the box doesn't have too much dust on it, though, protected as it has been underneath the table.

Around the top, where it isn't interrupted by the door, I see tiny patterns in gleaming gold. In them I see the careful work of my father's tiny brushes, the way he used to sit, barely breathing, painting figurines of houses or trees or people. It was the only thing I ever saw that narrowed and focused my father's world, altering the impression he always gave that he was thinking of something else or wanted to be somewhere else.

I know he wanted it to do the same for me, but it never did. Regardless, it was good to watch it work for him in a way I didn't realize was comforting until I was old enough to have filled my life with other things.

I trace over the strange symbols with my fingers, trying to make sense of them. They're all connected. They feel geometric, mostly, but the pattern takes a long time to repeat. And there are oddly placed curves and ornaments that don't look like they belong. It vaguely reminds me of alchemical imagery, though I'm not familiar enough with the subject to be sure. It's not a balanced enough design to be beautiful, and my father was never much for decoration, anyway.

I turn away from the unanswered questions and look to the handle. The key is in the lock, and the mechanism offers no resistance as I unlock and open it.

Inside is a stack of papers and books, taking up nearly half the space of the cabinet. No wonder it was so difficult to move. Though some sections look like they belong together, there's no sense of overall uniformity, except maybe that the material seems newer and in better repair at the top and gets older and more fragile as the eye travels down.

Sitting on top of the stack are two objects.

One of them is a lantern. It's delicate and seems composed of metal that's been cut and worked into shapes reminiscent of the markings around the top of the cabinet. Inside the lantern is a plain white candle. It's been burned previously, but it couldn't have been left lit for long. The formed point of the candle wax has barely been blunted.

The other object is a pair of seventies' style glasses with thick orange-brown plastic frames.

Groovy.

I stare at the contents, breathing in the deceptive peace of the attic around me. I reach in and pull out the lantern and glasses so that I can access the top book, part of a stack of three mid-century-looking bound volumes, each about two inches thick.

On top of the book, I find a sheet of loose notebook paper, covered in writing that I instantly identify as my father's. I set the book down, holding the sheet of paper carefully in both hands as though it's some precious thing that will fly away from me or shatter in my hands if I don't treat it gently. I read.

To whoever finds this box,

I am sorry this has come to you. I couldn't bring myself to destroy it, because I don't think it should be destroyed. But still, I pity you.

You'll probably think it's a joke, or that it's the ramblings of an insane man, standing on the shoulders of many more insane men. I did, too. But I assure you, everything contained in here is unfortunately real. At least, as far as I can tell.

I encourage you to read the letter in the beginning of the book on the top of this file. I found it illuminating. And though I am about to take measures that I'm certain will make me less reliable if you find out who I was, I hope this letter helps to influence you to take this seriously, and to consider walking away before it gets its hooks in you.

Sincerely,

David Baker

A letter as an introduction to a letter. How very helpful, Dad. I'm dismissive in my thoughts, but my grip on the notebook paper tightens. Every time I've seen my dad in the last eight years, he's been barely lucid, trailing off on tangents and never, never ceasing his endless quest to kill himself. I'd lost track of the attempts he'd made before he finally succeeded a week and change ago. But this was before that.

This is what started it. Maybe.

I force myself to set the paper on top of the box and pull out the first book on the stack. I can see now that there are orange sticky notes hanging out from the sides. My dad's favorite color. The thought stabs at me. The cover is plain gray cardstock, and it looks like it has been bound by hand by someone who didn't know what they were doing. It's a book, but just barely.

There's no title page or copyright page or any of the normal niceties, just a letter on the first page. I recognize the solid look of a typewriter font, with gentle indentations around each of the letters as though the writer had been typing on a manual machine with a deliberate intensity. There are no corrected errors.

To the human who finds this trove, I read, raising my eyebrow. I glance at my dad's handwritten letter that began a similar way, as though I could reach out through the years and gently tease him for copying. I continue.

I regret to inform you that unless the global situation has altered in ways too profound for me to believe likely, your understanding of nature and the laws thereof are deeply and inherently flawed. This is not a failing of your own, or of your upbringing, but rather a deliberate falsehood woven by the powerful to conceal reality from the powerless. It is in the spirit of ameliorating this wrong that I have preserved and bequeathed this trove of knowledge.

Perhaps it may be that you are skeptical of the claims that I make within this volume and those some three or four other volumes I intend to create in order to pass what knowledge I have gained over my lifetime to your care. For that reason, I have begun this volume with a few simple spells that, when you perform them, may yet convince you.

Spells. I shouldn't be surprised by the word, but I am. The ordinary quality of the book, the quaint language, and the smell of old paper feel so at odds with the thought. I continue reading.

It is a lie often told by one wizard to another that only those born wizards may perform acts of magic. In truth, any human being capable of carrying out the precise steps of a spell within the exceedingly slender margin of error may perform it. Wizards are at an advantage, as their sense of magic points the way toward performing these steps better and renders what is almost impossible into a simple matter of "going with the flow," as some younger wizards have of late begun to term it. But disadvantage does not determine ability.

As you discover and complete the spells laid out in this book, you will doubtless learn that intention—which in the non-magical world is an ephemeral thing—is the bedrock of much magic philosophy. This may help you understand why it has been a source of much speculation within myself, why I preserve and add my own knowledge to this trove.

There is a possibility that a certain measure of spite may be present in my actions. I grow near to the natural end of my life, and it seems likely I may die. I have convinced no wizard with the knowledge of longevity to pass that knowledge on to me, so that I may have the 500 years of life that most wizards can rely upon, barring misadventure. This is, for a wizard, the most profound of failures, and the most profound of betrayals.

To allay this fear, I can offer only the following truth: turning over this trove to other wizards may, with some cunning, have gained me the favor or leverage to obtain knowledge of the ritual of longevity. However, given the real effect that my motives in passing the trove may have on your success in using it, I encourage you to interrogate the long-lost motives of my heart as surely and as ruthlessly as you interrogate your own.

In the eighty-odd years of my life, I have seen the world change in incomprehensible ways. I have seen it grow brighter and darker, and I have begun to see old stalwart assumptions lose ground to newer, stranger thoughts and measures.

For myself, I can only attest that it is my opinion, as well as the opinion of those wizards who have in the past contributed their own knowledge to this trove, that revealing magic practices to non-wizards may help the world in ways yet unknown, ways as incomprehensible as the changes I have seen across my lifetime would have been to my grandfather, born in 1670 and dead on the day I was born. I believe it will be human hands who must take this knowledge and spread it.

I cannot offer you power or protection. I offer here only the tools by which to take it, and I wish you both good luck and safety. The potential danger inherent in this journey may be great, but so is the prize. And while you must bear the danger alone or with some few cherished others, the prize may, in a better world that I will not live to see, be shared among many.

In unknowing affection,

Stuart Dowley, Wizard. 1954.

I hold the book in my hands and try to imagine the man who wrote it. I hold him in his own unknowing affection. I read the letter again. I feel I don't understand it as deeply as he meant it. If this is real, I imagine I won't understand for a long time.

I find the part of me that believes this is all a fabrication of my breaking brain sliding away from me, but I cling on to it. I know why. Like any good fantasy, this story gives me what I want. It makes me a hero fighting against an unseen foe.

And, more importantly, it makes my father one. It takes away his mental illness and replaces it with glorious purpose.

It's an unfair tactic.

But it's engrossing. And I've got nothing to do anyway, so I turn the page and start reading.

The first page has a simple symbol—a dot with some asymmetrical swoops and lines and triangles positioned around it—drawn in ink. Instructions written on that same typewriter as the wizard Stuart's note appear below it.

1. *Cut a piece of material (paper may be easiest) to exactly square dimensions.*
2. *Transfer the above symbol onto the material. The symbol may be any size, but the dot at its center must be in the exact center of the material you intend to ignite.*

Ignite? Of course, ignite. How could it be anything different?

1. *Attain a state of Right Mind for the spell. For this spell, Right Mind is a sense of justified and unquestionable righteous fury.*
2. *Snap your fingers.*

Four steps to magically create fire. Sounds straight-forward.

Of course, it's also useless for my purposes. It's meant to convince the reader that magic is real, but it can't do it the way I need. After all, I've already seen proof. There's no middle ground where the wizard I met today was able to effect real magic, but this book is all bullshit.

But still, if I'm looking for a next step, this is it. No other next action gets me anything. Except calling a psychologist and making an appointment, which I probably should do but don't want to.

I gather up the book, the letter, and the objects, and head down to the room that is intended to be a home office that Faisal and I will share when we've settled in enough to unpack. It's mostly still in boxes, but I dig out some printer paper, a pencil, and a ruler, and follow the steps as carefully as I can.

I create a square by cutting the excess off the long end of some printer paper, using another identical piece of paper turned ninety degrees as a guide. Then I use a ruler to mark a dot in the center of the paper and align the dot on the thin printer paper with the dot on the page of the hand-bound book. If I squint, I can just barely see through the printer paper, and I thank the heavens above for Faisal's frugal insistence that we buy the cheapest printer paper available, seeing as we didn't need to print anything officially for work pretty much ever.

For a painful fraction of a second, I imagine my father doing exactly what I am. I imagine him using some of the tracing paper that he kept for his drawings, as I'm sure he must have. He would have applied the same patience and precision to this that he used to make his models. I try to channel him, and I find it easier to do it this time than I did when I tried to copy him with the train sets. Maybe it's because I'm fighting against something, even in a small way. I always *was* motivated by insurrection.

I finish and pull the paper back to survey my work, comparing the symbol I drew to the symbol on the page. I examine it carefully for a full minute and then sigh.

It's not right. It's not close enough. If we're working with the truly thin margins of error that the wizard Stuart claims, this isn't going to do it.

Okay, try again. I repeat the process, coming closer this time. And then again. And then again. Finally, I end up with something where I can't tell the difference between the symbol on the page and the symbol on my paper.

Excellent. Time for Right Mind. I start counting up the transgressions in the world. The things that shouldn't be, but are. Poverty, racism, inequality, anti-vaxxers… After a few minutes of cataloging every unjust thing, my stomach churns with rage.

What can I say? Getting worked up about things I can't personally go out and fix has never been an issue for me.

Then I snap my fingers.

And nothing happens.

My anger evaporates, leaving in its place a dull sense of embarrassment.

But that doesn't make any sense. If none of this is real, then that means I've been making it up. And if my brain is going to torture me with rude, arrogant wizards, it should at least let me set a piece of paper on fire. And if it *is* all real, then…

I'm not used to focusing the way my father was. I've started to tap into the side of me that takes after him with this kind of work, sure, but by the time my dad found this book, he'd probably been forcing his mind to focus for decades.

Am I going to be sitting here trying to set a piece of paper on fire for decades?

I look over at the box that contains the ancient PC Faisal and I use when we've both left our laptops at work, as though I could ask Google the answer to this very specific personal issue.

The computer.

Oh, god. Right.

I'm an idiot.

With a renewed sense of vigor and mild chagrin, I set back to work. I dig out the computer and get it booting up. Then I look through more boxes and find the old printer/scanner that works a solid majority of the times we aren't desperate, and even a few of the times we are. I dig it out, and it predictably takes me twenty minutes to find the right cable.

I have to cut the page out of the book to be sure it's

lying flat, something I would probably feel worse about if the book had been bound better, but I get it scanned in.

Once I know it is, I load up GIMP, the version of Photoshop priced to accommodate a public servant's salary—which is to say, free. Then I bring in the image of the symbol and blow it up large so that it almost takes up the whole of the paper. The bigger the scale, I figure, the bigger the margin of error and the easier it will be to execute.

It takes a fair amount of futzing around with it to get it to print so that it's going to be exactly in the middle of a piece of paper once I cut it down to a perfect square. But once I do, I feel confident in my results.

Stuart the wizard must have seen a lot of things in his life, but he didn't live to the age of convenient computers and printers, making easy work of his nigh-impossible tasks. I smile, momentarily proud of humans. And then wash that away in a flow of righteous fury.

Genocide, war, chemical weapons. Sexism, classism, disease.

I snap my fingers.

And nothing happens.

"Oh, fuck you," I say out loud to the paper, and then set it down.

I pull the book to me, now missing the page I had to cut out to scan flat. Part of me wants to go looking for something easier, but I'm pretty sure Stuart the wizard would have put the simplest spell at the beginning.

But what I do see, as I look at the next page, surprises me.

Helpful tips for the student:

This spell introduces you to the concept of Right Mind, which often confuses students. I, myself, when first learning, tended to lean toward nobler and wider-ranging motivations to call up what I believed would be Right Mind. I met with little success. Magic is the art of accepting your own failings, even as you surpass your own limits. This may mean recognizing that more personal triggers for emotion, which you may believe should be less effective, may be more so. This does not make you selfish. It only makes you human, which amounts to the same. Houses may be smaller than mountains. But they look bigger when you're living in them.

I stare at the writing on the page for a long moment, at first convinced that, *obviously*, it didn't apply to me. And then I sigh, and think, and come up with a sufficiently selfish reason for righteous rage.

The day my father died, just after I heard the news, I was driving to my sister's house. Another driver cut me off. A ratty-looking hatchback jumped right in front of me on the highway, crawling, and then accelerated to way above the speed limit. That guy was going to kill someone.

I focus on that memory, on that feeling. When I snap my fingers, I imagine snapping off that reckless driver's tiny little head, obviously barely filled with their tiny, rarely used brain.

And then I yelp as the entire sheet of paper in my left hand is very suddenly engulfed in flame.

I should have had something prepared for success—a bucket of water, maybe. I was expecting a small flame, commensurate with my small, beginning-student power. But nope. I guess when you do a spell right, the spell executes.

On instinct, I release the flaming paper, which falls into my lap and catches my clothes on fire. And then I do something that I never expected: I actually use stop, drop, and roll.

I roll for longer than I probably need to, just to be completely sure, and laugh with relief and delayed surprise and delight.

I stop laughing when I see that somehow a piece of the flaming paper floated onto the desk, where it caught a stack of printer paper offcuts.

I grab a random packing blanket and start smothering the pieces of paper. It works—luckily—and after a few terrifying seconds of intense action, the only visible remnants of my first magic spell are my ruined clothes and a scorch mark on the cheap IKEA desk that has held up admirably for its price.

I slump back into the office chair.

Okay. So that's magic. Magic is a thing.

FIVE

A
Search

I don't attempt any more spells for the rest of the day. Figuring out how to do one was plenty of detailed work. And though it felt good to focus on something that intently, it also feels like my brain is a little worn out. Instead, I head back up to the attic and start skimming through all the different hand-bound volumes and collections of pages.

I find myself most drawn to all the sticky notes. My dad went through all this stuff, and I feel like I'm spending time with him as I try to decipher his messy penmanship. He might have had impeccable fine motor skills when he wanted them, sure. But when he wasn't using them, he really wasn't using them.

Many of his notes were on potential uses for described spells, or potential negative side effects. He'd fully bought into Stuart's vision of a world with commonplace magic and had begun imagining what it might look like in modern times. As I read his notes, I begin to buy into it, too. Though my view of how some of these spells might play out is admittedly a little more cynical than his.

Hours pass. Every time I look at the time on my phone, it rocks me. Sometimes, it's because the time has passed too quickly. Other times, I'd have sworn it passed too slowly. I wonder if time magic is a thing, and if these books are enchanted somehow. But the easier explanation is my own unsteady mind.

Now and then, I tell myself to remember that this might all be imagined, that I could be making it all up. That I need to be careful not to do anything I'll regret too much if this is all a break from reality. That I should keep my eye out for holes and definitive proof.

But it's hard not to suspend that rational disbelief. It's so easy to get sucked in. All those reasonable, skeptical thoughts get pushed further and further back in my mind, adding an anxious layer to my mood.

I find the spell that Dad used to enchant the thick-framed glasses fairly early on—just before noon. It's one of Stuart's, near the end of his last volume. Looks like Right Mind for this particular spell is a spirit of intense curiosity, and it's not hard to see how Dad got that one to work. The glasses grant the ability for non-magical humans to see like a wizard, and my relief is palpable as I read that, once enchanted, no further magical input is needed to use them.

I put them on and look around the attic. Everything looks normal, except for the lantern and... me?

I can't tell what's wrong with my arm as I look at it, and it sends me down the ladder and into the bedroom, where I can look at myself in the full-length mirror affixed to the back of the door.

It's subtle—very subtle. I have a hard time nailing down what's actually different about me, except to think that this is what people must mean when they say someone has a "healthy glow." I look generally sturdier. Generally happier. Generally solid. My concern is righteous and warranted. My wonder is profound and joyful.

I can see why Max didn't notice it at first. To the uninformed observer, this might appear natural. But when I take off the locket, set it on the bed, and look back at the mirror, it shows me as I actually am without the effect of the locket. My face is stricken with worry and uncertainty. My arms and legs are too thin. It's only been a bit over a week of not eating properly, but it's already starting to show. The house clothes I put on after my work clothes got a little singed make me look dumpy and resigned.

I snap the locket back up, draping it around my neck and settling it under my shirt where it's already starting to feel like it belongs. I head back up into the attic.

Once there, I examine the lantern. Inside it, I see a lit green flame. I blink and remove the glasses. Same old, dull world with the dark lantern and its slightly used candle. I put the glasses back on and the candle is once again lit with a green flame. And that flame is leaning.

Huh.

I turn back to the books, picking up the pace. I'm reading with a purpose now, trying to find an explanation for the locket and lantern.

Neither of these objects are from Stuart's books. I find the locket first, in a group of papers by a man named Ezekiel who was writing in the nineteenth century. His handwriting, while immaculate, is even harder for me to read than my father's. This is going to be a problem. The farther I go back in time, and the lower in the stack I reach, the harder the writings will be to decipher.

Apparently, the locket is an "amulet of protection," and there's not that much on what it does other than that it "protects from injuries borne of harmful intention." That thin description prefaces about eight pages of detailed instructions on how to put it together and activate it. This is emblematic of Ezekiel's writings as a whole. From what I can tell, the man was big on the how, but not so big on the why.

I'm more than a little impressed that Dad managed to put this thing together. I remember watching him put together detailed dioramas, but nothing remotely this intense. I skim the sticky notes, looking for an indication of Right Mind for the activation. Apparently, it required Dad to feel "a spirit of affection and protective nurturing of loved ones." Even moving past the thought as quickly as I can, it still stings to consider how he must have achieved that.

I keep heading down the stack, mostly skimming. I'm delighted that the farther down I go, as the languages and handwriting get more and more obscure, there are more and more sticky notes from Dad. Many of them are rough translations of the purposes of the spells or why he won't attempt them. *Requires goat pus*, reads one. *Can only be performed on or by virgins (which?)* reads another.

The pages describing the construction and purpose of the lantern are a loose-leaf sheaf without attribution, in a language I don't recognize. They are peppered with sticky note after sticky note describing steps, with a lot of question marks, as well as crossed out and corrected bits. I do my best to decipher them all until I get to the one that tells me what I need to know.

Detects magic.

I raise an eyebrow and search the sticky notes around that one, looking for more detail.

Nope. That's all. Everything else is instruction on putting the thing together and activating it. Again, not much on what it's supposed to do, or how, or how well.

I'm sensing a theme. Maybe it's a common wizard

thing. I let the absurdity of that phrase hit me and ground me, just a little, back toward the insanity explanation. That explanation is far outgunned lately. I need to put my thumb on the scale if it's going to hold on.

I set the papers aside and look again at the lantern through the glasses. The green flame is definitely indicating a direction. I spin the lantern lazily and notice that the flame stays pointing the same direction no matter how I orient the object.

I lean back. The light outside the windows is waning. It'll be fully dark soon. Easier to see the flame if I…

I let the thought trail off, still pretending that I'm not going to do it—that I'm not going to grab this thing and follow it through town. I stretch out my back, sore from hunching over the papers for hours and hours. I listen to the sound of the oncoming evening through the open window. It's that glorious time of year when people are just beginning to cut their grass, and on just the right days, you start getting a sense that summer is coming on. There's some deeply rooted feeling of prosperity to come that's buried in these days, that just makes you feel good.

And here I go, about to ruin it.

I run through the best- and worst-case scenarios for what might happen, both for if this is real, or if I'm having a mental break.

If it's real, the best-case scenario is that I find someone who helps me figure out what's going on with the suicides. I may not be sure where the lines are, but that man from this morning and the suicides he dropped in my lap are just weird enough to land on the spooky side. And I'll need help if I'm going to figure out what's happening.

Of course, the worst-case scenario is that I find something magic that my amulet doesn't protect me from, and it kills me.

If I'm crazy, the best-case scenario is that I see something that I can't reconcile, and that makes me face the facts, and I call Faisal and get his list. The worst-case scenario is that I hurt someone.

Just as a bonus, I throw in a medium-case scenario for the crazy option: Someone spots me, recognizes me, and asks questions about why an employee from the mayor's office has lost her mind and is running around town in ill-fitting glasses staring at an unlit lantern.

Well, all right then. Just so long as I know where I stand.

I put the papers back in the cabinet, close it up, and notice the symbols around it again. I haven't come across those yet. They must be farther down in the stack. I'll check on them tomorrow, assuming this goes well. I push the cabinet back under the train set table, so that it's just behind the fabric. Still hidden, but a little more accessible than it had been before.

Satisfied that everything is as inconspicuous as it ever was, I close the window and head down the ladder. This time, I remember to put away the dining chair. Not that I'm expecting more company, but it seems like a prudent measure.

I go to my room to change out of my house clothes. Something a little more fit for strangers seems in order, and I pull on jeans and a T-shirt, hesitating.

Injuries borne of harmful intention.

It's impossible to say how wide or narrow that definition is, or how the mechanics of this work out. As grateful as I am for my happy little amulet, it seems safer to assume the locket won't protect me from everything. I feel like I need more protection, and my mind flicks automatically to what I think will satisfy that perceived need. It feels a little over the top without a clear and present threat. Should I give in to a generalized feeling of danger?

Probably not, but I do it anyway.

My sister got me a yellow leather jacket years and years ago. It was just before Dad got committed, and I was pushing my boundaries, excited to go out and see the world on the back of a motorbike. She told me that the yellow was as close to high-vis as she thought she was going to be able to convince me to wear, although it's more like a faded mustard color. Then Dad got committed and the world felt more fragile all around, and I canceled my plans and backed out of the deal for the bike.

I've never been the type to wear leather jackets in general, so this thing has never been worn. Not once. But they used to make armor out of leather. And if leather would have protected me from the asphalt, it's probably the closest thing I have to general protective gear.

I put it on now. It still fits, maybe even better now than I remember it fitting back then. It has exterior pockets but also spacious interior pockets in the lining that feel secure and useful. I like the wide lapels and the way it sits just above my hips.

I don't think I appreciated how much Olivia must have paid for this at the time. I should have thanked her better instead of rolling my eyes at the color and the implied worry. Teenagers. What can you do with them?

I consider bringing a weapon but discard the thought quickly. I've heard enough statistics to know that if someone untrained with a knife ends up in a knife fight, they're the ones who will end up dead. If I can't avoid a fight, I'm sure as hell not going to win one. Besides, crazy-person-walking-around-with-an-unlit-lantern is a whole lot better than crazy-person-walking-around-with-an-unlit-lantern-and-a-knife. Humoring myself with the idea that I could make use of a knife isn't worth the risk of actually bringing it with me.

Satisfied with my choices, I grab a messenger bag that I don't use often and make sure the lantern fits in it. Then I gather up my phone and keys and head out to the car.

SIX

An Introduction

L ooking at your phone while driving is a safety risk, so I'm going to go ahead and guess that looking through magic glasses at an invisible flame inside a magic lantern probably is, too. How am I going to do this?

I ponder while I get the car in gear and look around me, concerned that someone will see me acting strangely.

I pull up a map on my phone and compare the angle of the flame to it. I plot a course and decide on places where I'll stop to check and see if I need to readjust. At some point, it'll direct me back, and I'll zero in. When I've zeroed in enough, I should be able to get out and walk, and eventually see *something* out of the ordinary through the glasses.

I'm sure there's a better way to do this, but I don't know what it is right now. I'm anxious. Need more data. Need to see something that I can't discount. Something real that other people, who I *know* are real, see too. I'm adding up the evidence. It feels like a lot, but I need more.

The plan works well. It leads me to the Arts District, which seems right somehow. But it's an area that's hard to drive in, so I get out and walk sooner than I thought I would need to, and I end up doing more walking than anticipated.

It's a nice night. Still a little chilly, but warmer than it's been so far, which has brought people out in droves. I start getting used to ducking down alleys, pulling the lantern out, glancing at it quickly, and hoping it's not too suspicious. A couple of times I think someone recognizes me—I do press conferences occasionally—but I dismiss it as paranoia. I'm not famous. I shouldn't get too full of myself. That can't help me now.

It takes maybe an hour from when I leave my house to when I figure out what building the lantern is pointing at.

The Emporium. I've been here a couple of times before. I tried to get in the habit of attending a book club to get in some non-work-related social activity, but I ended up forgetting to read the book after a couple of meetings. It's a bookstore—mostly used books, if I remember correctly—but the front third of the building has a café that serves coffee and ice cream. Other assorted objects for sale also dot the aisles. I vaguely recall that some are antiques. I don't think I've seen any of them disappear, but I figure they must sell now and then. Otherwise why would they remain up for sale?

All in all, it's an effective combination. It's managed to cling on in a part of town where the buildings seem to have new signs hanging from them every year. That might be in part due to the ice cream. Though I haven't tried it, I'm sure I've promised I would to at least three rave reviewers.

I zip the messenger bag up around the lantern, though I'm not sure why. I can't make out the shape of the lantern underneath the fabric, but through the glasses the entire thing glows with a dull green light that matches the color of the flame. I wonder why Max hadn't been able to see the glow when he'd been in the attic. The symbols around the box, maybe? I'll need to keep searching through the books for those. They seem important.

Someone jolts me walking by, and I give and receive profuse apologies. That's what I get for standing still, lost in thought a few feet from the doorway. Time to stop stalling.

I step inside.

The Emporium strikes a perfect balance between coziness and elegance. One of my coworkers once called it "worn-in Art Deco," and that description strikes me as apt. Sometimes overly decorative spaces can feel fiddly or fragile, but neither of those terms fit the space. When I've visited in the past, I've always been left with the impression that nothing anyone could do could change it. The brass and wood bookcases and tables, the elaborate wavy staircase to the second floor, the overstuffed leather armchairs, the Tiffany lampshades hanging from the ceiling—all of it is just so. All of it is exact.

I look around the Emporium with new eyes. I'm not sure what I'm looking for exactly. I'm guessing some kind of glow like the lantern. God help me if it's subtle like the effect the amulet has on me. Making sure I'm out of the way, I examine everything carefully. I probably look crazy. Seems right, since I probably am.

I don't see anything glowing, and I'm about to head into the depths of the store, when I hesitate. Something is different. Wrong. I flip the glasses up and down a couple times and can tell what it is.

Everything is… less, somehow. Not black and white, but desaturated slightly. The glasses weren't having this effect when I was driving. I think I would have noticed, and I did check now and then to see if I could spot any differences.

An uneasy feeling tells me to run—tells me that what

I'm seeing is life being stripped away from everyone and everything around me. But that's nonsense. I don't *feel* any worse. The people around me don't look like they feel wrong, either.

And then I stop breathing for a moment as I see the owner of the Emporium: Gigi.

I remember her well from previous times I've seen her, which is rare enough for someone who has only served you coffee twice, but she's a memorable woman. She's tall—taller than most men. I doubt anyone who's ever met her hasn't had the word "statuesque" float unbidden into their minds. Maybe it's her certain similarity of spirit with the Statue of Liberty.

Through the glasses, she's the only thing that looks real. She's in full color, vibrant and sharp. She's also…

I blink and squint, suddenly not caring at all about how strange I look. I take a few steps forward involuntarily, transfixed.

She's *solid.* She looks like she's been carved out of stone, but the stone is alive. That's the only way I can characterize it. And she's got a pull to her like gravity. A *weight.*

And then she looks at me, and I see her eyes. They're diamonds. No irises, no pupils, no nothing. Just two eyeball-sized faceted diamonds that see through me in a way that only sounds nice in theory.

Her lips curl up in a smile so sharp and wide it could shear a continental plate in two. I shove the glasses back up onto my head, away from my eyes, before I bear the full, terrifying weight of that smile.

Without my glasses on, I just see a woman with olive skin, black eyes, and crimson hair. She wears a dirty apron with a nametag on it, holds an ice cream scoop, and grins at me warmly. Her eyes dart meaningfully from my face to an empty two-seater table in the corner of the café, squeezed between the table for lids and flavorings and the decorated plate glass of the storefront.

Without question or hesitation, I go. I have time to wonder if I'm doing it of my own free will or not, and I feel like I probably am. Maybe. I don't know. But my amulet protected me from being bossed around mentally earlier, so it should be saving me now, right?

I watch her with zero temptation to put my glasses back on. She's warm and courteous, and something she says as she hands a middle-aged man his ice cream cone makes him laugh—too hard for the relative humor of the joke, I'm guessing.

There are a few other people in line. She serves two of them quickly, but something she says to the third makes him turn away with a frown and leave without purchasing anything. When the line immediately in front of her is empty, she pulls out an antique telephone. I have no credentials except a misspent youth watching *Antiques Roadshow*, but it looks authentic to me.

When she speaks, her persuasive voice comes out of speakers in the corners of the room. Would that voice sound different if I put my glasses on? I don't test the theory.

"Attention customers, The Emporium will be closing in fifteen minutes. Please make your final decisions and bring your purchases to the front for checkout."

I check the time on my phone against the opening hours written in elaborate script on the other side of the window, and I feel the bottom drop out of my stomach. I don't know anything about Gigi, and I've liked her in spite of that each time I've come across her in the past. I'm pretty sure I even told someone approving applications for Arts District revitalization loans that they'd made a good choice by accepting her application. But now that I've seen her through my glasses, I'm horrified that she's taken an interest in me.

Motionless, I watch her as she rings up books and makes small talk I can't hear for the next fifteen minutes. In her position, I'd probably be looking over to make sure I hadn't left, but she doesn't seem to need the reassurance. Is that just because she knows I'll listen? Or does she have eyes in the back of her head that I can't normally see? I don't check.

When the crowd has left, I expect Gigi to come over to me, but she doesn't. Instead, she disappears for a minute into the stacks before reemerging, herding out a couple of teenagers with headphones on.

Eviction complete, she locks the door and… still doesn't come over to me. Instead, she heads back behind the counter and I watch closely as she makes a milkshake. Mint chocolate chip. Is it part of whatever mojo she has that she knows it's my favorite flavor, somehow? Seems like it would be a useful skill for someone running a café.

When she's finished, she walks to a table in the middle and sets the milkshake across from her.

She looks at me.

Her eyes lay heavy on me as I walk over and sit down in front of her. She's wearing that grin again, the very same one that's sharper and wider underneath than it is on the surface.

"Drink," she says. Although her voice is sweet and deep, and I've listened to the tenor of it at a distance since I've been in here, it still puts me on the defensive when directed at me this way.

"That doesn't seem safe," I say, my own voice hollow in contrast.

Oh, come on. Really? her face says for her.

Poison seems like some pretty intentional harm to me,

so I do as I'm told with my protection amulet in mind. The milkshake is delicious. I begin to relax even as I feel on display both to Gigi and to the dark street on the other side of the glass wall.

The recommendations for Gigi's ice cream didn't oversell it. If anything, the rapturous praise was woefully insufficient. It's balanced and rich, and it carries the kind of cold that seeps into your bones after a long day of sledding. My drink is thin enough to sip easily through the straw but seems to expand once in my mouth. It's whole-body satisfying in a way I associate with a very different sphere of my personal life. If this is magic, it's a kind of magic I don't mind.

"So," Gigi says, settling her chin down on one hand, her joy at my pleasure evident. "What are you? You're not a wizard."

I take another sip before answering.

"How do you know?"

"You're not pretty enough."

I try not to look insulted, but I must fail. Her voice sounds gentler when she speaks again, like she's talking to a child.

"My, you *are* new to all this, aren't you? It's one of the first things wizards learn to do. They transform themselves into something gorgeous."

I eye her warily. I should be wearing my glasses for this conversation, but I'm deeply unwilling to.

"Sounds vain."

Gigi smiles. "Vanity is one of wizards' many failings, yes. But it's practical, too. Humans trust pretty people. They like them."

"Is that why people like you?"

Her grin shifts to a smile. If I put on my glasses, what would her teeth look like? Would they be sharp?

"I'm more handsome than pretty," she says lightly. "And no. I don't think so."

I force my eyes away from her for the first time since I came through the door. The coffee shop and the bookshop behind it are well loved. Welcoming.

"Why do you think they like you?" I ask, as if one potential reason wasn't all around me.

"Because I tell the truth. And I think some part of them can sense that."

My eyes snap back to her. "Always?"

"Always."

"Why?"

I take a long drag through my large-diameter milkshake straw as she regards me. The only movement in her body is her deep, steady breathing. Even without my glasses, I can almost see the solidity underneath. She's deciding something. I hope she decides in my favor.

"Because it's what I'm for," she says, and I'm relieved. She heads me off with answers before I can begin to ask more questions.

"You know that old riddle—two gates, two guardians? One to doom, one to glory. One guardian who always lies, one who tells the truth. One question."

I nod, and her smile takes on a bit of the sharpness hovering underneath the façade of her grin.

"A long time ago, a wizard thought he would be very clever and made one for himself. *Et voilà, c'est moi*! He made me invulnerable, but he forgot to put a time limit on it. The gates crumbled, the wizard died, and I continued."

I open my mouth with a question but hesitate.

"Oh, go on," she says, a sudden exhaustion in her voice.

"What am I holding?" I ask, curling my fingers around the milkshake glass, and she rolls her eyes.

"A milkshake. No, I'm not my sister. And yes, she still exists. I assume. I'm very pleased to say I don't know where she is."

Her gaze goes somewhere far away, but only for a moment.

"So that's me," she continues. "What are you? You found me somehow. And you're protected. Spell or amulet?"

"Amulet," I say unsteadily.

"Where did you get it?"

I should just say I found it. It's true. But I don't. "My father gave it to me."

She sits stock-still. "Father by blood?" The question seems to bring her back to life, though I don't know why it would.

"Yes."

"So, not a wizard either."

Her eyes light up, and I try not to think what *that* would look like through my glasses.

"He had a *trove*," she breathes. "I was really beginning to believe the wizards had found them all."

I don't ask any questions, and I don't confirm or deny. I'm pretty sure all that would be pointless.

She gives me a sharp, quick nod. "Right," she says. "There's a wizard in town. A young thing. You'll want to avoid him, although I'm pretty sure he'll find you. Especially because of all that business with the train… accidental?"

I stop sucking on the straw of my milkshake just long enough to answer. Cold sinks down into my body in a way I'm really hoping isn't symbolic. "Very."

"Right," she says again. "So that's that. Why did you come looking for me?"

I lean back in my chair, struck by the question. I

wonder what she does in situations like this, where there's more than one true answer. I guess she gets to choose, just like I do.

"There's something I need your help with."

I tell her about the suicides. About how harsh and unnatural they seem, and how regularly they happened.

"Unlikely," she says, like it means more than it does. "But not impossible."

"No," I say, feeling like we're having two different conversations. "Not impossible. What does that mean to you?"

She's far away again when she answers. "It means I may know who's responsible."

She looks down at my milkshake, and I question again the wisdom of drinking it.

"If you'll finish that, I'll take you to meet him."

With pleasure.

And fear.

But mostly pleasure.

SEVEN

An Altar

I try not to rush finishing my milkshake. It's just as good as I near my final sip as it was on my first. I wonder briefly if my amulet would stop narcotics. Is that harm? What constitutes harm? Why are the borders of magic so fuzzy?

I'm pretty sure Gigi can't read my mind—the conversation with her had felt too natural for that—but her expression as she silently watches me drinking and thinking doesn't support that theory too well.

When I've almost reached the bottom of the glass, she begins going about the business of closing up the bookshop café, and I'm struck again by how mundane her actions are and how well she does them. Part of the allure of magic, I've always thought, is an escape from the mundane. But here she is, wiping away counters, putting an insulated cover in the ice cream counter to seal out the heat, cleaning out milk jugs, filling up a commercial dishwasher somewhere in the back, and putting chairs up on tables.

I can't help but like her, watching the contented grace of her easy, practiced motions. She likes our world, doesn't she? She likes me, doesn't she? It feels like she does. I don't want to know if I'm wrong, though that seems like pretty relevant information.

When I've finished, she swiftly whisks my glass away to the dishwasher that has been waiting on my contribution to start. She turns off the lights while she's back there, and I'm left sitting in the dark. I can see the people walking by out the window now. None of them know about any of this. How is that fair?

"What was your name?" I hear Gigi call from the back, a hint of surprise in her voice. She'd been so interested in what I was, she didn't ask who I was. Maybe she *doesn't* like me.

I interpret that question as also calling me to her, so I get up and walk toward the back as I answer. "I'm Elizabeth."

When I come through the doorway to the little dish-washing and prep area in the back room, I have that same weird feeling of seeing something I wasn't supposed to that I've had all day, just in a more mundane way. Gigi glances at the door as though judging the sight lines, and then she nods, apparently deciding we are sufficiently obscure.

"All right, then, Elizabeth. Take my hand."

I do. Her eyes sparkle. She takes a step.

When her foot comes down, it lands on the chill dirt of a field. It's too early for whatever crops are going to be grown here to come up yet, apparently. A thin, cold breeze blows my hair away from the back of my neck.

"Holy fuck," I blurt out involuntarily, and Gigi's laugh rings out in the night air. I look up at her and see the harshness of her smile and the brightness of her eyes, so different from who she'd been to me just minutes before. She's lit all from one side, and it grants her features an intense drama. I drop her hand like it's a snake and turn toward the source of the light.

It's a palace. Or a temple? Or an exceptionally old, grand hotel? It reminds me of nothing so much as the Taj Mahal, though it's much smaller than that. I think it's the onion-shaped dome that does it.

The building isn't glowing with unearthly magic. It's just really well-lit with enough bright, vintage-looking incandescent bulbs to murder a rainforest all by themselves. Red pennant flags on either side of the entrance flutter lazily to the left in a breeze I can't feel. There's a grand, wide staircase leading to the entrance, and a few couples walk up it, with one figure taking the other figure by the arm. In each case, the leading figure is dressed formally, with tuxedos on the men and long, slinky black dresses with slits higher than I would dare on the women. The other figure in each couple looks casual. Normal. Aggressively plain in the dazzling surroundings. They remind me of American tourists along the French Riviera. Or at least what I think that would be like, since I've never actually been.

I slide my glasses into place over my eyes and note the differences. The grand building stays the same, and the casual figures are still there. But their escorts disappear.

One thing that doesn't change is a tall, lone figure standing at the base of the stairway like a welcoming host. He's got his eyes on Gigi and a smile brighter than any of the bulbs around him.

Gigi strides toward him with a dancer's rhythm, and I stumble along beside her gracelessly, like I'm being pulled forward by a string. When we get close enough, the man opens his arms in a genteel welcome, revealing the precise, careful, *expensive* styling of his tuxedo.

"Gigi," he purrs, his accent unmistakably upper-class

British, even just from those two syllables. "It's been too long."

Gigi accepts his greeting, stiffly exchanging a double-cheek kiss that I would never be able to execute without looking out of place.

"Has it, though?" Gigi asks, with a gentle lilt to her voice that I hadn't heard back in the café.

The man turns his gaze to me appraisingly. He's handsome in a refined way. Indian, I think, or somewhere near there, though there's no trace of it in his voice. If I had to guess his age, I'd say… I'm not sure. Grown. Older than me, probably. Or maybe around the same age? He looks human even through my glasses, but I can feel down to my bones he's not. He's a few inches taller than Gigi, which makes him much taller than me.

"What have you brought me?" he asks. The question is clearly intended for Gigi, but he doesn't take his eyes off me.

"A human," Gigi answers, still with that lilt. "Nothing more, nothing less. I think you'd like her if you got to know her. I'd encourage you *not* to."

The man rolls his eyes at me at Gigi's words, like we're sharing a secret aside, then he fixes her with a cool gaze.

"As always, Gigi, you are delightfully consistent."

Turning back to me, he offers his arm.

"Shall we?"

I look to Gigi, hoping to see some indication of whether I should take it or not, but the stone she's made of looks like it's lost its life.

I take the man's arm and let him lead me up the grand staircase, with Gigi coming around to flank my other side. I feel like a child between parents. Or maybe more a worshipper between pillars in a church.

"I'd take it as a personal affront," the man says in a

casual, friendly tone as we approach the entrance, "if you keep those glasses on. I'm welcoming you into my home. You should see it as I intend you to."

"This is your home?" I ask as I comply with his request, pushing the glasses back up onto my head with no hesitation.

"Among other things," he answers.

Just as he does, I begin to hear familiar noises. The sound of… slot machines? The dings and blips and cheerful ringing that bring me right back to hazy memories of the handful of times I've been to Atlantic City.

"Aloysius here is a chance demon," Gigi says.

I look up at the man, cold with fear. He still appears so unacceptably human.

"Demon?" I say. Then, softer, as I try to sort out how incongruous his name is with his face. "Your name is Aloysius?"

I want to withdraw my arm from his but don't feel I have the option.

The demon smiles. "That is the name she knows for me. And demon is a terrible term. Pay no mind to it. It's the label some give to things they don't understand."

His voice sounds reassuring, but I don't feel reassured. There's no time to linger in the thought, though, as we step up the final stair into the warm half-circle of light from the open doors.

We enter into a small lobby, all polished stone. Little space is stolen from the casino floor, full to bursting with slot machines near the entrance. I try to nail down the style, but I can't. There's something old-world Vegas about the grand entrance doors and their surrounds, and the small table laden with a too-large vase of glittering flowers. But some of the slot machines seem very modern— crass and flashy. The double set of staircases I can see farther back leading to a grand interior balcony are all polished glass and metal, like a Fortune 500 company trying to intimidate you into not asking too many questions about their business practices.

We stop in front of the vase of flowers. I don't know if it's because the demon wants me to admire them, or if he's just used to people doing so. They're exquisitely crafted. The stems are various precious metals—some I can identify, some I can't. The leaves and petals are gemstones of different kinds, painstakingly cut into the thin proportions of the real things. I'm not sure how they're held together, as there don't seem to be settings, at least not the way I would think of them.

Magic, I guess. It's all just magic. I can't feel it, exactly, but the whole place reminds me of a dream in the final moments of waking, when you know you're about to forget it and cling hard to the details as they begin to slip away.

"Would you like one?" The demon's voice drips into my ear, suddenly very close.

"Would you give me one?" I ask.

I don't look up, but I can feel the smile curling his lips as he answers, "Perhaps."

Then we're moving again, through the rows of people on slot machines. No one pays us any mind. They are all transfixed by what they are doing, glassy-eyed and hungry.

"They're human," I say.

"Yes," Gigi answers in a measured tone.

I have a sudden ridiculous thought, and I laugh out loud at it. I'm pleased by the surprised expressions on my companion's faces. The demon looks at me questioningly.

"Is this legal?" I ask. "Where I'm from, gambling's against the law."

I smile at him like we're the co-conspirators he pretended we were earlier when rolling his eyes at Gigi.

He laughs, and despite myself, I like the sound of it.

"Aloysius doesn't bother with laws," Gigi answers for him. "*Anyone's* laws."

I'm not surprised, but I continue, still curious about the mechanics of it.

"Right. But we're still… on Earth, right?"

"Yes," the demon answers, sounding for all the world like an indulgent, approving teacher.

"Not far from Springfield?"

"Correct," Gigi says, adopting the same tone.

"So… won't the police notice? Or won't someone report it? How do you handle that?"

Gigi answers, her voice ringing with bitterness. "The people gambling here won't remember it in the morning."

"Sure," I say, like I'd already figured that out, which I guess part of me had. "But won't they notice when their money is gone? How do you hide the paper trail?"

The demon throws an overacted long-suffering glance at Gigi, and this time, I'm the one left out of the joke. It doesn't feel as good on this side of it. I stare at her until she explains.

"They're not gambling with money."

I feel the motion of my own breath like it's a hard-fought thing. Like I'm breathing liquid.

"What are they gambling with?" I ask. Her face is hard-set, and it's the first time I see not even a trace of a smile on her lips. She doesn't answer me.

"With the only thing humans have of value." The demon's patient, practical voice washes over me like a lava flow. "Their souls."

My eyes dart manically around the room in mounting horror. The slack-jawed expressions. The single-minded purpose.

We've reached the bottom of one of the staircases leading to the balcony.

"And they lose them?"

The demon's hand is on my chin, directing me to look up at him. His face fills my vision.

"Sometimes they lose them," he says. The jovial, casual sense of welcome that he's had up until now is long gone. His intensity drowns out the chaotic roar of the machines around us. "But sometimes, they win. Have you ever met someone who seemed to be *so much* of what they were? Who had so much to give and so much of themselves to use and to risk? Who poured everything of what they are into everything they did, but somehow never ran out?"

I had. Of course I had. I blink. "But if they lose, they die?"

His fingers on my chin relax, no longer holding so much as cradling.

"Rarely," he grants. "If they bet everything. Very rarely."

I take advantage of his weakened grip to break away from the intensity of the exchange, and I look around the room again. My heart feels heavy, and the scene before me feels distant—doomed.

"Poor bastards," I whisper.

Aloysius looks at me like he's never considered this before.

"Eventually," he says, "I suppose. But much can happen before eventually."

I try not to let him win me over. I can't tell if I'm succeeding. I think I am.

"But they *can't* know what they're risking."

The demon's voice is light again as he moves us forward, up onto the staircase. "They don't *know*, no, but they feel it. They know the weight of it, and they keep going anyway."

There's a warmth in his tone. Admiration, maybe?

"You say that like it's a good thing. Like the ones that lose are your favorites." It isn't a question, exactly, but it plunges him into thought. We walk in silence while he considers.

"Not my favorites," he says at last. "A true gambler doesn't stop when he runs out of his own stake, and we don't grant house credit here."

I shake my head, suddenly feeling very small and powerless, even as Aloysius leads me up the stairs and I rise above the casino floor, step by step.

"But even so, the house always wins," I accuse, looking up at the demon's face. He's staring off into the distance at something that I either can't see, or that isn't there at all. For the first time, I notice a casual gauntness to him, like he's malnourished but so used to it that he doesn't notice anymore.

"Yes," he says with a disarming sincerity and a smile that could dry wet winter socks. "I do."

We climb in silence for a few seconds until we reach the balcony. The balcony houses card tables, mostly, and stretches back farther than I can make out. I identify black-jack and poker at a glance, but there are some others I can't. Some games involve tiles; some others involve unfamiliar tokens. I glance up and see the demon surveying this part of his domain with unbridled affection.

"Yes, yes," Gigi says beside me with an unimpressed air that even *I* can tell is feigned. "She's very intimidated, I'm sure. But we did come here for a reason."

Aloysius starts us moving again, cocking a questioning eyebrow at Gigi. For a second, I'm afraid Gigi's going to make me explain things to him, and I'm relieved when she doesn't.

"There have been some statistical anomalies in Springfield, one of the closest towns to this crossroads," she says.

Crossroads?

"Too many suicides, too perfectly timed. And beginning right around the time the Casino comes around. It all seems very… *improbable.*" She levels the word at him like it's a weapon, but he doesn't react.

"Tell me you don't still think I meddle with probability, Gigi," he says reproachfully. And then, like I wasn't just angry with him, he makes me the one in on the joke with him with a wink.

Gigi isn't swayed. She purses her lips. "Is this you?"

We walk silently for a few seconds, routing around a blackjack table full of rapt, agonized faces.

"No," he says at last. "Though I do feel very lucky to be here as it's happening."

Gigi nods once, stopping short. "Good to know. We'll be going."

But the demon keeps walking forward at a steady pace, placing his free hand on mine in the crook of his arm to belay any thought of stopping or pulling away. "And miss the fight? I wouldn't hear of it."

I look back at Gigi while she decides whether to do as she wants and get out of here or not. I could resist the demon's inexorable march forward. She'd back me up.

But I'm curious, and what was the point of going out in search of mystery if I turn away as soon as I find it?

So I go with the flow, leaving Gigi to give up fighting and trail behind us with a look of disappointment. And when the demon brings us to an ornate, antique-looking elevator that opens with a clatter of wrought iron, I step inside.

EIGHT

A Cheat

The elevator takes us up. I look for a dial telling me floor numbers, but I don't find one. I think we're up three floors based on the glimpses I get through the elevator cage, but I wouldn't bet my life on it. When the elevator slows to a stop, the demon has something new on his face: absolute authority. He no longer has my arm in his, and when I step out of the elevator with Gigi, it's behind him, not beside him. We have no status here. I feel abandoned, even though I'm luckily not alone.

It's only seconds before we've lost him to the crowd.

And it *is* a crowd. They all look human to me right now, but I'm sure they aren't any more human than Gigi or the demon. They're entirely too at ease, and I have the distinct feeling of entering a party where everyone knows everyone else, but no one knows you.

"Aren't you going to put your glasses on?" Gigi purrs, and she's not trying to hide the sharpness of her grin anymore. My fingers on one of my hands tracks up to one of the arms of the glasses, tucked safely behind my ear.

There's no trace of annoyance on Gigi's face that I didn't stand with her and insist on leaving, but I have a feeling it's underneath.

"Seems like a bad idea," I say, only partially thinking of what the demon told me about my glasses at the entrance. Gigi's eyes flare, and she leans down so that I can hear her as she lowers her voice.

"*Terrible*. But you want to see everything, don't you? And I must admit, I'd find it entertaining. I do get bored so easily."

The problem with people who take things personally but don't tell you about it is that there's no way to make amends. I shake it off and ask, "What is this?"

Gigi doesn't answer. She just wades toward a drinks table and lets me choose whether to follow her. I do.

I think we must be in the onion dome. Little glittering lights hang like glow worms somewhere far above. I'm not sure what they are, but I like them. The room itself is dim, mostly lit by torches on wrought-iron stands, which are incongruent with what looks like a modern boxing ring raised in the center.

The people milling around are no more consistent. They wear clothes from different eras, going back further than I can identify. About the only thing that unites them is that they all seem to be the formal version of whatever time period they've come dressed in, and they all seem very comfortable and natural in them.

"Is this a costume party?" I ask Gigi, who rolls her eyes but at least answers me this time.

"No," she says. "If anything, it's the opposite."

I stare, waiting. She'll continue, or she won't. I'm not going to beg for every little dribble of information, and I don't think she'll try to make me if I stand my ground.

She caves before I do.

"All right, newbie. There are some things you're going to need to know if you somehow stop the local wizardling from wiping your brain. First: what you see when you look at us—any of us—is a lie. A kind of illusion magic that the wizards some thousand years or so ago threw in as part of the deal when they made a treaty with us. Mainly it's a 'we don't bother them, and they don't bother us' sort of deal, but the illusions made it possible for us to stay generally out of the limelight, which was something they cared about. A lot, apparently.

"But any decent illusion has to be flexible if it's going to last. It works more with what the viewer expects to see than it does with the original wizards' ideas of where fashion would go in the future. Make sense?"

I nod, but don't interrupt.

"Right. So when what *you* would call a supernatural creature is out and about in the world, their intention is to fit in. The illusion was made to portray that intention in a way that's congruent with what they are and what they're doing. You see a loaded vampire out on the town, you're going to see in-season Armani. You see a couple of dryads hanging out at an environmentalist rally, you're going to see hand-me-down sundresses. If they attack you with magic, chances are you'll think it's a knife or a gun. It's a marriage between what is, what's intended, and how you can perceive it without breaking the illusion."

I don't comment on the implicit polygamy in her figurative language. I have a thousand quibbles and questions, and I'm pretty sure I'm going to come up with more— mostly to do with what-ifs and edge cases. But I only allow myself one.

"So, your apron's not real?" I ask, remembering how

real it looked lying on the dish sink at the Emporium, not attached to her body in any way.

Gigi rolls her eyes. "Nothing's ever all one way or another in magic, newbie. Some of us also buy clothes. It's…" I get the sudden certainty she's remembering something else while she speaks. "… a compromise."

I want to push, but I don't. Alienating the closest thing to a friend I have here seems like not such a good idea. I redirect to the scene in front of us.

"So right now, they're not trying to fit in. They're trying to be comfortable but formal. Dressed up in the way that they want to be. But they still look human to me, and anything magical they do will look as normal to me as it can. So when they get in the ring…"

Gigi smiles. I think she's starting to warm up to me again.

"The fight will look very different to you than it does to anyone else here, yes."

I look around the room, considering, trying to absorb what Gigi has just told me.

"Seems like a pretty big disadvantage to the humans in a fight," I say, more to myself than to her.

Gigi answers at a similar volume. "It was a *deal*, human. Wizards got what they wanted. We got what we wanted."

"And humans weren't in the room." Do I sound mad? I might.

Gigi fixes me with a stare, and answers as though it had never occurred to her before. "No, I guess you weren't. Do you think you should have been?"

I'm formulating an answer when the torchlights dim, and the conversation around us quiets.

"Ladies, gentlemen, and everything in between and on all sides, I welcome you tonight to my humble domain."

Aloysius the chance demon stands on a pedestal I hadn't noticed on the other side of the ring. Was it there before, or did he rise up on it like a leading lady with a flair for the dramatic? He's speaking in a normal conversational tone, but I hear him as though he were directly in front of me.

"Tonight, for your viewing pleasure, I present a battle to death or dismemberment. For the first competitor, I select…"

His eyes rove over the crowd, as if searching for something I can't see.

"You." He indicates with one hand, and a beam of light much like the one around him comes up around a nondescript man in a plain brown houndstooth suit with a pair of thick tortoiseshell spectacles. He looks dull and inevitable. And very, very afraid.

"Oh, that's unfortunate," Gigi says under her breath.

"Why?" I ask, terrified on behalf of the man. He may have come here knowing the possibility—unlike me—but he's too scared not to feel sorry for.

"That, newbie, is a graveling. Big on rules. *Loves* order and permission. Manmade, natural… whatever kind of order they can get their roots on. But they usually shun combat. They're fragile by our standards, so they find other ways to get what they want."

I scan the crowd. Few other people seem to agree with Gigi that the graveling's selection was "unfortunate." Too many faces look far too eager. It's disgusting.

"And for the other competitor," Aloysius continues, "I select… you."

This time, he indicates a bright-eyed woman wearing stylized armor. Her eyes light up with the floor around her, and her mouth is set in a grim smile.

"Well, that's the graveling done for," Gigi says. I look at

her questioningly, and she answers my glance. "Valkyrie. You should have heard of them. Famously do *not* shun combat."

I note the change in her body language. I hadn't noticed she was tense exactly, but it's clear she's loosened up—if stone can loosen.

"Were you nervous Aloysius would pick you?" I needle her.

She doesn't look at me. "I don't like killing," she says, like she's talking about craft beer. "And I don't like dismembering. It always creates *such* grudges, and those never end well. I don't like having to remember them."

Even if I didn't know she was telling the truth by nature, I'd believe her.

"Place your bets," the demon says, and the hum of conversation that followed the selection process dies to nothing in an instant. Around me, everyone closes their eyes, including Gigi. It reminds me of the time on vacation when I was a kid that my aunt's family carted us to Mass along with them. That same feeling of prayer in the air. The same sensation of being an anthropologist standing on the other side of the glass, observing and torn between wanting to belong and being afraid of what belonging would mean.

"Very good," the demon says, and as one, everyone raises their eyes and turns them to the competitors.

I haven't looked at either of them since the selection, but now they're both in boxing outfits, which I suppose makes sense. I wonder how much of what they wore has changed underneath. Do they wear clothes? What are they?

My hand slips up to the glasses on my head, but they meet Gigi's fingers instead.

"Don't," she says. I obey.

The fight isn't formalized. There's no official "go," no referee in the ring, no bells. Just fists, blood, and chaos. It turns out a lot of immortal beings are tall—or at least a lot of the ones around here going to a fight night are—and I have trouble seeing the action. I wouldn't have minded, but Gigi notices and leads me up to a series of risers that I hadn't noticed before. I end up a little farther away from the fight, but with a better view. One of those things bothers me more than the other.

I've never been to a boxing match, but I don't think they're very long, are they? But this one feels like it goes on for an eternity. Death or dismemberment with fists. Or, at least, with whatever a thousand-year-old wizard illusion interprets as fists. I don't have an appetite for violence, and my disgust grows with each hit.

The man with the tortoiseshell spectacles is doing well, all things considered. His heart seems to be less in the offense, but he's defending admirably, I think. The expression of fear that came over him with the selection light never fully leaves his face, even when he's landing a hit.

And the crowd is *into it*. I can tell who each bet on without a shadow of a doubt.

I hate them all. I hate their bloodlust, even directed within their own faction. I hate their casual acceptance of the coming death. I hate their yearning for it. I hate the game they make of it.

I look at the chance demon, ready to hate him for his joy in the proceedings.

But I don't see joy. I don't see fun. I see a clenched jaw and sharp eyes that dart to mine a split second after I start looking.

I look away from him. I don't want to look at the ring,

but I do. If he can look, I can look. Someone should witness this with something other than glee. The man in the tortoiseshell spectacles deserves it.

More blood, more hits, more pain, more screaming. It's monotonous. Until the blonde woman pulls out a dagger and sinks it into the frightened man's side.

I stop breathing. There are gasps and cheers as the man stumbles. He's trying to say a word, but I can't tell what it is. He's too far away. There's too much happening.

Another stab, in his other side. The man's mouth gapes open like he's trying to scream.

I scramble down the risers and dart through the crowd toward the ring. Everyone feels bigger than me. Stronger. Even the ones that don't look like it. I shouldn't shove. I shouldn't upset anyone. People really shouldn't get mad about being shoved in a crowd, but probably not a great idea to put human-based assumptions on… whatever these things are.

Cries of joy and despair rise through the crowd. He must have been stabbed again. It disrupts the solid mass of bodies enough that I can weave through to the edge of the ring, so I can hear his words. His last words.

"Cheating!" I make out finally as his eyes search the hungry crowd, looking for someone to listen. His gaze is angry and desperate. "She's cheating!"

Holy fucking shit, I hope my amulet works against… everything here.

I climb up into the ring, breathing harder than I should, trembling with fear. My feet are unsteady on the ring, and I wonder what material it is underneath. Some people are motioning to me to get out of the way. I'm causing an upset. Well, more than an upset. Confusion at my presence in the ring—a human where a human does *not* belong—travels out through the crowd like ripples in a lake.

"She's cheating!" I scream in the loudest voice I can, throwing a snowball at an avalanche. "She's cheating!"

And then it all stops: the fight, the sound, the rolling beads of sweat down the faces of the shouting mass before me.

"Is she?" the chance demon says. I look up at where he stands, still on his pedestal. Is it the pedestal that gives him the powers he's exhibited standing on it, or is it just him? I don't ask.

"I think she is," I say. "I've been watching them fight with their fists, and she pulled out a knife. The wizard's illusion—"

"Is a lie that reveals the truth, I know," he says lightly. His gaze rests on the bleeding man on the floor of the ring. I feel like a child explaining a playground fight to a teacher. I was always a teacher's pet, so the feeling comes natural to me.

"He's lucky a human was here."

I look at the crowd.

"Was I lucky I was here?" I ask.

The demon smiles. "Yes, Elizabeth, you are. I have a sense about these things."

I don't remember telling him my name.

And then I stumble back as the screaming of the crowd hits me again. I hear the demon's voice again, but the quality of it is different than it was a moment ago. He's back to his artificial magical amplification tricks again, so everyone in the room can hear him when he says, "I declare a draw. The eight individuals who predicted this outcome may collect their due later tonight in my office. For the rest of you, make arrangements to pay what you owe… or I will collect."

Hundreds of pairs of hateful eyes pin me. What was it Gigi said about grudges? I look down at the pool of blood on the floor of the ring where the frightened man had been. He'd fled so quickly; I hadn't even seen how.

I hope he was worth it. But then again… I couldn't have done anything else, could I?

NINE

A Gift

I sit down in a clean portion of the ring and wait for the room to clear out before leaving. I'm physically exhausted, which I wouldn't expect, considering I didn't do much physical exertion. I guess adrenaline doesn't care if you put it to use or not—it'll take what you owe it either way.

Regardless, I'm not muscling my way through a crowd of supernatural creatures who—except for the eight whose bets I won for them—all hate me.

Gigi has no problem wading through the teeming masses, though, and she comes and stands next to the ring, folding her arms and leaning them on the ropes. I can't tell whether I'm reading pity or amusement on her face.

"Do you think that was wise?" she asks.

I shrug. "I don't know. You tell me."

She regards the thinning crowd. "I don't know, either. You made a lot of enemies, and I don't think the man you saved will be helpful to you. But you do look more like yourself."

I'm too tired to stop the expression of wonderment

from crossing my face. "You say that based on what, exactly?"

Gigi shrugs. "Instinct."

I join her in watching the crowd, and neither of us speak for a long moment.

"This is real, isn't it?" I say at last, defeated and exhausted. "Magic. All of it. It's real."

"Yes," Gigi says. "It is."

We don't talk for the ten minutes or so it takes the crowd to grow thin enough that I don't mind making my way through it. Just before I leave the ring, I take a second to flip my glasses down, making sure I only look at the pooled blood—all that remains of the man with the glasses.

It's rich, dark dirt.

Huh.

Gigi seems to know how to operate the elevator, which I'm grateful for. She takes us all the way to the first floor, so we avoid the poker players, but I have to go through quite a few rows of slot machines. Back here, underneath the balcony, the hard stone floor of the casino gives way to lush, expensive-looking carpeting. If it were real, I'm pretty sure a room of it would set me back more than anything I own, other than my house and maybe my car, with a generous buyer on a good day.

When we get to the lobby, just in sight of the big vase of jeweled flowers on the little table, Aloysius is waiting for us.

We stop a little farther from him than I would usually stop before someone who clearly wants to talk to me. Maybe I'm afraid of him. I don't know. He pulls a small, blue sapphire chrysanthemum from the vase and closes the excess distance in a few long strides.

"You did well," he says with a gentleness and familiarity he hasn't earned. "Go on. Take it. It belongs to you."

He offers me the flower, and I do take it. Maybe I shouldn't, but I do. I don't know why. In any case, taking it makes him smile and step out of our way, so we can get out of the casino and head back into the field surrounding it.

As soon as I clear the last step, the jeweled flower in my hands transforms into a real chrysanthemum, but it's dead and dry and brittle. I'm not sure it'll survive in the pocket of my jacket, but I tuck it away regardless. The demon could still be watching.

"So," I say, trying to turn a page in my mind. "I guess now would be a good time to tell me how the fuck we got here and how I'm getting home?"

There's a shift in Gigi, a loosening much like when she wasn't chosen for the fight. This must be what relief looks like on her.

"This is a crossroads," she explains in a teacherly tone, looping her arm through mine and leading me farther away from the casino, toward where we appeared in the field. "It's a gathering point. All supernatural creatures can use them. Whichever of the eight points of the compass we step toward, it takes us to the closest crossroads in that direction. We can walk between the crossroads, but if we go from one to another, we lose our starting point. And most crossroads are in the middle of nowhere. They bother humans, though they can't put a finger on why, so they don't tend to build or settle near them. Generally, it's much more convenient to keep to the closest eight. That's why there were so few people there tonight. It was mainly just those whose closest crossroads in one of the directions was this one. We call that the crossroad's *catchment*."

Seemed to me like a lot of people were there tonight. I

do what I should have done when we first got there and pull out my phone to look at where we are on the map.

"A hundred miles?!"

Gigi smiles at me and steps forward. When her foot comes down, we're standing where we were before that whole… adventure. Or whatever it was. The industrial dishwasher is still diligently sloshing away, and the scent of disinfectant fills my nose.

I'm not ready to leave the world of explanations quite yet, though, so I keep questioning Gigi. No longer standing in the field with the casino lighting us from one side, the questions feel more outlandish. "Why don't you live by the crossroads? Why don't any of you? Does it bother you, too? The way it bothers us?"

She walks back behind the counter. "Because all sorts of things use the crossroads, not all of them friendly."

"Like wizards?"

She shakes her head as she reaches down somewhere I can't see and pulls up a very well-kept vintage purse.

"No, not wizards. They're still human. Sort of. They can't use the crossroads unless we take them with us, the way I took you. But other things. It's a wild world out there, newbie."

She grins that grin that I know what's behind. Before I can respond, she's ushering me toward the front door. She's faster than she should be. I don't know why I didn't notice it before. Maybe she's been holding herself back?

Then we're outside.

"It's closing time," she says, and she's gone. Not in the blink of an eye like she's walking the crossroads, but she's walking away so swiftly. I blink my eyes. I catch her just before she's out of earshot of my slightly raised voice.

"Do you think Aloysius was telling the truth? About not being behind… what we asked him about?"

She turns, and I'm mostly sure it's my imagination that her skin gleams like marble in the orange glow of a streetlight. Her thoughtful expression strikes me even at this distance. "You can never be sure with him. But yes, I think so."

"That's bad, isn't it?"

She's perfectly still for a long moment. She nods her head once, and then she begins moving again—out of sight in a matter of seconds.

I blink, alone again in the cold air. I start to put myself back together and take stock of my surroundings, free from the mental glare of Gigi's presence. How long were we at the casino? It hadn't felt like the entire evening, but the Arts District has emptied out considerably.

I look at my phone. It's after ten. Three hours. The casino must be wrong with time somehow. I'm impressed and confused, but not shocked. The whole thing still feels like a dream to me, and dreams never play by the rules of time.

I head home, trying to put together the pieces of what I saw. Trying to remember the faces under the great dome. I want to be able to identify them if I see them again, but the whole thing feels a little fuzzy. Am I going to forget about it all come morning? Do I want to?

Max wants to wipe my memories of all of this. Maybe I should let him.

Maybe. If it weren't for the fact that people are dying, and I trust him to do something about it about as far as I can throw him. Plus, I think I just pissed off hundreds of supernatural beings—most of whom probably live somewhere in my general neck of the woods.

God, I'm tired. I want to go to bed when I roll back in through my front door, but I know I won't sleep. Instead, I drag out the chair and climb up into the attic.

Without any light coming in through the windows, I have to rely on the one bare, dust-covered incandescent bulb dangling from the ceiling. It's not enough, so I supplement with the light from my phone.

Paging through the trove already feels familiar. It takes a few minutes to get everything out and find where I left off earlier. Then I start going through it as fast as I can. I know what I'm looking for.

With what I saw tonight, I need protection. The amulet is something, but I need more. Whatever the wards around this box are, I'm pretty sure they're something I want.

It's an hour of searching, feeling arrhythmic pangs of grief at my father's handwriting as they cut through the dull monotony of skimming, startled at how close his mind feels yet how far away he is. I can't pay too close attention to any one spell or any one description of a supernatural being. Pretty sure I don't want to know too much about the supernatural beings described and recorded in here… it's too easy to imagine them behind the faces from the fighting hall. I find a bound book by someone named Wilhelm that seems, based on the illustrations and my father's notes, to be solely devoted to describing supernatural beings. It's not what I'm looking for right now, though, so I only have enough spare attention to notice a page is missing before I move on.

Finally, I come to it. The instructions for the wards are blessedly short. They're not in English, but my father's scribbling on the sticky note is in quotations, so I'm pretty sure it's as exact a translation as he could manage.

Place these wards around that which you would protect from harmful intentions toward the rightful owner. The ends must meet.

Intention, again. Why does magic have to run on intention? It makes for such fuzzy boundaries for something that otherwise seems so clear-cut. At least there's no activation involved in this one. I just get the wards in place, and that's it. I think. But the careful, precise strokes around the cabinet—that my father was capable of executing but that I didn't inherit—tell me it's probably going to be easier said than done.

This is in one of those sheaves of some kind of parchment, held together incongruously with one of those alligator clips that always reminds me of my stint as a temp worker at various midmarket, somewhat backward offices near Philly. I pull the slim page out. The only other sticky note on it, other than the translation of the instructions, says one word: *Basement.*

Of course. Down there they won't be disturbed. And they'll protect the house, right? In theory? I don't know much about magic—not yet—but my dad clearly spent a lot of time reading what's in here, and if he thought it would work if I put these wards around the basement, that seems like a good idea to try. At least until I find something that tells me different.

I run my cleanup routine, tucking the trove away in its cabinet and hiding it behind the table skirt. Then I turn off the bare bulb and head downstairs. I have to go outside to reach the basement—it's one of those with a metal hatch on the side of the house and no interior access—so I set the paper down on the kitchen table. I don't know why I don't want to bring it outside, but I don't. I snap a quick picture with my phone in case I need to reference it when I'm down there.

It's cold out, and I wish I hadn't taken my yellow jacket off when I got home. Some safety blankets are dual-purpose, and my yellow jacket is one of them. The hatch to the basement has a lock on it, but this one I have the key to, unlike the one holding up the attic. The lock is rusty, and it fights me, adding a measure of frustration to my pile of exhaustion by the time I descend into the darkness beyond the hatch.

I feel like I'm in one of those archeological horror movies when I'm finally standing in the space, using the light from my phone's flashlight in lieu of the burnt-out lightbulb that no one had thought to replace, and that I'm pretty sure I should turn the breaker off before I mess with.

But despite the dim light, I find what I'm looking for: my father's attempt at protecting our home. There are three lines of wards. They must have taken him forever. They're careful, and to my eyes, they look perfect. My father was an artist. Why didn't I realize that when he was alive?

They're not perfect, though. If they had been, Max wouldn't have been able to come in. I'm certain if there's a test for harmful intentions, he'd fail it.

"Your mission, if you're willing to accept it…" I joke aloud. It isn't funny, but I laugh. Jesus, I'm tired.

When I finally go to bed, I keep my amulet on and tuck the parchment with the instructions for the wards underneath the mattress right below me, where no one could take it without disturbing me. It's the only way I can sleep.

And even then, I dream of glowworms lighting mounds of blood-soaked dirt laced through with bloody coins. I'm digging through the mounds, pulling out coins and piling them up behind me. But every time I turn around to look at the stack, it's gone.

TEN

An Accessory

I sleep until after eleven, but I'm still tired when I wake. I could have slept for a year longer and not minded. But even if I don't have the return of normalcy to propel me forward, at least I have a task today.

I'm pretty sure I know how to do this. I just need a few things, but they should be easy enough to get. At least, I think they will be. But I have to get a shower and some coffee in me quick to make it to the library in time to catch my sister on her lunch break.

The Springfield Public Library isn't called the Springfield Public Library, but the name of the old dead guy it's named after is hard to pronounce, so no one bothers trying. For a while after she started working there, my sister Olivia corrected people, but she gave that up years ago. The building itself is grand, comprising four over-height stories with a lobby that spans all the way up three of them. It's brick, but the kind of uniform brick that manages to look modern. There's also a basement below that I've always had the sense went on forever, but I've only convinced Olivia to take me down there twice, and both

times she watched me like a hawk to make sure I didn't
wander off and get into something I shouldn't. Completely
unfair. I'm very responsible.

I wander deep into the stacks on the fourth floor in the
southeast corner of the building. It's all non-fiction up
here, and I know she likes to eat her lunch surrounded by
volumes on the history of Siberia and Central Asia. There
is a break room tucked behind the circulation desk, but I
don't blame Olivia for avoiding it.

Olivia is bookish in the best possible way. I think if she
were ever not in a cardigan, one would emerge fully
formed from her skin. She's only six years older than me,
but she's reading her eyes into an early grave, and she
always has a pair from her ever-growing collection of
reading glasses around her neck on a silver string. Today,
it's the green ones.

I've always thought her features are prettier than mine,
but mostly because there's more kindness behind them. As
her two daughters have grown and ventured out into the
world to go to school and playdates, there's more worry
back there, too. But she wears it well.

She has a Tupperware container full of some kind of
casserole that smells amazing. Faisal left some meals for me
in the fridge before he headed overseas, but both Olivia
and her husband are better cooks than he is.

"Here to steal my lunch?"

"I would *never*," I reply with mock offense and pull an
apple from my purse as I sit down.

Olivia smiles and shovels a little bit of her casserole
onto the Tupperware container lid, which she then slides
over to me. When I start picking at it with my fingers, she
raises an eyebrow and slides over the paper towel she's
brought as a napkin.

"What, like you have a spare fork?" I respond to the silent admonishment.

"I'm surprised you didn't bring one."

I gasp, turning my mock offense from earlier up to eleven. "How presumptuous do you think I am?"

She laughs. I feel closer to her than I have in a long time. There are so many of the same things I have in me hiding behind her laugh. I don't ask her how she's "holding up," and she doesn't ask me. Instead, she tells me about some drama that happened earlier at the Young Learners and Readers group, which she knows I devour like our grandmother used to devour the latest episode of her favorite soap opera. I've never met the mothers and fathers involved in the drama, and I hope I never do. They could never possibly live up to my image of them.

"I thought you were back at work this week?" she asks eventually, having exhausted the juiciest morsels. I *could* come visit her on my lunch break when I'm working, and I sometimes even do. But I dress better for work than the assortment of mostly clean clothing I've tossed on. She doesn't comment that I'm finally wearing the leather jacket she bought me over eight years ago, but I'd like to think she's glad about it.

"Nah, going back next week," I say, hoping she pretends to buy my casual tone. She does.

"So, other than the tuna, what brings you here?"

I don't begrudge her the assumption—it's accurate. "I was wondering… do you still have the scanner you used for that digitization program you were working on a few years ago?"

Her brow furrows. "I think so. We don't use it for anything anymore, but it's there. Sitting in a box."

I nod. "Do you think I could check it out?"

Olivia's not a senior librarian by any stretch. She's

been working here almost fifteen years now, sure, starting with summer jobs in high school. But there's a group of women and a couple of men who have been working at the library since the concept of time was the hot new thing. She could still probably help me, though. She has the authority that only comes with competence in an environment that recognizes it, however begrudgingly.

"Sure, I could slap a barcode on it. We rent out those DIY tools, and cake pans, and the 3D printer. Don't see how it's any different."

"*Awesome*," I exaggerate. It's not *that* big of an ask, but still. Good to know somebody.

"What do you need it for?"

I'm not going to lie to my sister, but I'm not going to tell her the truth, either. "I found some of Dad's old papers in the attic that I want to preserve."

I can't tell whether she's surprised or not, or whether she feels any kind of way about it at all. When we were divvying up what was left of Dad's life, it made the most sense for me to get the house, since her girls were in school, and the house would put them in a different school. Plus, it's smaller than their current place, and more run down. But anything to do with Dad, and she shuts down in a whirlwind of practicality.

"Well, if you want help archiving, I'm pretty good at that. I've got a very expensive paper that says so and everything."

"I'll keep that in mind."

She fixes me with a stare and raises an eyebrow. "So… what else do you need?"

I go to say, "who says there's anything else?" but fuck it. Life is short, and I'm tired. "Do you loan out any of those cutter things that people use for crafts?"

She thinks for a second, and when she doesn't answer

immediately, I know the answer is no. My sister may occasionally forget my middle name, but she never forgets anything that enters her domain.

"No…" she says after a moment. "But you know who would have one? Mr. Thompson across the street. His wife got one back when they first came out, remember? Maybe he threw it out after she died, but I've always thought he was the kind to hold on to things."

"Oh yeah," I say, not doubting her assessment. If anyone would recognize someone who wants to hold on to things, it would be Olivia.

She finishes her lunch, talking about her girls and her husband, Peter, and the last time she talked to Mom. She's a little spare on the details of how Mom's doing, probably because she doesn't have many. When we lost Dad to the hospital, we lost Mom to Florida. We try to keep in touch, but she always feels so much older than she should be, and it hurts to hear how much she doesn't want to remember about our entire lives. I've told her about Faisal multiple times, but she always seems to forget his name by the end of the conversation.

On a trip down to visit her, we were able to convince her to see a doctor to be evaluated for early-onset dementia or Alzheimer's. Neither of us knew how to feel when the results came back clean in every quarter. She has the capacity to remember us. She just doesn't care, no matter how much we try to lure her in with rosy pictures of our lives. She just listens to us talk and gripes about Florida. She never minds when we call, but she never calls either of us. Olivia's better about calling her anyway and forcing through it than I am.

When we get up to head downstairs, I slip my apple into Olivia's bag. She likes them, and I only *think* I do when I'm grocery shopping. She notices but doesn't acknowledge the gift. We step up to the circulation desk, and I make small talk with a kid from the high school across the street who's manning the desk as part of a work-study period during the school day. Olivia disappears off to somewhere to find the scanner. I can tell by the way the student talks to me that she thinks Olivia walks on water, and I do nothing to dissuade her from that notion. She's right.

Olivia checks me out, rolling her eyes that I don't have my library card with me, forcing her to look me up manually before we say our goodbyes. She offers to help me with the scanner, but I refuse. It's not heavy, and I'm starting to feel the weight of all the things I'm not telling her. We let each other go with a slightly too-long hug, and I head for home.

On the way, I stop in at the hardware store to pick up some construction adhesive. I know nothing about what I'm looking for, and I'm nervous the salesman is going to try and ask me questions about what, exactly, I'm trying to affix permanently to my basement wall. But thanks to the glory of capitalism and the soul-grinding nature of retail, he's not the slightest bit curious. I load up on more tubes than the rough calculations he helps me figure out say I need, and I buy a caulk gun. I'm only a little disappointed that Faisal isn't here so we can giggle at the word like children.

Not that I'd tell him what I'm using it for so he could help. I don't think? I push the thought back.

When I get back home, after I stash my treasures away in the house, I head across the street to Mr. Thompson's house.

Mr. Thompson moved in across the street from us when I was twelve. He's easy to talk to in the way a wood stove in someone's house makes a neighborhood feel like camping: it's not the main point, but an unavoidable side effect. He's as solid a man as I've ever met. He's only somewhere in his forties, but he *feels* older, especially if you've ever experienced the comedic joy of watching him attempting to interact with technology. I always think I smell sawdust any time I get near him. I don't know if the sawdust smell is real, or a remnant of being in his shop class for a semester back in high school.

When he answers the door, he has a grim smile on his face that I remember well from when I used to live here. Back when I didn't have a crazy dad—and certainly not a dead one.

"What can I help you with?" he asks after our hellos, and I'm grateful he doesn't offer me condolences. He already has, but I've noticed some people like to double up. I don't know why. Gives them something to say, I guess.

I explain what I'm looking for, and true to Olivia's assessment, he still has whatever of his late wife's crafting supplies no one's asked for since her death twelve years ago. He informs me that the device I'm asking after is called a Cricut as he leads me to the exact right box in an impeccably organized storage unit.

Mr. Thompson was younger than I am now when his wife died. It hits me as I watch him treat the box containing the Cricut cutter with measured care. At the time, I knew it was unfair, the way things that you can't really grasp that happen to other people are unfair. But I didn't realize until now just how *wrong* it was.

On the way back out, I realize what's bothering me about Mr. Thompson's house. It feels exactly the same as it did last time I was in it. That couldn't have been long before Dad lost his mind.

They were friends, right? Is everything really so exactly the same, or is my memory just not that great? Eight years is a long time for nothing to change at all. Eight years is a long time to be in stasis.

"Offer stands," he says, when I've passed back through the front door and he lingers in the doorway. I'm confused at first, but then he shifts his eyes toward my house and back, and I understand. He came over with condolences and a houseplant not long after Dad passed. I didn't think more responsibility was what I would want at the time, but some new life hadn't gone amiss in the end. In that brief, painless-as-possible conversation, he offered his DIY guidance in fixing the place up, when I was ready for it.

"You really don't remember how badly I did in woodshop, do you?" I make the joke I hadn't been able to make a week ago.

"Oh, I remember. But I also remember how hard you tried. People who try can get their way through anything." He gives me his most exuberant smile, which is still pretty subtle. I don't cry.

"Thanks for this," I say, holding up the box. He smiles in return, and I turn and walk across the street back toward home.

ELEVEN

A Necessary Measure

I don't realize until I get the Cricut back home and look online to download the right drivers—yes, this model is *that* old—just how expensive this thing must have been back in the day. I'm surprised no one asked Mr. Thompson if they could have it sooner, but I guess you can't ask for what you don't know is there.

The internet seems to think this thing is intuitive and user-friendly. Maybe that's true for newer models, but it takes me well over an hour to get this one set up and ready to start cutting the wards pattern out from the spare vinyl sheets that Mr. Thompson provided. I cut out the fire symbol as a practice shape and stash it in the back of a drawer.

The vinyl feels like sturdy material, and I'm cautiously optimistic about how well it'll hold up. It seems like a simple task to make these permanent, but it's an important one. I don't want these things falling down unexpectedly because of water or rats or whatever destructive forces of nature happen to basements and keep home insurance companies up at night.

I've got the image of the wards scanned in, and I'm amazed again at how clean and perfect and straight the lines are, written in ink in the book. They were clearly done freehand in unhurried strokes—and well before computers—but when I blow the image up just the right amount, everything lines up to nice round inches or fractions of inches. I could probably make this thing a vector, I think. I'm about eighty percent sure I understand what vectors are, and that seems right to me.

When I can avoid it no longer, I head down to the basement and start making measurements. Measure twice, cut once seems like good general-use advice, but for these purposes I measure three times. I even break out a level app on my phone to determine that my dad's lines of wards are level, and that I can use them as a basis to measure the total length I'll need to cover to encircle the basement.

And then it's time for the math. The patterns at the end have to line up perfectly, which means that I need to make sure that the size I make them—as large as I can get away with to maximize my allowable margin of error—needs to wrap perfectly around the basement and meet with the ends at the exact same place in the pattern. This is straightforward in practice, but I triple-check my calculations and try to make sure I'm taking everything into account, especially in the corners.

It feels like I've been working on this forever by the time I'm ready to start cutting. In comparison to everything else, the actual cutting out of the patterns, taping them together, and gluing them to the wall with construction adhesive is kind of fun in its simplicity. I'm not an artist like my dad, but that doesn't mean I don't enjoy creating something with my hands. The adhesive doesn't even smell bad after the first few minutes. I think I'll screw in some boards to hide the wards from view and sandwich them securely onto the walls at some point, but I don't have to do that right now.

I try to think of a good way to test the wards. I could get something I *know* has harmful intentions toward me and see if it can get it here. My slightly loopy mind, still haunted by the pictures I saw yesterday, thinks of getting Gigi to kidnap a tiger from the zoo. And then it makes that idea slightly more reasonable by imagining her using the ferocious German Shepherd down the street instead.

But that sounds like a bad plan. Even if Gigi wanted to help, these plans sound fun and innovative, which I've learned is a sign that I'm having a terrible idea. While I'm casting around for better ones, something occurs to me.

I go up into the attic, wishing not for the first time that this house had been built with more sets of stairs and fewer ladders and exterior access hatches. I bring the lantern up with me, still in the bag from the night before. Sitting in front of the cabinet, I flip my glasses down. That green glow still permeates the bag when the lantern is inside it.

I fish the lantern out of the bag, place it in the cabinet, and shut the door. Nothing. The cabinet wards block the magic. A smile, all the more welcome for all its rarity these past weeks, stretches my lips. I grab the lantern and head downstairs. At first, I figure I'll carry it down to the basement to test it there, but then I think better of it. I want the wards to protect the whole house, so I may as well test it on the first floor.

First, I set the lantern outside on the back porch and close the door behind it. From the inside, with my glasses on, I can see the door glowing green.

Okay, time to switch places. I step outside and put the lantern in the house. No glow.

A thrill of excitement runs down my body. But I'm not

satisfied yet. I open the door and look through my glasses at the lantern.

No flame.

I reach my hand in to grab the lantern and run the test again, and notice that as soon as any part of me crosses the threshold, the magic of the object is visible again.

I grab the lantern and head back up to the attic, feeling pretty pleased with myself, to be honest. Without a bag to sling over my shoulder, getting up the ladder with one hand is a little awkward, but I manage. Once up there, I make my way over to the part of the attic that overhangs the porch. The basement, I feel sure, having gone down and looked at it twice, doesn't go underneath the porch. I'm not sure this is all kosher from a code standpoint, but it does seem like an interesting little space to have—inside the house but outside the wards.

I set the lantern outside the wards and confirm I can still see it. I don't doubt that I will, but it feels thorough to check. Then, just as I did downstairs, I trade places with the lantern. The second all of me is out on the space over the porch, the lantern flame disappears. When I put even a toe back over where I assume the wards must be, in an even line with the inside of the walls, I can see the light again. As always, it's leaning steadfastly toward the Arts District, presumably toward where Gigi stands, scooping out ice cream and pressing espresso grounds.

By George, I think I've done it! A part of me wants to call Gigi, to show off what an accomplished little non-wizard I am. But that part of me is outweighed by the memory of the sharpness of her smile when seen through the glasses. She may have been the least intimidating person I met yesterday, but I shouldn't be lulled into imagining she's harmless, however tempting that lie may be.

I can't shake feeling like I'm the unpopular character

being invited to sit with the cool kids in an eighties teen movie that isn't as funny in retrospect as it was meant to be at the time. It's just a matter of time until the joke is revealed, and Gigi… I don't know… eats me or something.

But if she wants to do that, the wards will stop her now. Maybe. Probably. I think.

More importantly, the trove is protected, and any magic I manage to do in here should—I think—be harder for Mr. Wizard to sniff out. Both of these things are a relief, and I head down to the living room and sit down heavily on the couch, smug and self-satisfied and a little tired.

There's so much dust in here. Is there always so much dust in here? I watch it glitter in the afternoon light coming through the living room bay window. All this busy work distracted me, and I had more lined up. I have the scanner with its shiny new bar code sitting right by the ladder to the attic. I could spend the rest of the day methodically scanning in the trove so that I can more easily analyze, translate, archive, and search it.

But I know what I'm trying to distract myself from with it, and I shouldn't give in to that impulse. The option to hide is a mirage, and I know it.

I pick up the phone and dial Angela's desk. She sits on the other side of the room at work, but only lives a couple of blocks away. The joys of a small town. Well, small-*ish* town with a limited number of neighborhoods that are both affordable on a civil servant's salary and safe enough to appeal to the kind of people who become civil servants.

"Good afternoon, this is Angela! How can I help?"

The phrase hasn't changed since the time four years ago when I sat next to Angela for a while, and it annoys me now just like it did back then. I appreciate Angela's cheerfulness. I appreciate that it's useful. I just think it's best taken in manageable portions. Sitting five feet from her for eight-to-twelve hours a day might have overdosed me on it.

"Hey Angela, it's Elizabeth."

I can hear her expression of intense concern when she replies. It's probably genuine, but it's always struck me as hollow in a way I feel guilty for thinking. "Hey, Lizzie." No one calls me Lizzie. "How are you holding up?"

I try to sound hard-pressed but determined. "Oh, you know. I'm hanging in there."

"That's good," she says, drawing out the O-sound just a little too much.

"Hey, Angela. I just realized that I accidentally left some stuff on my desk yesterday, and I was hoping you could bring it back home with you so I could swing by and grab it from your place. There's a file and some really delicious cookies Linda made me, and…"

I hear a voice in the background on the other end of the line. A familiar voice.

"Hey, Angie, that's not Lizzie, is it?"

Ice water runs through the veins. What the fuck is Max doing there? Why the fuck is there a wizard in my office? I find Angela annoying at times, but a fierce feeling of protection over her pulls me up off of the couch as though I were going to run there and beat Max and his nonconsensual mind-mojo off her with my deeply inexperienced fists.

"You know… it is! What are the chances? Do you want to talk to her?"

Her cheerfulness sounds a little less hollow when she's talking to him. Maybe it isn't usually as genuine as I think.

"Sure, that would be great! Haven't heard from her in ages." I hear the muffled sound of the phone changing hands as my heart pumps. "Lizzie, you know, I had no idea you were working here."

My voice sticks in my throat. "What are you doing there?"

"I think it's going to be so great to be able to work together again. I had no idea our fields would overlap so much, but as long as they are, I'm happy I'll get the chance to be involved with whatever you're doing."

Jesus, he doesn't sound even remotely natural. How is anyone buying this?

"You just walked in and took someone's job?"

"Yeah," he says. "I'm a special assistant. I pitched a special project to Sharon, and wouldn't you know, she loved it. I just have that effect on people, I guess."

I feel helpless at a distance. I know the office isn't my home, and those people aren't my family, but I brought a snake into the nest, and now I can't breathe.

"Did you fuck with Sharon's brain?"

He chuckles. "Something to be said for natural charm. I don't know. People just like me."

"Natural charm that's not so natural, is it?"

He chuckles like I've just shared an old inside joke with him. "That's right." Before I can say anything else, he keeps going. "Say, there were some cookies on your desk. I hope you don't mind, but I ate one. You left a file out, too. You wouldn't like me to bring them to you, would you? I'd love the chance to catch up."

"Absolutely not."

"Great, great. I'll head over there soon."

At least if he's coming here, he won't be there. That's something. He hasn't outright threatened any of my coworkers, but he doesn't have to. His threat is implicit in his presence.

"Fuck you," I say.

He chuckles again—that same cheerful, intimate sound. "You too, Lizzie."

TWELVE

An Impostor

Rationally, I know this is an excellent chance to test the efficacy of the wards I just put up. It's reasonable. But two things make me scramble to throw on my jacket and my shoes and head out onto the porch.

One: I don't know the limits to these wards, or even if they have limits. Max couldn't hurt me through my amulet, but are the wards the same? Are there strength levels on these kinds of things, or what?

Two: If I do have protections that won't keep him out but will hide me from magical sight, I don't want him to know about them. Both because that seems like a strategic advantage, and because I don't want him to think too hard about where I got the information on how to create them. Right now, he thinks my adoptive wizard father made me an amulet and put together a voodoo train and then died, and that's as far as it goes. The longer I can keep him in the dark about the trove and anything else I know, the better.

It's not a long drive from the office, but panic makes

me move quickly, so I'm already sitting on the porch swing when he shows up, moving it gently back and forth with my leg.

I haven't seen his car before. He rushed into my house without warning, jumped out the window, and hobbled away, so there hadn't been a chance. But the thing he drives up in feels like a prop. I don't know much about cars, but it's shiny and electric blue, and it has the smooth lines and loud engine of something my mechanic wouldn't know how to fix.

He gets out of it smoothly, wearing another perfectly tailored business suit, this time in a light gray with pinstripes. If I weren't already sure that he'd messed with Sharon's mind to get himself into my workplace as a new hire for a special project we don't have the budget for, this would confirm it. Sharon doesn't trust men wandering into her office in suits that nice.

"Anyone who spends that much time at a tailor spends too little time with people who matter," she sometimes says to me when the right reporters are around to overhear. I never point out that tailors are people, too. That's not the point of the sound bite.

Max doesn't let preserving the carefully crafted lines of the suit restrict his boyish energy, though. He jogs up the front path and takes the porch steps two at a time. Then he smiles like he's actually the old friend of mine he's been passing himself off as. He sits down on the railing across from me, and for an unflattering second, I wish it were in worse repair and crumbled under him. He has the Manila folder with the horrifying photos in one hand.

"No one calls me Lizzie," I say without preamble and without stopping the motion of the porch swing beneath me.

"Angela does."

I roll my eyes. "No one other than Angela calls me Lizzie."

He shrugs, and I notice again the striking strength of his jaw as he looks down the street. For all my generation is supposed to hate suburbia—and I've taken my turn railing against it, too—it does have a certain nostalgic peace a surprising amount of the time. I wonder what Max looked like before he got his appearance upgrade. How old was he? Does he even remember what it was like to land within the normal range of attractiveness in which ninety-eight percent of people fall?

I don't think he can read my mind, but the look he fixes me with for a second makes me doubt that assumption.

"Still protected, I see."

Okay, so I just decided not to tell him anything, but it *does* seem like it'll be easier if he's not working under the assumption that my protection is a spell that's just going to wear off if he waits it out and keeps tabs on me in the meantime. If he knew that hanging out at my office would be a long-term thing, maybe he wouldn't think it was worth it.

I fish the amulet out from underneath my T-shirt and hold it up, steadying the swing with my foot while I do in order to make sure he gets a good look.

It's hard to parse the full range of emotions that Max goes through in one overstuffed moment. Surprise, greed, jealousy, and… I'm not sure. Sadness? Regret?

He leans back a little. It wouldn't take much to overbalance him and send him falling backward. Just saying.

"Well, that complicates things."

I shrug. "I don't think so. Seems pretty straightforward. I'm protected. You can move on."

He raises an eyebrow. "You sleep with it on?"

I laugh. "I do now."

I reconsider telling him about the wards. Would that help him just give it up? Is there a snowball's chance in hell he's going to? I doubt it.

"A lot of wizards have died who own amulets, you know."

I try not to be curious. "How?"

He gives me a big, garish, sarcastic smile. "Take that thing off, let me get you safely out of all of this, and you won't ever need to find out."

He looks like a ghoul. Not that I've ever seen a ghoul. Unless I have. Hard to say.

I lean back in the swing more deeply, kicking off again. I drop the subject. "I feel like I should be giving you sweet tea," I say.

"Wrong side of the Mason-Dixon line," he mutters. For a long moment, we give in and embrace the peace of early evening. He left the job he doesn't really have early to come bother me, and the end-of-day rush of activity isn't here yet. But I can feel the first tendrils of it starting to pull at the edges of the quiet.

"You didn't bring the cookies," I observe drily. He looks down at the folder in his hand.

"You weren't interested in the cookies."

Not accurate, but I don't push it.

"This is some grisly stuff," he continues, as though something is occurring to him. "Of course, you probably don't have to worry about it. I've heard a rumor that the Casino of Lost Souls is in town, so it's probably just a chance demon messing with people's fate for his own sick amusement."

He's trying to intimidate me, what with the *Casino of Lost Souls* of it all. What I *want* to say is, *Oh, nah, I don't think*

Aloysius is behind this. He seems pretty well amused by his own thing he has going on. But that's just giving in to temptation and giving away more than I need to for the sake of trying to show him he isn't getting the better of me. I might not see the hidden traps, but I should at least try to avoid the obvious ones.

But I don't, at least, try to force myself to look scared. "Probably better to investigate, though," I say. "In case it's not?"

He nods, slowly. "Maybe you should join me in investigating this. You'll see what this world you think you want is really like. Maybe even meet a demon if you're unlucky enough. And then, by the end of it all, you'll recognize the gift I'm offering for what it is."

I fix him with a long, languishing look. It's what I want. I think? Will he really leave me alone if I make it to the end of this and haven't come around? He speaks before I do, and that feels like a victory in a game I wasn't playing.

"Those are some snazzy glasses your dad left you," he says.

"Why, thank you," I say, flipping them down over my eyes like he's given me an invitation. Which... maybe he has.

His features don't change, which tracks. Gigi said the whole appearance upgrade is a transformation they work on themselves, not an illusion. And he doesn't glow, not exactly. But he looks crisper, somehow, than he does in my normal vision. And disjointed—like he's a high-res image that's been Photoshopped onto a background, but the artist hasn't worked whatever digital voodoo they do to make him look like he belongs.

I flip the glasses back up and stop the swing with a foot for a second and final time. "Sounds like a plan. Your car or mine?"

He looks over at my little sedan, looks back at me dramatically, and then looks at his car.

I stand up. "You don't have to be a dick about it."

THIRTEEN

An Investigation

I expect Max to ask me to navigate, but he seems to know exactly where he's headed.

"Where are we going?" I ask. I don't appreciate how I assume he got the money to buy the car, but I appreciate the results. It's silent enough in here for us to hear each other think.

"The house of the first victim. I think we should talk to his wife."

"And you know where it is?"

"I looked it up."

"And you know how to get there?"

He smiles, and it's one of the few expressions I've seen on his face that's not for my benefit. "Of course I do. I glanced at a map of Springfield years ago. Wizards don't forget."

Bullshit. "What?" I blurt out.

He shrugs and smiles, this time very much for my benefit.

"We don't forget anything. Ever. One of the first spells we learn."

I feel like if I could find out whether it was the memory spell or the prettification spell they *actually* do first, I would know a little more about a wizard's mindset. But probably not. Both those things just tell me they're very practical.

I bite back the urge to ask him how useful he thought a spell like that might be to Alzheimer's patients. Or detectives. Or students. Or scientists. Or, fuck it, *anyone* who thought about it and made the informed decision that the benefits outweighed the costs. Education would be turned on its head, and I'd bet money on it that would be a positive change. But that conversation, I feel sure, is a nonstarter.

"That's handy," I say instead, and let the jealousy he's looking for in my voice show.

We pull up to the house after what I'm sure is not a long enough time for safety's sake. It's nice. A nicer neighborhood than mine by a decent margin. I recall the photo from the file and realize that this neighborhood must somehow still be in the catchment for Lakeview Elementary. I feel a little sting of pride that my neighbors are co-opting these people's property taxes to educate us poors.

That's unkind, and it isn't warranted. But I'm not sure how to deal with the hell these people are going through, and I'm defaulting to snark and othering. It's a bad habit I know I have, and one I'm usually more successful at fighting.

I should know how to deal with what they're going through. Of all people, I should know. My dad killed himself three days before this guy did. But I knew Dad's suicide was coming. These people must have been blindsided.

Wordlessly, we get out of the car and climb the very well-kept steps flanked by professionally chosen and maintained plantings. There's a concrete stoop in front of their door instead of a porch, and I feel both exposed and forced to stand closer to Max than I'd like.

I don't ask Max what our story is. I'm sure he's going to do the talking, anyway. And hey, wouldn't you know it, I'm right.

The dead man's wife looks tired. Fair enough. The kids are at school, though, so she invites us in. At a meaningful glance from Max, I slide my glasses on so I can see… anything, I guess. Anything relevant.

I don't. It's all tasteful furnishings and a house in mild disarray that the woman keeps apologizing for. Won't stop, for some reason. Max makes up a story about us being from the city—which I guess is kind of true if you squint at an angle—here on a kind of community outreach. He asks her questions about her husband's life and how she's coping.

He's not bad at this. He has a way of winding things around to get at useful information without seeming to do so. The conversation is long and polite, but also somehow so personal and useful.

Most notably, the widow tells us that the dead man came home early from work after a lunch meeting three days before his death and that he seemed different—like something was bothering him. She'd thought maybe he'd done something, or that something had happened with the finances, but that she'd looked into everything and it all checked out.

Had she notified the police? No. Of what? Nothing was wrong. The colleague that he'd met for lunch was fine. Said her husband had been fine during lunch.

It seemed like useful information, sure, but I still hate that we're invading this woman's space for that.

"You say he was 'different' for the three days before his death. What do you mean by that?"

Max has strained the believability of our story. I can see suspicion growing in the woman's face. But she answers the question, however hesitantly.

"It was like his mind was somewhere else. He kept searching the room like he was looking for something. He started going for long walks through the neighborhood. At first, I thought he was just trying to shed a few pounds, but he walked until he had blisters on his feet. I found his bloody socks in the hamper, and—"

She cuts off, looking at Max with a fire in her eyes. We've found the edge of her compliance and I feel a fierce, incongruent pride well up in me.

"Why are you asking me these questions?"

Max doesn't try to repeat the lie or defend our position. Instead, he stands and holds out his hand for a handshake.

"Thank you very much for talking to us. We know this is a difficult time, and we appreciate it."

And with Max having backed us away from the edge, the fire in the woman dissipates. Never underestimate the power of manners. The woman stands up and accepts his hand. And, as she does, Max pulls her close and moves in for a kiss on the cheek.

I should stop him, right? I can't tell what's going on. If I didn't know what Max was, it wouldn't look predatory—just socially inept and/or deeply European.

But in the few seconds Max holds the kiss on her cheek, the tight concern on the widow's face fades. Her shoulders loosen, and she stands up straight. When Max pulls away, she breathes deeply for the first time since we've been here.

"I'm very sorry for your loss," Max says. After the last week, I consider myself a connoisseur of that phrase. He says it well, with gentle sincerity.

The woman smiles. "I appreciate that. He was a great

man, and the kids and I will remember him as he was before the last few days. He deserves that."

"You've still got each other," Max says, warmth in his voice as he looks at some portrait-studio-produced pictures of her children. I didn't know those were still a thing, but I guess they have their place.

The woman's face shines as she follows his gaze to the same pictures. "Yes, we do. And we're going to be all right."

When I say those words, I say them like I'm wishing it into existence. She says them with certainty.

"I don't doubt it," Max says. "Thanks again for speaking with us. We'll be on our way."

I'm not sure what to think of that. Horror and righteous rage vie with jealousy. I follow Max back into his ridiculous car.

"Showing me the horror of it, huh," I say, when we're on the way to the next family. He shrugs, ignoring the accusation in my voice.

"Showing you how it is. Anyone ever tell you you're a little bit judgy?" he asks.

"Anyone ever told you there are worse things to be?"

I want to scream and rail at him about the sanctity of minds. I want to tell him it's not his choice—that grief is a brutal burden, but it's a sacred one. I try to find the right words—they've got to be the right words—and I can't find them in the short drive to the second victim's house. The husband of the second victim is so broken. He's old, as she was. I remember her crumpled body twisted around the electric fence. He was there, he tells us. He cries. They were high school sweethearts.

So I don't stop Max when he leans into the man and gives him that same kiss on the cheek. And I don't stop him when we've finished talking to the college girl's parents, although I momentarily worry that he won't manage to pull it off, since there are two of them in the room, and wife number one seems very taken aback when he kisses wife number two on the cheek.

I'd put good money on it that he wouldn't have been able to get his lips on either of them if their daughter hadn't died two days ago. But the polite confusion that the exhaustion of grief brings is a powerful thing. He gets his hooks in them both, and I'm relieved to see that the icy sheet anyone could perceive between them during our visit has melted by the time we walk away.

What's Right Mind for that spell? Going by his face, it's something sweet—kind, deep, and affectionate. What kind of ego must it take to go into someone's brain and rearrange it to your liking, all the while holding on to those kinds of feelings?

"Don't ever do that to me," I say when we're back in the car and Max has started backing out of the driveway. His foot goes to the brake pedal, and it occurs to me that this is the first time today I've felt like I've affected him. He fixes me with a confused look.

"I mean, I know you're trying to get in here and do some erasing. But even if you do, don't do *that* to me. Don't mess around with my emotions."

Max's face flashes with rage before he gets it under control. He takes a long breath in and lets it out slowly. I can just about see the wheels turning from here, but it only takes him a few seconds to dismiss me.

"It's telling that you only say that when I've finished."

He's right. I ignore that.

"How did they die?" I ask, catapulting away from the subject, weaponizing my rage to get him to answer the question he wouldn't before.

Max didn't follow my movement, so I add, "The wizards with amulets. How do they die?"

He seems as relieved to change subjects as I hoped he would be. "I don't know a ton about it. Amulets get destroyed if their wearer dies, so there aren't many around. But mostly, you just have to confuse it by introducing a degree of separation or offset the harm with time."

I raise an eyebrow.

"The story that probably explains it best is this. Once there were two wizards who hated each other: Cayden and Sampson. Cayden had an amulet, so Sampson arranged a celebration and didn't invite Cayden. Then Sampson gave directions to the caterers to poison the food in advance. He did this knowing it would kill all in attendance, but that Cayden was not slated to be in attendance. At the time, as it stood, that action couldn't be of harm to Cayden, and it wasn't even Sampson doing the poisoning.

"Most people agree that would have been enough, but Sampson wanted to be sure. So instead of disguising himself as someone Cayden knew and inviting him himself, the wizard chain-linked the action. He invited people who he thought would invite people who would eventually invite Cayden. And Sampson wasn't even at the party when everyone died—he was on the other side of the world. Removing the action that caused the harm by making it less direct and also displacing it in time. Cayden died. Sampson caused it. But the amulet couldn't track the intention through all of those steps, so it didn't save him."

I nod, absorbing. Traps I don't see coming feel like an awfully large blind spot to have. I don't think I pissed anyone off enough by ruining their bet last night to go to those lengths, but who knows? Maybe I did.

"Sampson killed a lot of people in the hopes of killing one," I note.

Max shrugs. "A lot of our history is like that."

A lot of everyone's history *is* like that, I guess.

"It was a brutal time," I say, searching for some kind of agreement to close off the subject and move on.

"What, the seventies? I'd say the fashion was, anyway."

The seventies? That could have made the news. They had film. They had reporting. They had social mores. And Sampson didn't care about any of them. Wizards gonna wizard.

"Where are we going now?" I turn from him to look out the window, all business again. We're not headed toward my house. He matches my practical tone with the ease of someone who's had a lot of practice glossing over conflict and hoisting himself out of intense emotional states in an instant.

"I figure we should go see where it all went down. All the families tell a similar story: weird for exactly seventy-two hours, then they offed themselves. Seems unlikely where they did it made that much of a difference, since the timing's so precise. But hey, who knows? Maybe there'll be some residue or something. Closest one is the bridge."

Max doesn't know I didn't get to the final picture in the file, so I don't know how the college student killed herself. But there's only one bridge close to us, in the direction we're heading, so I take a guess.

"Good," I say. "I could do with a walk in the park."

FOURTEEN

A Chance Encounter

I see I'm right as we pull up to Skyway Park. Unfortunately. Skyway Park was one of Sharon's first initiatives as mayor. I don't like that all this shit has now tarnished my memory of the project. It used to be an old railway bridge, abandoned when the railroad company deemed the tracks it connected to more expensive to maintain than they were worth.

The options at the time were to spend money destroying it, spend money making it safe for the public to access, or spend money keeping the public from getting out onto it. The third option would have been the cheapest, but Sharon ran the numbers and read all the research I did for her, and she concluded that turning it into a unique park would be a good draw for some of the struggling businesses in the area, as well as the city as a whole.

And thus, Skyway Park was born. It has grassy spaces, sculptures, and enough safety measures to keep anyone from falling over the edge accidentally while not obscuring what I still think is a pretty amazing view. It passes over a rocky valley with a seasonal stream running through it, and it runs north to south, which makes sunrises and sunsets incredible.

Twilight falls as we pull up to the bridge. If the suicide was widely reported, it doesn't show in the attendance. The place is pleasantly thrumming along with a happy crowd of people when I untangle myself from Max's low-slung automotive contraption. In the distance, a strong male voice drifts to me on the breeze. It feels familiar, somehow, but I can't place it.

Without waiting for Max, I stroll forward, pulled toward the sound. The last few hours have been rough. I could use a little levity.

Max follows along behind me like he's hesitating. The park runs for a good 250 feet, but it all feels pulled toward a center point. Toward the singer. Toward…

The man who gave me the folder. He's standing up on a wooden box that improbably supports his weight. He's in the same worn-out layers, looking even more imposing and still more haphazardly put together than he had in the lobby of the office building. Had that really only been yesterday morning?

I can't place the name of the original artist of the song he's singing, but it feels familiar to me. It feels like a song I used to hear every night when I was a kid, even though we didn't have any kind of tradition of singing like that in my house growing up.

Maybe it's a folk song? It has that kind of lilting, repetitive movement to it. But it's not one I can nail down to a specific memory, or a specific name, or a specific time. I stand, gathered in a group that, over the last few minutes, has clogged the bridge and prevents anyone from getting by. No one minds. Everyone's listening. We're deep in the song.

He sold me leather, boy

When I had none
I shot the wind with my father's gun
Gave up forgiving at the rising sun
I'd be right back to see

I don't know what it means. But the song snags a strand of my heartstrings hard. The facial expressions I can make out in my peripheral vision tell me I'm not the only one.

Hold up.

I flip down my glasses, and the experience shifts. The man I'm staring at has the same bedraggled look, but he's a little bigger now—probably the better part of seven feet tall. His nose is bigger but also stubbier. His chin juts out. His teeth aren't yellow, but they are uneven, and I think slightly gray. His hair is wild and uneven, long and free.

He smells like the wet dirt around a melting brook on a cold mountain. The melody he was singing is gone, replaced by a deep rising vibration I can feel in my bones. Like a musical version of an elephant's gait—solid, shaking, in rhythm but too slow. My world rocks back and forth for a few seconds until I begin to distinguish the other noises: a whistling of wind, like air is passing through gates in the sky all around me, out in the empty space away from the bridge, out over the valley. And now I can hear whispers in my ear, so quiet that I can only make them out if I focus.

"You have to look closely," they say.

"What did you think he felt when you said that?" they say.

"Go down and ask your mom if we can eat up here," they say.

They're my father's words, but not my father's voice. They're no one's voice. They're puppet strings without fingers attached to them.

I try to listen. I feel certain the whispers will remember things he said that I can't. I feel certain it's my last chance.

The sound of applause surrounds me, telling me the music has stopped. I try to blink the tears out of my eyes until I give up and wipe.

I don't carry any change to place in the comically over-sized hat that sits on the sidewalk in front of the man, but I see now he's got a little stand holding up a laminated paper with a QR code. I wait in line, and scan the code when I reach the front, moving away to the side quickly so that others can do so, too. Max is right behind me, though he looks more annoyed than enraptured as he scans the code to pay.

I give the suggested donation: three dollars. It's not much. Glancing at other people's screens with a curiosity I should probably try harder to restrain, I notice there are different suggested amounts. Maybe it's random, but I doubt it.

When we've finished, Max and I stand off to the side. Too many onlookers to start asking the man questions now. Besides, he's busy with his adoring fans. One of them asks him about YouTube, and he points to the phone in her hands. She reacts with shock, so I can only guess he's made his account appear there.

"That's quite a magic trick," one of them says. I can't help but smile.

My eyes trace farther afield, and I see some people wandering away that look… wrong. It takes me a moment, but I realize they look black-and-white through the glasses.

Maybe I'm seeing ghosts? Wouldn't put it past myself at this point. I flip the glasses up momentarily to confirm that I can see them at all with my normal eyes. Yup, still there.

"They crossed the bridge the troll made for them and

didn't pay him," Max whispers in my ear, only a little louder than the voices in the music had been.

"What happened to them?" I murmur.

Max hesitates. He's close to me. I want to shove him away, but more than that, I want to know the answer.

"They're going to find it very hard to get to where that bridge takes them in the future."

I shudder. "Seems a bit harsh," I say a little louder, a little clearer.

Max steps back slightly. He shrugs. "They knew they were supposed to pay. It didn't have to be much, relative to what they have. It just had to be something. They could feel the same pull you and I did. You have to decide not to give in to that pull. They decided."

Makes sense, I guess. Still, I make a note: *Always pay street performers*.

"So that's trolls," I say, leaning back to find the railing behind me. I stare at the man—at his wild hair and his careless clothes. And I breathe in how crisp and clean he smells.

"That's trolls," Max says, venom in his voice.

It takes a good while for the crowd around the troll to dissipate. Everyone who talks to him seems to feel that same confusion of intimacy and strangeness that I did, trying to navigate a way out of that tender, close space he'd brought us all to. By the time the last of his admirers has wandered away, the sun is waning hard, and I'm glad of my jacket.

"I told *her*. I didn't tell you," the troll says to Max. With my glasses on, his voice still feels like it's vibrating up through the bridge—like he *is* the bridge. I take my glasses off.

"Why did you tell her?" Max asks.

The troll laughs, and I'm glad I have my glasses off. That laugh is a little overwhelming even without them.

"You don't know much."

"Enlighten me." The words are dull rusty knives, and I see the troll feel the threat of them.

"That young girl brought death to my bridge," the troll says, rather than answer the question directly. "I saw her die. Saw something in her eyes."

Max nods, his eyes shining with something ugly that looks almost like lust from this side of it. "What was it?"

The troll shrugs, his lips twisting up into a grim parody of a smile. "Don't know. Get off my bridge, wizard."

There are lines drawn that I can't see, and the troll seems to have crossed one of them. Max draws himself up to his full height, and I only now realize he's been slouching just a little all afternoon. He's always given me the impression that he's a kind of quick, darting thing. But standing against the troll, he's the tide.

"I'm a wizard. I stand where I want."

"Lot of wizards stand. Lot of wizards die."

The troll's words aren't loud. I'm not sure they'd even sound harsh if the word "die" weren't in them.

Some part of me feels like I should jump in and say something snarky about *boys and their egos*. But these aren't boys, and what they've got between them goes deeper than me.

Plus, only one of these things is nominally human, and it's not the one whose side I think I want to take. A little tricky to figure out where you want to stand when you can't even rely on species solidarity.

"You going to kill me?" the troll asks, and I don't know why it sounds like a threat.

"You said you told her about it. The pictures were from you, then?"

If the troll is surprised that I didn't tell the wizard he gave me the pictures, he doesn't show it. "It's a public health problem. I told the mayor's office."

His explanation is missing pieces, and Max knows it, too. "Why take something like this to the mayor's office? You know it's magic. They won't do much for you."

"Where else?"

I've seen a lot of expressions on Max's face in the short time I've known him, but I haven't seen him look personally hurt before.

"To *me*."

The troll shakes the bridge with his great big laugh again, and I wonder if maybe we should have allocated an even greater proportion of the Skyway Park project budget to structural enhancements to ensure public safety. Max winces.

"I know better," the troll says.

Again, that hurt expression. "You don't know me."

"I know enough."

Another long, intense moment. Under different circumstances, I'd have expected some passerby with hero complexes and/or de-escalation training to step in, or at least to hover nearby. But something about the conflict is triggering their "this is a natural disaster, you can't fight it" reflex, so no one does. I know this because it's triggering the hell out of that impulse in me, too.

There's a sad quality to their standoff, though. Maybe. I might be making that up.

"Do you have anything else you're going to tell me?" Max says, his voice level and low.

"Get off my bridge."

Anger flashes in Max's eyes. If he'd snapped his fingers, he could have started a fire. And that anger sparks the reaction in me that I've been struggling all afternoon to keep nailed down.

I hate his arrogance. I hate the way he demands. I hate the way he assumes. Digging around into the contents of people's souls. Pulling out their sacred grief. Taking liberties they never would have given him.

He doesn't have the right. No one gave him the right.

He looks at me, jerks his head in the direction of the parking lot, and starts walking. It takes him longer than it should to realize I'm not walking. He turns back and fixes me with a cold glare.

"Are you coming?"

"No."

I think he's going to bicker with me more, but he doesn't. He just clenches his jaw, turns around, and heads for the parking lot with long strides.

The fabric of his suit has a slight sheen to it, and it catches the warm rays of the fading sun like gold. Even with his back turned, his muscles clenched, and his hands shoved hard into his pockets, he's got a beauty to him.

"Angry young men," says the troll.

I look up at him, surprised and overwhelmed by the absence of fear.

"Angry *old* ones, too," I shoot back at him. He laughs yet again, but lightly this time. Less like an earthquake and more like the fresh rumbling of a car engine on a cold day.

"I'm Wilbur," he says, holding out one massive hand.

I take it. "I'm Elizabeth. But you know that."

"Need a ride home?"

I look back after Max, so small now with the distance.

"That would be nice."

FIFTEEN

A Relevant Question

I shouldn't be surprised that Wilbur disappears over the side of the bridge when no one's looking, but I am. I know, I know… troll. But still. When he reappears, vaulting back up with no more care or attention than if he had just come upstairs, his milk crate filled with performing accoutrements has been replaced by a laptop bag.

"Doesn't anyone ever see when you do that?" I ask, and he shrugs.

"Sometimes. Bothers wizards. They want us to hide more. I hide enough."

I shoot him a skeptical look. "Climbing up and down bridges doesn't seem like hiding."

He shrugs again. "Humans can climb on bridges. Sometimes they ask. I say I'm a troll, and they laugh. It's always nice. Sometimes they take a selfie."

I laugh, and it carries away a ton of the stress of the heavy afternoon. Together, we start heading for the same side of the bridge Max had stormed to minutes before.

"So, while we're on the subject…" I say, feeling out

whether the barrage of questions I want to ask him is going to be welcome or not. He greets the implicit question with a generous gesture of his hand, as if to say *go ahead*.

"You live under a bridge."

"Yes."

"But you also… build bridges? Metaphorically?"

"Older a troll gets, the more symbolic he gets."

I absorb this and analyze it. "So, your bridge is music?"

I feel his shrug more than see it. "Not just music. Lots of things that bridge the gap and carry you somewhere that's hard to go otherwise. All kinds of art. I also like computers a lot. I make connections."

I stop dead still in my tracks.

"You don't have to say it," he says.

I grimace. "I kind of do, though."

He looks back at me, the shadows on his face getting long. Then he nods, the picture of the long-suffering saint.

"You're an internet troll."

He looks disappointed with me, and I can't blame him. "I'm a troll who likes the internet. Most of us do. It's different."

He turns his head back toward our destination and begins walking again. I follow. When we reach the entrance to the parking lot, he leads me to a silver BMW. I guess life is pretty good when people *have* to pay you, and you have no housing costs. He hunches up more than I would think he would have to as he gets in. The wizard's illusion I've unknowingly lived my life within is impressive, but it can't actually compress space. I slide into the passenger seat and dip my glasses down just enough to see his true form scrunched up like we're in a clown car.

"I need a bigger car," he says, like an apology. I don't think he wants a bigger car.

"This one's pretty nice."

He sighs. "Too nice to get rid of."

We head toward my house, and I don't think too hard about the fact that I didn't tell him where I live.

"Do you get cold?" I ask. For the first time since I've been hanging around with supernatural creatures, I'm thrilled that I get a chance to ask about the little things. It feels good.

"Nope."

"How about hungry?"

"Always."

"Do you eat people?"

"Not lately."

Another thing not to think about.

"If you're all metaphorical now, why still live under a bridge?"

"Tradition. And it's a nice bridge. It has Wi-Fi now."

"Do you hang upside down to sleep?"

That gets a good hearty laugh that fills up the space. "Am I a bat?"

"I'm asking the questions here, mister."

He shakes his head. "I lay on a crossbeam."

"Aren't you afraid of falling?"

"I've got good balance."

I pause for a bit.

"Why is your car so nice and your clothes so…"

He looks down at his layers. "I like my clothes."

"No offense."

"You think I get offended easily?"

I very carefully don't think of Max. "I'm still the one asking the questions. Do you have any troll children?"

"No. Now ask if I have half-human children."

My involuntary shock and horror make me glad he doesn't get offended easily.

"Do you have any half-human children?"

"No."

I'm more relieved than it would be polite to admit.

"How come my magic-finding lantern found Gigi and not you?"

His eyebrows shoot up. I think he's impressed. "Gigi's made out of magic. She's a stronger signal. If she goes far enough away, it'll point to me."

"Is there anyone else it would point at?"

"Probably only the wizard. Unless someone's hiding. People hide sometimes."

"What do they hide from?"

"Wizards mostly."

"Why?"

He takes his eyes off the road and looks at me, incredulity etched on his face. Then he turns his attention back to the road, shaking his head in disbelief.

I stop sharply, like he'd answered yes to my people-eating question. The question comes to my lips: *Why do you hate wizards so much?* I swallow it down so it can't escape. But another related question slips out instead. "What are the terms of the treaty?"

He doesn't answer right away. Instead, he tilts his head in thought. His tone is gentle when he eventually speaks. "It's a long document. Took months to negotiate. A lot of rules that the different kinds of us have to live by. What of our culture is allowed, what of our culture isn't."

I reflect silently for a second. "You're not allowed to kill humans?"

The troll's laugh makes me grab at the handle of my door like the car is crashing.

"No, no, we can do that. Wizards wouldn't try to stop that. But we have to keep it quiet. Can't kill too many at once. That kind of thing. All very…" He pauses before spitting the final word out like spoiled yogurt. "Regulated."

"And what do you get out of it?"

Wilbur winces. "A few things. They made the illusion that keeps us hidden. They keep humans in line. Out of our world. They're responsible for you."

I don't have enough context to tell if that's a fair trade. Maybe it is now. Maybe it wasn't a thousand years ago. It wouldn't take a perceptive person to tell what Wilbur thinks of it.

"If it's such a bad deal, why did you make it?"

When Wilbur answers, his voice is soft and low—I feel it in my bones as much as I hear it. "Treaties don't happen when both sides think they're winning. One day, ask that wizard why you'll never meet a member of the Fae. Or a god."

The words hang in the air until they dissipate. I'm not sure what to do with them. I don't speak again until I can find my way back to steadier ground.

"How old are you?" I ask.

"Very," he answers, his voice steady and light again.

"Do you just age really slowly, or did you get to a certain age and you'll stick at it for the rest of your life?"

"Neither. Aging is human. We're small trolls, and then we're grown trolls, and then we stay that way."

I pepper him with every tiny, mundane little question I can think of for the rest of the trip, only breaking to think of more. He answers every single one with good humor. Never impatient. Never unwilling. I get the feeling he'd never stop me. As long as I don't ask him anything more about wizards.

"How do you know where I live?" I ask as we pull into my driveway.

"I looked you up," he answers, but I barely hear him.

I'm looking at the light shining out from the window of my living room.

"Who's in my house?" I ask under my breath. I feel Wilbur the internet troll tense up beside me, and his voice carries violence in it with his answer.

"That one, I don't know."

SIXTEEN

A Breakthrough

I must have done the wards wrong. Either that, or this person doesn't mean me any harm. I don't know which is more likely. No way Faisal cuts his trip short with no warning; he takes his job seriously. My sister would have texted, as would any of my friends. And most of them don't know my new address yet. And while it doesn't stop wizards, usually human beings have the courtesy to not break into your house.

I weigh the pros and cons of carrying a weapon again, though it's too late now. Besides, I have an actual real live troll sitting beside me. And an amulet of invincibility. Come at me, burglar.

My self-talk is a little bolder than I feel. Maybe a lot bolder. But it gets me out of the car and heading toward the front door.

It's unlocked. I step inside and immediately relax. From my front door, you can see clear through my house to the back door, interrupted only by the side of the living room and the other side of the dining room. And there, standing at my dining room table, looking as out of place as a diamond in pea soup, is Gigi.

Now would be the time I lower the gun I don't have. I step forward, and Wilbur follows me inside.

He has no trouble getting through the wards, which doesn't surprise me. But, if I'm completely honest, I *am* a little surprised they didn't stop Gigi. I'm not sure why exactly.

The woman—is that what she is?—looks up from what she's doing and smiles that smile that makes me glad my glasses are off.

"Wilbur!" she says. "Welcome to the trove party!"

Wilbur's eyebrows shoot up, and he strides forward like a lava flow. I'm a little insulted that the trove—which is now sitting on my kitchen table, in *clear* view of the street from the open door and possibly even the living room window if someone stood in the right place—is so much more interesting than I am. But I get it. I'm just a human. This is, apparently, important. I shut the door behind me and quickly go pull the blinds.

"A trove…" Wilbur says softly as he approaches the table.

"I found your machine," Gigi says, putting a hand on the overhanging arm of the scanner that I borrowed from my sister a thousand years ago this morning. It's an expensive thing, and technologically advanced, what with its super-fast high-resolution scanning and built-in character recognition software. Olivia told me all about it way back when. But, dear god, it looks like something from the late nineties.

"This is what you got it for, yes?"

I stifle the urge to scream at her. Breaking into my house is one thing. Finding the trove and bringing it down here and rifling through it is another. An obsessive, jealous instinct runs through my body, seeing her hands on the papers.

I dial it back—or try to, at least. Picking a fight with Gigi feels ill-advised. Especially since she's already inside my wards and seems friendly with Wilbur. I don't think she stole anything. I don't *think*.

I shouldn't be surprised that Gigi was able to figure out how to get the scanner up and running—the woman owns what is evidently a successful business, after all—but I am a little impressed. As I get closer, I can see she's almost gotten through the wizard Stuart's volumes.

"Are you—"

"Scanning twice, the second time with the sticky notes removed so that we can see what's under them? Yes. Yes, I am."

I stare at her. Annoyed. Impressed. Not sure what to say. Standard interacting-with-Gigi feelings, I'm beginning to think.

"It's rude to come into a human's house uninvited," Wilbur says, picking the cabinet that contains the trove up off the table and setting it on the floor, making room for his own computer.

"Yes," I say, biting back a comment about her digging into my trove. "It is."

She fixes me with an incomprehensible gaze. "I was worried."

That hits me wrong. She can't lie, but that hits me wrong. "For my safety?"

"In a manner of speaking."

That's more like it.

"What worried you?" I ask. I like this whole asking-questions-expecting-answers thing. A lot more productive than the overawed silence that I found myself stuck with for much of last night. But then again, last night was a different thing altogether.

I go to the fridge and get a beer. I don't drink, but Faisal does now and then when he can't figure something out on one of his side-research projects. I steal one of his. It feels right in the moment.

When I come back to the table, Gigi has followed Wilbur's lead and put away the scanner for the time being. She's sitting at the table, sipping a beverage that I assume she must have somehow made out of the things in my kitchen. I'm just not sure what combination of things I have that could have produced something quite that *blue*.

It's possible she drinks drain cleaner. It wouldn't kill her. And maybe it tastes good to her nonhuman tastebuds. I don't ask. We're sticking with useful questions right now.

Instead, I sit down like it's a dinner party, and I'm shocked by how comfortable it feels. Gigi is a terrifying force of nature, but all the same I feel welcomed home. Wilbur, by his own admission, used to eat people, yet I'm glad he's here, too. It feels like we've gathered together like this a thousand times before. The familiarity comforts me, though I'm well aware it's a lie.

I made a mistake yesterday. I thought it was an either/or between the supernatural world being real and me having lost my damn mind. Turns out both was an option.

"Okay, Gigi. Why were you worried?"

She swirls her drink with a stainless-steel straw. I make a mental note to wash both well after she's gone.

"I was… keeping track of where your lantern was."

"You can do that? Keep track of magical objects?"

"Magical objects that I know about and that are actively tracking me? Yes. I could feel it once I saw it.

Earlier today, it disappeared. And then reappeared. And then disappeared. And then reappeared. And then disappeared again. I thought it was a signal. I was impressed you *could* send me a signal like that. But either way, I figured the wizard was getting to you. Figured he got the trove."

I tap the wards on the side of the cabinet.

Gigi raises an eyebrow. "Yes, I saw that. Clever, but not you, I imagine."

"No, that was my dad," I admit. "I did the house wards, though."

Gigi lets out a jeweled laugh. "Now that's a useful first foray into magic. You may survive longer than I thought."

I don't think through the implications of that compliment. I'll take my wins where I get them.

"The wizard did find her, though," Wilbur contributes.

Gigi's smile fades. I'm struck by how unnatural her face looks when it isn't smiling. I don't think it was made to frown. "Oh?"

"He found me before I met you," I say.

"You didn't mention," Gigi says without a hint of forgiveness.

"You didn't ask."

Gigi shrugs it off.

"He's looking into the suicides." Wilbur ignores any uncomfortableness. "Probably going to blame the chance demon. He's near."

"Yes," Gigi says, "but I don't think he did it."

Wilbur's laptop chimes its readiness. I stifle the urge to go grab him some Mountain Dew and pizza or something.

"'Course not," Wilbur says. "Why would he?"

"Wilbur, why did you bring the photos to me?" I ask, as much to head off any potential confrontation between the two powerful immortal supernatural beings in my house as to avoid facing the thought that's been gnawing at the back of my mind.

He looks at me like a disappointed teacher. "Because your father was the first death."

"No, he wasn't," I say coldly and quickly.

"He died at twelve oh seven. Whatever we're dealing with, it attacks at twelve oh seven."

I didn't know the minute of my father's death. I hadn't asked. "Afternoon," they'd told me. And that was more than I'd wanted to know.

Twelve oh seven. It bites at me. It's too big a coincidence not to be related. That doesn't make me want to accept it.

Wilbur doesn't try to convince me. He lets the facts speak for themselves. Instead, he begins typing away idly on his computer. Gigi, meanwhile, rifles through Wilbur's laptop bag, finding her own assortment of printed details about the case. I can tell at a glance that some of the things she's looking at are the photos I saw yesterday morning, much as I try not to look.

"No," I say. "That's not when it attacks. At least, it's not when it enters them. It enters them three days before."

Both creatures fix me with uncomfortably intense stares.

"Max and I talked to the families today," I answer.

They stare, confused. It hits me: They don't know Max's name.

"The wizard," I clarify.

"Oh," Gigi says. "Right. He's barely a wizard, really."

"Wizard enough," Wilbur grumbles, barely audible over the sound of his fingers on his keyboard.

"True," Gigi says, in a way that makes me desperately glad she's not talking about me.

We're getting off topic.

"When we talked to the families, they all said that their family members acted strangely for three days before the attack. Long walks, weird conversations. One of them didn't know exactly when it started, but the other two said it started around noon, when they got back from lunch for one, and a shopping trip for the other."

"Noteworthy," says the troll.

"What about your father?" Gigi asks. "Did he act strangely before he killed himself?"

Other than the eight years he was locked up? I want to spit at her.

"Yes," I say instead. "But for a lot longer. He'd been on suicide watch for eight years."

"Oh!" Gigi said. "That explains it! Something was stuck in him, but he let it out, and now it's attacking others. We've solved the mystery. 'Go team!' I think we're supposed to say."

I ignore her delight at my father's condition. Honestly, it's only marginally worse than reactions some other people have had.

"That's not enough," I say. "We know why it's attacking now, but we don't know where it came from, and we don't know enough to stop it. That's what counts. Where's the connection? The first victim must have given it to the second victim, and so on, and it takes three days to kill them. Exactly. Every time."

The sentences feel foreign coming out of my mouth. But if there are rules, I can learn them. And if I can learn the rules, I can solve the puzzle. It's easier to think of it as a puzzle, anyway.

"If it's transmitting from one to another, then the next victim must always have been at the scene of the previous victim's death. Or nearby, at least. Right? And my father died in a controlled environment, so…"

I look at Wilbur. His face—or at least, the version of his face that I can see—is riddled with concern.

"Doesn't work," Wilbur says. "I looked at the visitor logs for your father's institution before I gave you the pictures. Wanted to see if there were any connections there."

I deflate. "Nothing?" I ask.

He shakes his head.

"I take it back," Gigi says, between sips of the blue whatever-it-is she's drinking. "Bad job, team. Also, Elizabeth, you don't seem to have noticed, but I think he's building you a bridge, no?"

I shoot her a confused look.

"He's building a bridge over the internet between you and whatever information you're asking him for," she continues, voice dripping with patient condescension. "When trolls let you cross their bridges..."

I sit up straight. "I should pay him."

Gigi nods.

I remember the urge I had a minute ago when his computer turned on. Would it have gotten stronger when he'd finished his work? Would I have forgotten payment? Would Wilbur have reminded me?

"Are you hungry?" I ask Wilbur.

He smiles. "You asked that before," he says. "Always."

"I could eat, too," Gigi purrs as I rise from the table and head into the kitchen.

I look through the fridge at the meals Faisal made me before I left, a gesture of contrition for abandoning me a week after my father died to do a silly little thing like his job. That thing that sustains him and, before we moved in here, paid half our rent.

I pick out a small lasagna that he told me to warm up in the oven. Sorry, Faisal. Most of the people eating this aren't going to be human. I think we can safely make some sacrifices.

I figure there are four servings in here, which should just about do for one of me and two supernatural creatures. Maybe? I'm deep in guesswork territory now. I punch the buttons and the microwave starts humming away, conspicuously mundane.

Once I'm satisfied that payment is underway, I return to the matter at hand.

"So if they're not connected to each other that way, they must all be connected to something else, right? There must be something they have in common? They all died in different places, but what about where they were when the thing got into them? You could check—"

"Credit cards," Wilbur says. "On it."

He alternates between typing, scrolling, and reading for a couple minutes.

"Are you hacking into the credit card companies?" I ask, a little concerned for the sanctity of my internet connection.

Wilbur looks at me with almost as much disappointment as he did when I called him an internet troll.

"Of course not. That would take too long. But I keep beacons in useful places. I'm just telling them to go find the data I want when they check in and feed it out to me in tiny chunks. It might take a minute. There are a lot of companies, and I have to keep the pieces pretty small to avoid anyone noticing the exfiltration."

Gigi's eyes crinkle around the edges with her smile.

Exfiltration, she mouths at me, and I laugh.

"That sounds like something a spy would say," I say, turning back to the microwave, watching the cheese start to bubble up around the edges.

"Only someone who has never been a spy would say

that," Gigi says. I don't take the bait and ask her about it. She'd only be cryptic about it if I did. See? I learn. Eventually.

I open the microwave on the first beep, congratulate myself for having timed it right, and plate up the servings. Given his size, Wilbur should get the biggest serving, I figure. And I must have figured right, because no one complains when I set the plates down along with silverware and napkins I'm not sure they'll use. Everyone tucks in, Wilbur in between bursts of typing.

Gigi's looking over Wilbur's shoulder, and I realize I missed a low-volume conversation while I was plating up dinner. Because apparently what an immortal, invulnerable bookshop owner really needs is to gain a basic understanding of computer hacking.

I keep my hands clean of their discussion. It might be better if I *didn't* know how it all worked. I do work for a politician, after all. For now. Assuming no one catches me doing crazy things that don't make sense. Like, say, wandering around town harassing the families of recent suicide victims.

"All right," Wilbur says when the lasagna on my plate is half gone, "I've got a charge for the first victim around the time of your father's death at CJ's Bar and Grille."

I try to place the restaurant and can't.

"Where is that?" I ask Gigi, who is already pulling it up on her phone.

"Oh, it's out at that new development they built a few years ago on those failing dairy farms east of the corn museum."

I stop chewing momentarily, and not just because no matter how many times people mention it, I still can't believe we have a corn museum.

I could try to tell myself it's a coincidence, but that

would be disingenuous. I don't say anything, but Gigi notices the look on my face. She doesn't ask me—yet. Wilbur continues with evident pleasure in his discovery.

"Which makes sense, because the second victim was tagged in an Instagram post with her niece at the Sunglass Hut franchisee out there. And the third victim…"

Gigi's staring at me now, presumably because my face is growing paler by the second. I finish chewing my bite of lasagna and swallow.

"Yes," Wilbur says, surprised for the first time I've seen him. "People really spend that much in one day?"

"Do you want to share with the class?" Gigi asks me. Wilbur looks up from his computer.

They're patient. I guess that's one thing about immortal beings—they've got time.

"My dad owned some of the land that the development out there was built on. Just this little, random field in the middle of nowhere. He left instructions before he was committed that we should hold on to it and not use it, but…"

"But the developers offered a lot of money, and you sold it," Gigi guesses.

I clench my jaw, feeling defensive even though I seem to be the only one at the table who has leaped to the conclusion that this whole thing is my fault for not standing up for my father's wishes and refusing to sell the land.

"His care was expensive. He left instructions for us to use the rent from the house to pay for it, but the roof needed replacing…" I murmur, trailing off.

"All right, so our working theory is…" Gigi says, moving bits of lasagna around her plate with her fork. "Something nasty that makes people want to kill themselves was hanging out in dearest daddy for eight years. And he knew in advance that he was going to come down with it, because he went out of his way to buy a plot of land and bind it to it, and he tried to keep people away from it. He gets locked up, procedures fail, it gets set free. And the land the spirit or *whatever* is attached to now has a mixed shopping-dining-residential area on it. So it's been jumping into people and making them kill themselves three days later, and then getting sucked back onto the land to find another victim."

Jesus, is that really our working theory? It seems to fit, but I'm getting whiplash from trying to rewrite eight years of emotional processing about my father's condition.

"Do I have that right?" Gigi asks, and I start to nod, but then—

"No, I don't think so," I say. "The things the people did weren't random. They were going on long walks. Walking until their feet bled."

"Always on the same route or always different routes? Could they have been searching for something?"

She's looking at Wilbur, but he shakes his head.

"If I had a beacon anywhere that could get me their location services on their phones, I'd have used it to start with. And the CCTV network here is so flimsy. I can get some video doorbell footage, maybe try and track them from their homes, but we don't have time to sort through it all."

We don't? Why don't we?

My blood runs cold.

"Someone's going to die tomorrow if we don't stop it," I say. I'd been feeling a sense of urgency, but I hadn't put together why until now. Hadn't let the weight of it sit on me. Another horrific death from something *my dad* let loose was going to happen in less than seventeen hours if we didn't do something to stop it. And I was complicit. I sold the land. I helped.

"All right," Gigi says, her tone as bright as the drink in her hand. "Let's not bother, then. Elizabeth can go to the shopping mall and see who it jumps into tomorrow, and we can get more answers from there. You know, I was skeptical about getting into this kind of thing again, but it really is fun."

I stare at her.

"We have to figure it out before then," I say, daggers in my eyes. "People are going to die."

My eye daggers bounce off Gigi just as harmlessly as real daggers would. She shrugs. "Humans die. It's one of their most reliable characteristics."

I look at Wilbur, who has closed his laptop. He gives me a regretful smile. "Gigi's right."

I rack my brain while the two of them eat the meal made with love I'm now thinking they don't deserve.

"The lantern!" I say the second it comes to me. "Can't we use the lantern to find it?"

Gigi frowns and swallows before speaking. "The lantern points to me."

"Yes," I concede, "it does right now. But if you go to a crossroads, maybe it won't anymore."

Gigi exchanges a glance with Wilbur that doesn't feel flattering to me. But they both stand and take a step into the crossroads.

The stillness of the house when they've left it feels sharp. Without them, the house is full of my grief—the grief they'd kept at bay. I grab the lantern from where Gigi set it on the floor beside the trove. I pull down my glasses and look at the flame of the candle. It points in the same direction Gigi stepped to enter the crossroads.

Then Gigi and Wilbur are back, and I scramble to take off my glasses before I have to see Gigi through them again.

"Well?" she asks, and I note the cutting edge of her disapproval.

"Try another direction," I say, unwilling to concede. Gigi rolls her eyes and steps off in another direction. Wilbur, I notice, doesn't pick the same one.

I flip the glasses back down and look at the lantern. It's followed her again.

I take the glasses off and lay them on the table, rubbing my eyes.

"No success?" Gigi asks when they return, pulling out her chair to sit down.

"You need to go farther," I say. "Can you walk a couple of steps to different crossroads so it doesn't point to you anymore?"

She doesn't move to stand. "No," she says.

"We're talking about a human life…" I trail off. It's useless.

"The closest crossroads is fifty miles away. I'm not getting a cab back from there for your fool's mission when we've got a perfectly good option. Chances are the lantern would only find your wizard, anyway."

I don't like that Max has become "my" wizard now. Pretty sure that means that I'm falling fast in her estimation.

"But if you would just—"

"I said no," Gigi reiterates, casually resting her hands on the lantern on the table between us, sending another jealous surge through me. The words aren't sharp or angry, just final. "I don't do things I don't want to, and I don't want to do that."

"You did something you didn't want to yesterday," I said, remembering her reluctance to go upstairs at the casino and witness the chance demon's fight.

"Are you an ancient immortal demon with powers

profound and motives obscure?" Her words went their way around in the air like a poorly folded paper plane.

"No."

"I didn't think so. I don't do things *for you* that I don't want to do."

The evening has soured. Wilbur tucks into his payment, and I pick at what's left of my serving. I'm not hungry anymore.

"Well," Gigi says after a moment, "I'm not going to go with you tomorrow. I've got a shop to run. And besides, I don't like the idea of getting something stuck in my head that tries to make me kill myself. Can't imagine what it would do if it got frustrated."

I look at Wilbur, who isn't volunteering one way or another. I don't think he wants to go. I don't know why. I guess he just seems more like a background person. He looked happier on his bridge.

"I'll take the wizard," I say, noting how Wilbur stops chewing for a second after I say it.

Gigi raises an eyebrow. "I suppose that works. Possession is inherently harmful, so your amulet should protect you. Maybe the spirit will go into the wizard. One can only hope."

In short order, Wilbur finishes his food, and the two of them head to their cars and disappear—less magically this time—into the night.

The grief is heavy—heavier than it was before. I go through the motions of putting away my leftovers and getting ready for bed. I move the trove to the corner, where it can't be seen from the street, but I leave off putting it back up into the attic until the morning. I don't like that it's down here, but it's going to take a lot of strength to get it back up there, and I'm tired.

Before I head for bed, I notice a slip of paper where

Wilbur had been sitting with his precise, distinctive handwriting on it. It reads:

Maxwell Jones

18 Mayflower Way

I hadn't asked him for this, but I'd needed it. I hope he was paid sufficiently. I think the meal did it. But how would I know? What would I find harder to reach if I didn't? The internet? Information about Max? Addresses in general?

I'm not used to everyone knowing the rules but me. But one lesson seems clear: Always feed the trolls.

SEVENTEEN

A Visitor

I wake up tired, grief settled into my bones, in a bed that always feels too big when Faisal's not in it. No matter how often he's away, I never get used to it. It's good he wasn't here last night, though—I would have bothered him with all my tossing and turning.

I can't think of a way to find the person currently possessed. I can't stop the next suicide from happening. All night I kept running down different options in my head. Other than announcing to the general public what is happening and insisting that everyone keep eyes on one another and report anyone they know who has been going on long walks over the last few days, I am at a loss. At this point, I would try the mass public appeal if I had even the slightest hope that it would work.

But no one would take it seriously, especially given my family history of mental illness that's always just a Google search away. If I used Sharon's platform to try and get the word out, I'd ruin my career, too.

I thought of going to Max last night, but it would have been useless. If he had a way of hunting down whatever this is, he'd do it with or without my help. He'd probably do it better without me. I don't have any info that would help him.

Plus, given the things Wilbur had to say about wizards, I feel a lot better about showing up on his doorstep during the daylight.

I feel powerless, so I focus on doing the things I can. I move the trove back into the attic, though that means removing most of the papers first, shoving the box up through the hatch, and then carrying the papers up stack by stack. I shower, get dressed, and try to put myself together. And then I bring the scanner up to the attic, too, and comfort myself with the pleasant monotony of scanning in the pages for a couple of hours.

The ravenous curiosity I had the first time I looked through these pages has faded, and I have to move quickly. But there's already a familiarity in the materials that feels like a scaffold for my frustration.

Given the great big coincidence of my dad ending up with something murderous possessing him with these books nearby, the pages also take on a sinister feel. These books are mine. These books got my dad killed. Both things are true. Both things matter. Neither changes the other.

I get the hang of the scanner pretty quickly and notice that Gigi had set it to only save the scans locally. Nope! Always have a backup! *Especially* when you are dealing with a rare trove of ancient and forbidden knowledge. That's just common sense.

I go to set the scanner to save to the cloud and then hesitate, remembering Wilbur and his beacons. Instead, I retrieve an old external storage drive from the office and let the images of spells and supernatural info settle in between archived photos from back when dedicated digital cameras were more of a thing, and PDFs of old tax returns.

My back is a little stiff when I come up on the deadline I set for myself to leave the house. I want to make sure I have enough time to tell Max what we're doing before our 12:07 p.m. appointment at the mall.

I don't leave early. I don't want to give myself too much unallocated time around him. I may not have Wilbur's hate for wizards, but I feel certain I'm safer the more distance I keep, even as useful as it might be to have backup out there today.

I drive to Mayflower Way. This being Springfield, there's very little traffic, and I make good time. His electric-blue car is in the driveway, and I'm not surprised. I'm not due to be back at my workplace until next week, so why would he bother showing up there?

The wizard's house is up on the side of a hill, and a series of immaculate stone steps meanders up to the front door. It's an old Victorian, in a neighborhood comprised of both houses of similar vintage, and more modern creations of architectural exhibitionism. Any second, I expect some kind of community watch is going to walk up and ask me what exactly I'm doing in the area. The place *smells* like money. Expensive plantings, trees down the middle of the street. The whole shebang. I expected it would, based on the breakdowns by neighborhood I see now and then on tax revenue and spurious complaints, but I'm still floored.

And, hell, why not say it: I'm annoyed that Max lives here.

Nothing I've read so far would make me think wizards *wouldn't* use their magic to enrich themselves. Probably the third spell they learn, after eidetic memory and beautification.

I climb the stone stairs to the wraparound front porch,

ducking my head to avoid an out-of-place sprig of blooming jasmine.

"Lizzie!" Max's enthusiastic voice greets me. "Welcome to my humble abode."

He's grinning like the cat who ate the canary. Not sure if he thinks it's impressive that he knew I was coming before I knocked on the door, or if he thinks me being here is an admission of guilt for our tiff yesterday—or whatever you'd call it. A moment of annoyance? I don't know. There had been a lot of magic involved just a moment before. I don't have my feet under me in those kinds of situations yet. It's all too new and overwhelming.

Which is why I'm here.

"Won't you come in?" he asks, opening the door wide and stepping aside.

I think harmful thoughts and walk through the doorway without an ounce of resistance. Huh. No wards then. Amateur.

"Aren't there all kinds of fairy tales about not walking into wizards' houses when they invite you?" I say after it's already too late. If something horrible were going to happen to me just from walking inside, Wilbur would have warned me.

"You're thinking of witches," he says. "Those are the baby-eating bitches."

"That's a little sexist," I say, and he shrugs, moving to lead me out of the entryway and into the house proper.

"Wizard is a gender-neutral term. There aren't any witches. We can say whatever we want about something that doesn't exist."

I follow him, and try to take it all in. The entryway feels like a continuation of the outside of the house—a perfect recreation of the Victorian aesthetic, but with a modern color palette and more durable modern materials.

But inside, Max has filled the Victorian living room, complete with gleaming wooden floors and perfectly restored trim, with aggressively modern furniture.

There's a huge glass coffee table in the living room that almost seems to float, so unobtrusive are its supports. A misspent childhood watching *America's Funniest Home Videos* reruns prepares me for it to break. The sofas are leather and look comfortable, but also like they shouldn't be able to support themselves, either, on the steel legs that purport to hold them up. I almost ask Max if there's magic involved in their construction, but don't. That isn't the kind of magic that interests me.

A huge, curved TV hangs on the wall opposite the largest couch, and gaming consoles sit on a floating shelf beneath it. I wonder how often he plays. *Mario Kart* can't be as interesting as unraveling the mysteries of the universe, can it? But I guess he must have a lot of extra time on his hands, what with not contributing to society in any meaningful way.

I go over to the couch and sit down like I own the place. Max perches on a similarly styled armchair nearby. I could sleep on this couch. I want to sleep on this couch. I wish I'd slept better last night.

"Make any progress?" I ask him, the picture of innocence.

"Did *you*? I figured you'd get something from the troll after we put on that show for him."

Is he really that fucking arrogant? Could he really not imagine that watching him digging around in people's heads without their consent might make me a little miffed?

I think I cover well, not showing my shock, but it's hard to be sure. It's also possible that he might be lying— crafting a polite alternate reality, where any disagreement between us had just been a ploy, so that we can slide past it without discussion. If that's the case, I'll take it. If it's not the case, then no need to fight with someone that delusional now.

"I did, in fact, get more info."

I lay out a version of what we put together last night, editing out anything to do with my dad.

"Any idea what the thing we're dealing with might be?" I ask when I'm finished explaining.

"Plenty," he says, standing. He starts walking toward a door that must lead to the kitchen.

"You want something to drink?" he calls back over his shoulder.

"I don't think we have time," I answer, but he's gone. I roll my eyes. I should have timed it even closer.

He comes back with a beer and something fruity and—given the smell of it—deeply alcoholic.

You know what? Maybe I do want something to drink. Might make this all a little more tolerable.

"Is this a magic potion?" I ask, accepting the drink and taking a swig.

"Nah. A harmful one wouldn't work on you, anyway," he says, returning to his perch on the armchair.

"That's why I accepted." I raise my glass in a toast. We probably don't need to keep restating the fact that I have an amulet, but it makes me feel better that we are. You gotta take any reassurance you can get when walking into the lion's den.

"Okay, so your plan is, what, exactly?" he asks after a deep drink. "Just go to this mall where we *think* all of the victims were when the one before them died, and look around?"

"I was hoping you had something for that. Don't you have some kind of spirit-catching something or other?"

He considers. "It depends what kind of a spirit it is. I

have a bottle that can contain some spirits, if we could find a way to get it in there."

"So how do we get it in there? If it does turn out to be the right kind of spirit to contain."

He looks at me, annoyed. I take a long drink. This stuff isn't bad.

"Would have been helpful if you'd told me about this last night. Given me some time to prepare."

"What happened to your perfect memory?" I ask, to Max's answering eye roll.

"Doesn't mean I think faster. Maybe we could—"

I glance around myself. Suddenly, I need to go look outside. I have to go see what's there. Something's coming. Something bad.

I narrowly avoid standing before I realize this isn't a natural impulse. I look at Max in accusation.

"Warning wards," he says. "They usually don't go off that strong. It must be…" A look of realization comes over his face. "Oh, *shit.*"

He jumps up, nimbler than I've seen him move before. In a fraction of a second, he's leaning over the coffee table, lifting the edge of it up.

"What are you doing?" I ask, rising to my feet. I doubt he hears me. His eyes are cast down to the empty floor beneath the coffee table. I maneuver my way beside him so I can see what he's looking at from his angle.

A glass box hides underneath where the tabletop had been, unable to be seen from any other angle. There are a few assorted items in it: a flashlight, a box, a bottle, and a few other shapes I can't identify.

"Get in," he says, his voice deeper than it has been up to this point. I open my mouth to protest, but he looks scared. It unnerves me. I want to say something dumb like *glass is transparent, idiot* just on impulse, but it seems safe to assume magic at this point.

Would my amulet stop him from trapping me? I have my doubts, but I make the call to trust him and climb inside.

There's plenty of room inside the box. If it's a coffin, it's a spacious one. My corpse would have plenty of space to stretch out in the afterlife.

He lowers the lid down over me, and the finality of the way it closes makes me imagine a rabbit as a trapping loop tightens around its leg. I can see the living room perfectly clearly still, but it's another world now, completely separate from my own. I don't hear Max's footsteps as he climbs up onto the floating shelf holding his gaming gear and adjusts something behind the TV. I don't hear anything at all. I don't even feel or hear it when Max sits on the couch and puts his feet up on the coffee table, just above my hips.

He sips his beer, doing a convincing impression of someone without a care in the world.

Seconds later, a man and a woman walk into the room.

No. They're more than that. They have the flawless beauty I thought Max had when I first met him.

The woman is tall—just a little shorter than Max and the man. She's got those perfect proportions it's impossible not to associate with pinup girls on the sides of airplanes, not in the least because she has that same aura of surface beauty wrapped around impending violence.

I'm almost completely straight, but she's hitting that with a sledgehammer. She's wearing one of those contour dresses in a rich purple, and black wedge heels that I'm sure were made by someone with three first names and a thick accent they're rich enough not to need to minimize. Her luscious brown hair falls in long, even, hair-commercial waves. If I didn't think she had magical shortcuts, I'd wonder how she had time to get anything done around her haircare routine. Her beauty feels cookie-cutter—like the front cover of a romance novel. Constructed. Which, I suppose, she is. It does nothing whatsoever to lessen her appeal.

The crisp, Scandinavian man next to her is a little older and embodies the word *distinguished* in a way usually reserved for George Clooney. Despite the difference in skin tone, something in the wideness of his mouth reminds me of Faisal. But that's where the resemblance ends. Faisal's features always seem to be fighting for real estate in a way I've always found charmingly goofy. This man's features are perfectly balanced. I've heard that beauty is closely related to symmetry, and the way I feel when I look at him amply supports that theory.

His glossy white-blond hair is long for a man's, but not what you would call shoulder-length. It's more that there's just enough of it to show a slight wave that would be easy to ruin with too much gel. Naturally, he doesn't.

It's clear his perfectly tailored suit came from the same place Max's did. Around his neck, he wears a purple cashmere scarf hanging down like a priest's stole that matches the woman's dress. They're a matched pair in every way. They go together.

I feel drawn to them like a spectator to a red carpet. They're the important people. They're the ones everyone cares about. Just looking at them, you know they float through life. And, when they don't, their failures are epic tragedies, not unfortunate, embarrassing episodes.

When Max looks at him, fear is written on his face and in the way he holds his body—in the tension there. He may be trying hard to project a casual air, but I caught the look of a cornered animal in his eyes the moment they walked in.

My breath comes in ragged gasps as I try to balance my physical reaction to their beauty, my instinctive sympathetic fear seeing Max's tension, and my curiosity. I want to know what they're saying so, so badly. But a part of me is glad I can't—it would be too much to handle.

They don't seem pleased with Max. This is a lecture, I think. My best guess watching their faces is that he's disappointed them in some way, and he's trying to play it off.

I pull my glasses down off my head and over my eyes, pretty sure I know what I'm going to see.

Yup. They have the same cut-out-and-Photoshopped-onto-the-background look that Max does.

Goddamn fucking wizards.

I relax a little, pushing my glasses back up. Nothing I've read has *said* that I'd get a headache if I stare at them too long through the glasses, but it feels like a thing that could happen.

They're beautiful because it's a trick. That's not real. It's not them. Max is terrified of them because they're dangerous and—probably—evil. They're likely older than they look.

Ask that wizard why you'll never meet a member of the Fae. Or gods.

I wish I could read lips, but I read the interplay between them, and that serves me well enough. The dynamic never changes. Max never gets any less terrified, although once he plucks up the courage to say something that must have been a risky little semi-affront, and he gets his metaphorical hand slapped for it.

At one point, the woman comes up to him and strokes his cheek, and I see Max fighting with himself. She has the distinctive look of a snake about to swallow its prey whole. And Max, despite himself, looks like prey that wouldn't mind being eaten. My eyes shoot to the man, looking on.

His sky-blue eyes are sharp. Grim. Proud? Something about him tells me that he has all the power here. Always has. Always will. I don't know what he is, or what he does, or what he can do. But I hate him. Impossible not to.

Finally, Max's excuses or apologies or promises must be enough, and they prepare to leave. How long has it been? I kind of want to pull my phone out and look, but I'm not sure how this thing works, and I wouldn't put it past the weird world of magic for looking at my phone to give me away somehow. I'm not sure why. Maybe it's paranoia at being so lost in all this. But still, I leave it in the pocket of my jacket. Instead, I look at the very stylish clock on the wall—one of those digital-analog hybrids where the numbers are formed by rearranging sticks that turn themselves into the letters that spell out the time. It sends a spike of panic down my spine. We're running out of time.

Max shepherds the other wizards to the door to the entryway, looking like he's pulled by strings. Just before they go, the man holds out his hand, and Max kneels and kisses the signet ring on it. The man withdraws his hand, but before Max can rise, the woman leans down and kisses his lips. I see the jolt of desire and terror run through Max's body. Then the woman pulls away, smiling like a well-fed tigress, and the two of them are gone.

Max watches the door impassively. His hands shake ever so slightly, and he clenches them to stop the motion. He swallows. He calms his breathing with three long, overexaggerated breaths. He closes his eyes and shakes his head ever so slightly, a motion too quick not to be well practiced.

And it's back—the bright, chipper, unstoppable air that he's had every time I've seen him. He strides over to the box, and I take care to note exactly where he puts his hand this time as he lifts up the side of the tabletop. I finally know how the food in vacuum-packed jars feels when you pop the lid.

"Your girlfriend's pretty," I say, unable to resist poking at the sore spot, however bad I feel about it the second after I say it. It's satisfying to see how quickly it punctures his air of invincibility. It makes me feel at less of a disadvantage as I sit up in my glass box, gently stretching out to release the stiffness that has set in from being held still in the same position on a hard surface.

"Those are my mentors," he says, and I shoot him a disbelieving look. He misinterprets it, wincing. "All right, those are my *masters*. It's traditional."

"Oh, she looks like your *master*, all right."

I feel mean. I'm tired, and I resent him, and it's making me mean. I don't want to be.

But he doesn't seem wounded—just worried. He fixes me with an intensity I didn't know he possessed, and I feel caught by the perfect green of his magically beautified eyes.

"She's dangerous," he all but whispers. "So is he. Don't meet them. Don't ever give them a reason to know who you are. You don't want to be on their radar."

"Or what?" I ask, sliding the words into him like a knife. "They'll erase my brain?"

"No. They don't do a lot of that," he says, settling back onto the floor, showing an exhaustion that a young, spry, well-rested man really shouldn't have before noon. He sits in a puddle of sun from the skylight above, and I can just about feel the warmth of it on his skin. If the Right Mind for messing with minds is what I guessed it was from watching Max do it yesterday, it doesn't surprise me those people don't do it often. I wonder if they even can.

Max doesn't look at me as he continues talking. "They'll find something you love and hold it over you to make you take your amulet off. Then they'll kill you, and probably do what they threatened you with anyway. You'll be dead, and for nothing. I'm sorry. I should have returned their call yesterday. They heard about the train. I should have kept them from getting interested."

He looks at me again, pleading. "Don't let them meet you."

I nod. He shakes off the conversation with that same subtle breathing technique that he used in the doorway. He stands up with an easy, graceful strength, back to himself. He smirks down at me as I much more awkwardly work my way up and out of my box.

"Of course, I could make that much easier for you to do."

"Oh, fuck off," I say. "Let's get to the mall. We're going to be late."

EIGHTEEN

An Encounter

I hate the development built in part on my father's land. I hated it even before the events of the last couple of days. At least Max's shiny blue jealousy magnet fits in with the general feeling of excess and materialism and gains us looks of approval when we park.

This place used to be fields not so long ago. And then, almost overnight, there was this stand of perfectly formed buildings and a deliberately planned-out "user experience" that feels like someone's very large, very financially motivated dollhouse. It doesn't have the vibe of a classic mall. It's outdoors, with buildings that are technically different, even though they were all built at the same time and probably rely on each other structurally. Shops and chain restaurants occupy the bottom two floors, apartments not worth what they cost sit above. There's even a movie theater that has a kind of corporate hipster quality to it. I resent how much I enjoy going to it now and then when Faisal's home and we decide we want to mark something with a designated date night.

I pop my glasses down, searching for anything magically amiss. Nothing jumps out at me.

I pull up a PDF of the site map on my phone. I got it in an email from an email address that was a random collection of letters and numbers. I feel confident I know who sent it. The site map tells me where the borders of Dad's land were.

It was a pretty small patch—half an acre right in the middle of all this. I try to figure out how to tell which of the buildings and streets we see before us falls into that patch. I frown. I can guess, but two guesses are better than one. Especially with only three minutes left, going by the clock on my phone. I speak quickly as I match Max's pace, heading into the expensive rat maze.

"Okay, so I think what we're looking for is going to happen within this patch of land. Where do you think…" I trail off as he lifts the phone from my hands to examine it closer. He clenches his jaw in what I know now is annoyance with me, and he quickens his pace such that it's hard to keep up.

"I think it's under the Walgreens. And maybe…" He looks up. "Maybe the alley behind?"

There's a question in his voice, but not in his step. Max clearly knows this place better than I do, and I accept the phone back from him, having to jog faster than he does with my shorter legs. Still, I trail behind.

Three minutes gets us close. I keep my glasses on, searching around me as we break into a run.

And then I see it.

At first, I think someone's just started a fire—that someone has burned something that gave off a lot of smoke. But there's no fire, and the smoke is changing colors from black to white to gray as it moves, like one of those color-changing fish that catches the light and reflects it back in strange and beautiful ways. Its movements are erratic, but I see it go around the corner of the building, heading back into the alley.

Max and I run after it. I have to hold my glasses on, but the fear forces me forward, helping me keep pace with him. Together, we round the corner, and…

Find ourselves in a crowd of people. My heart sinks. An exit door from the back hallway of the theater releases into the alley. One of their morning matinees of carefully chosen obscure-but-not-really-obscure movies must have just let out.

"Look in their eyes," Max hisses at me, as he starts going up to people, grabbing their faces in his hands, and examining their eyes. It's not making him any friends, but he doesn't care about that, and neither do I as I do the same.

I start working my way through the crowd, spreading out through it, covering people he hasn't examined. I don't know what I'm looking for. Maybe smoke of some kind? Something that looks like the creature I just saw, if I can even call it that? I'm guessing I'll know it when I see it.

But I don't see it, and the crowd begins to thin out.

"Wait!" I hear Max yell. "Let me look at you!" But they don't listen to him. He must not have a spell for that. If we were in an enclosed space, maybe he could have locked it down the way he did my house when we met. But his desperation makes it clear he's out of options.

"I work for the mayor's office!" I try, my voice sounding weak and harsh. "I need everyone to stay put for a second."

That gets a few looks, but then they look between me and Max, at our casual clothes and desperate demeanor and lack of badges. The inclination to credit me with any kind of authority doesn't take hold.

We chase after people as we can and spend the next twenty minutes searching the area and the route between the alley and the parking lot for any familiar faces to examine, but it's too late.

We lost it.

Whatever that was, it rode someone's body away. And that body is going to kill itself in three days. Just like the person who must have died somewhere out in Springfield for the spirit to reappear here, ready to start the whole cycle again.

Max and I don't give up easily. I get thrown out of two restaurants that I try to get into to see if I can recognize anyone in them who might have gone for a meal after the movie. I imagine he probably has been, too. We didn't prearrange somewhere to meet—didn't know what was going to happen. But he's half-sitting-half-leaning on the hood of his car when I get back to it, finally accepting that whoever the spirit rode out is lost to us now.

I don't think his anger is directed at me any more than mine is directed at him. He doesn't blow up at me, and I don't blow up at him, though either of us could probably have found an excuse to blame the other. If I hadn't… if he hadn't… maybe we'd have gotten there sooner. Maybe we'd have been in the alley quicker. But then, maybe we'd have been inside the Walgreens. No way to know if we'd have guessed right if we'd had more time. Maybe we'd have seen nothing at all and been in even worse shape.

I hoist myself up onto the hood next to him, sitting with my feet on the front bumper.

"How'd you know the exact area?" he asks with no preamble or playfulness. He doesn't expect me to try and keep it from him, and I don't.

"My dad was the first suicide. He started the pattern. Everyone else was probably here or possibly here at the time the person before them died. And he owned the plot of land in the plat map I showed you."

He breathes in and out, slowly. He doesn't yell at me for holding back.

"What was that thing?" I ask with the same expectation of forthcomingness, which he fulfills.

"A vampiric spirit."

I crook an eyebrow. "Like a vampire?" I ask, dismissing the thought of how natural Max's master would look in in-season Armani.

"No. Vampiric spirits have no more to do with vampires than vampire bats do. Something any vampire would be happy to tell you if you ask. Often in those words. And before you ask—no, that thing won't fit in my bottle."

He's trying to make light of it with that comment about vampires, but his tone of voice doesn't quite get there. He's haunted in a way I'm not comfortable with.

"What does it do?" I ask, fearing the answer.

"It's kind of a curse, kind of a weapon. I've heard some wizards can cast them, but I've never seen it. A bunch of different kinds of supernatural beings can do it, too. Probably more than I know about."

I've been assuming Max is older than me. Most of the time he looks like it, but right now, he looks so very young.

"So, someone cursed the land? Or someone cursed people? A person?"

Max's voice is soft as he answers. He's watching the muddled tide of humanity moving around us like ants in an ant farm. "A person. It's always a person. A person did something to upset a creature, and the creature cursed them. But the target avoided it somehow, and now the curse—the spirit—is looking for them. I don't know how it got bound here, but that's the only thing that makes sense.

The spirit's only goal is to get to the person it was created for, so it jumps into someone to get free of the binding to go look for them. That must be what all the walking is about."

I nod and pick up where he left off. "And then it gives up after three days and comes back here to try it with someone else. Why three days?"

Max shrugs. "I don't know. Might be part of the binding. Might be something about vampiric spirits I've never heard about. Might be an arbitrary decision on its part. I don't know a lot about them. And I might be wrong, but… I don't know. It fits, mostly."

I try to imagine either of Max's masters saying, "I don't know," but I can't.

Neither of us says what we're both thinking: It would sure help if we could ask my dad.

"We should ask your dad," Max says.

I stare at him. At least, I didn't *think* either of us was going to say it.

"Oh, sorry," he says. "We should ask the man you thought was your dad."

I no longer feel bad about being mean earlier, after his masters came to visit. "He's dead. You know that."

He rolls his eyes. "Yes, obviously. But where did you bury him? And was he a retina donor?"

NINETEEN

An Exhumation

Max didn't want to let me come along. He tried to convince me that I didn't want to see what he was going to do. I countered that the whole reason he was "letting me tag along" was to show me something to convince me I didn't want to be a part of this world. But as I stand in my father's grave, digging down, my pigheaded resolve wavers.

"And, to think, you wanted us to do this during the daytime," Max says.

I roll my eyes. "Forgive me for assuming you have more useful skills than you do."

How was I to know he couldn't hide us from view? Wizards once crafted an illusion so strong it covered all supernatural beings for a thousand years and allowed them to change with their environment. Was a little disguise in a rarely used graveyard so much to expect?

They just don't make wizards like they used to.

I'm out of breath and sullen. Other than a call from Faisal, during which I struggled to sound like a sane human being and found an excuse to get off quickly, I spent the entire day reading the trove and scanning in pages. Or, at least, reading the English portions and my father's notes on translations. I found nothing in them that would prevent another body from piling up on my already-crowded conscience.

We hit the coffin just after midnight. Digging up a grave is more work than you think, even when there are two of you and the grave is less than two weeks old.

"And to think, you wanted to do this alone," I say, as we maneuver ropes under the coffin, using both our strength to get him up to our level. We aren't successful. The coffin slides back down, and I get the horrible feeling that I've dropped my father.

"Are you sure we can't just do this down there?" I ask.

He shakes his head. "I'll be tired and sick after. I won't want to climb up."

"We have to fill in the grave anyway. You're not getting out of that just because you're tired."

I'm not going to let Olivia hear about Dad's grave getting looted. She doesn't need that.

"Fine. But you're right—we don't have to bring him all the way up."

Good. The man can change his mind. Sometimes. About something.

"I just need his eyes."

What the fuck.

"What the fuck?"

"What did you think we were here for?"

I shake my head. "You need to look in his eyes—okay. That's fine. But they stay in his head."

The moon is not enough light for this work. Not really. But it's just enough to see the queasy look on Max's face. "I'm not going to look into his eyes. You can go home if you want to. You should want to."

I stare at him for a long moment. An owl sees a prime opportunity to enhance dramatic tension and hoots. Neither of us move.

People are dying. My father is dead. Dead men don't need their eyes.

I nod, and Max jumps down into the hole. I lay on my stomach, leaning over the side of the grave.

We paid a lot for this casket. I didn't want to. I didn't think Dad would have wanted us to, but Olivia thought it would be better for the girls. It was going to be traumatic, she said, for this to be the only time they ever saw him. She wanted for it to feel as nice as possible.

"Oh, not *nice*," she had said. "You know what I mean."

I did. The funeral director with the dollar signs in his eyes understood, too.

The casket is polished wood, but after over a week in the earth, it doesn't gleam anymore. But the split lid does allow Max to sit over where the bottom half of my dad's body lies and open the top.

"You can look away," Max says. "It's all right."

It isn't. The least I can do is hold my cellphone flashlight and watch as Max opens my dad's left eye and slides a spoon—a fucking spoon—into the socket and removes his eye. I don't feel sick. Or sad. It all feels more like a prop than a body. When a wave of revulsion finally comes as Max turns his attention to the second eye, I tell it to fuck off. The sick, angry shudder that rips through my body doesn't listen, but I keep my dinner down.

Max pulls a small glass jar out of the front pocket of his hoodie, places my father's eyes inside, and puts it back. He closes the lid of the coffin and reaches for my hand to help him out of the grave. I give it to him.

We fill the grave and pack the earth down on it hard. It doesn't look exactly like it did before, but I think we do a decent job. The grass hasn't begun to sprout yet, so that helps.

"Can we go somewhere else for this?" I ask Max when we're done. I'm tired of this place. I remember the funeral. I remember Olivia, and Peter, and the girls. I remember the dull throb of knowing that Dad was gone, back when I hadn't started getting used to it yet. I remember feeling Mom's absence. I don't want to be here anymore. I don't want to stand in this place anymore.

"No," he says, as if just remembering himself. "We can't get that far from the body. It needs to… it needs to be close."

He maneuvers onto the freshly packed ground, right over where my father is, six feet below. He looks… I'm not sure. A little sick already, maybe? More than a little afraid. He doesn't want to do this—whatever he's about to do. He places the open jar with my dad's eyeballs in front of him.

He closes his eyes and takes a deep breath, and then opens them. He reminds me of a character in a war movie. He's got that same "Okay, we're doing this, with me, men!" look to him. The safe distance of practicality. He reminds me of Olivia.

"This is a long spell. It's going to take a couple of minutes. I mean a full couple of minutes, not what people think a couple of minutes feels like. If I do it right—and I am going to do it right—then I'm going to be brought into all of his negative memories to experience them. They won't be in order, and they won't be fun. I'm going to start shaking like I'm having a seizure when it happens, so if I don't get myself on one side, I need you to turn me. If you want to come along for the ride, you just have to touch your skin anywhere to my skin. It won't be as intense for you, and you won't be able to control it, but you also shouldn't shake or anything. And you shouldn't get sick."

I keep looking at the ground beneath him like I should be able to see through it. Like I should be able to ask Dad if this is okay. He'd say it was. I think. The last time I spoke to him as himself was eight years ago, but he was a good man, right? He'd approve if he knew.

I hold on to that belief and nod dumbly.

"I'm going to try and do this quietly, but if someone comes up, do *not* fucking leave me. Tell them I'm having a breakdown and try to get them to call in as few mental professionals as possible. Don't let them call the cops."

"Sheriff's office," I say quietly, with a hint of a smile. I almost wink. I mean it as a joke—a little callback to calm him down or lighten his mood. But it's ill-advised, and he doesn't go for it.

"Sheriff's office," he agrees. "The fewer people I have to clean up, the easier it will be. But if I have to clean up anyone after I'm finished with this, it's going to be a pain. You need to get me back home."

It's almost as bad an idea for him to rely on me as it would be for me to rely on him, but he's doing it anyway.

"You should start. It's cold."

It is. He does.

There's a lot of chanting in a language I've never heard and can't identify. The closest I could guess with the reference points I have is somewhere between Arabic and Chinese. I try to pay as much attention to the sounds as I can, even trying to repeat some words to myself after the fact. Not loudly. I don't think anything I do could interfere with what he's doing, but I don't want him to notice.

There's a lot in the trove about spoken elements to spells, but a language you don't speak is difficult to get across without the benefit of being able to record sound. The wizard Stuart could have recorded something but apparently he did not. All the other trove contributors have different ways of trying to get across how to pronounce the words—which, like everything, must be done *perfectly*. Dad straight up gave up on performing any spells with spoken elements.

Maybe if I hear Max speak enough, I'll have a chance. I surreptitiously start my phone recording while Max has his eyes closed. This could be a helpful night in more ways than one.

I watch his motions carefully, too. If it came to it, I would have no trouble convincing anyone that he was having some kind of a breakdown. They're jerky and seem uncontrolled, although I know they must be perfectly executed. He's like a modern interpretive dancer with a particularly masochistic choreographer.

And in there, underneath all this, there's a Right Mind. I'm never going to execute this spell—I'm certain after the first ten seconds—so I don't put too much thought into trying to work out what it is based on the look on his face.

But it isn't good.

A couple minutes is a long time. Such a long time. My focus on him is so absolute that I wouldn't notice someone if they did come up and ask what we were doing, and it lengthens my sense of the passage of time further. It could be almost dawn, for all I know, when Max reaches into the jar and pulls out my father's eyes.

And eats them.

"Holy fuck," I say, his spell on me broken as the spell he's putting on himself comes to fruition, sending him into the apparent seizure.

I hadn't let myself think he would do that. I hadn't let myself believe that was the aim. It was too wrong to be real. It was too far.

Max is on his back. He'll choke on his own tongue. I

can't move. He ate my father's eyes. He's seeing my father's life.

People are dying.

I crawl toward Max, fighting revulsion. I shove him roughly onto his side. I want to kick him. I want to scream in his face.

I could have left.

I lay my hand on the side of his neck.

And I, David Baker, feel pain. A deep, intense, physical pain. And I see my worried wife telling me I'm going to be all right. I feel her hand on my arm, and I trust her.

And I feel embarrassed. People are laughing at me for some reason. Young boys. They look young, but I think they're so big and intimidating. And I feel like screaming at someone, and I feel like beating someone.

The experiences are all passing too fast. I can't keep track. It's bewildering and confusing enough that I start being able to assert a sense of self—a sense of difference between me and the things I'm feeling and thinking.

Max is driving, and he gets the car under control.

He starts flipping through memories at an easier, measured pace. A sense of order emerges from the chaos. He lets each one play for a bare few seconds before flipping forward. We don't come across any more embarrassment, which seems privacy-preserving. Likewise, we're not seeing anything from when he was a kid anymore.

Max seems to have oriented himself to time, and everything becomes more recent.

And then we're in Dad's mental hospital. I recognize the floor tiles.

I almost scream and break my grip, but I force my hand to maintain its lock on Max's neck.

Oh god, I need to get out of here. I need to go searching. I need to run. I need to find. I need to die. I am a failure. I need to die. I am not useful.

The memory is gone, but the one it slides into is almost identical, just with a different patch of floor tiles and a different light. The same sense of failure. The same desperation. The same struggling at restraints.

It's gone. And then it's back. Carpet now.

Then more tiles.

Then a softer room. I wasn't ever allowed to see him here, but the staff at the hospital reported it was sometimes necessary.

Then carpet.

Then tiles.

And then that desperation is gone, replaced by sadness. By regret. I'm standing in a field just out of town, holding a hula hoop, and Mr. Thompson is in front of me.

"Are you sure?" Mr. Thompson says. I barely recognize him. He's younger, sure—eight years younger. But he's unsteady in a way I don't ever remember seeing him. He's shaking.

"It has to be done if you want to be free," I hear myself, David Baker, say. I believe my own words, but I hate them. And then I hold the hula hoop steady and make sure it's aligned right, just at the edge of the property that I own. And reach out to him and pull him toward me.

Then I'm not in the field anymore, and I feel a different kind of anger. I feel someone else's anger—Max's anger? Did he lose grip? Why didn't we stay? We needed to watch…

I see a piece of paper in my shaking hands. I, Elizabeth, recognize Wilhelm's Big Book of Monsters, as I've been calling it. I, Elizabeth, can't read the German it's in. But I, David Baker, read about vampiric spirits with rising rage. I tear the page apart, and I hate that it exists.

No. I hate what it says on it. I hate what I have to—

No. I hate that it's there. I hate that that man had it.

This isn't right. This isn't Dad. There is another intelligence.

And then I, Elizabeth, am in my body again, feeling Max throw me off of him. There's something greedy in his green eyes, flashing in the light of the moon like they're illuminated from within. Maybe they are.

"You have a trove," he forces through a tight throat, his voice horse and veins popping out the side of his neck and appearing on his temples.

"You have a trove," he says again, reaching for me.

His hands find me, and he's trying to claw at me—to *hurt* me. But his fingers aren't allowed to. They slide off with only enough pressure on my skin to register.

I scramble away. I don't know what went wrong. I don't know where he got lost. I don't know if he'll come back, but I know I don't want to be close to whatever he is in the meantime.

"Give it to me!" he finds enough voice to scream as I start walking away before breaking into a run. "I'll kill you for it. Give it to me! I'll take it!"

TWENTY

An Interrogation

Thank god we drove separately to the graveyard, so I've got my car here to drive myself home. I'm even grateful that I parked a few blocks away in front of a convenience store, so it didn't seem quite so strange to have two cars parked in front of a graveyard in the middle of the night. The walk gives me a few minutes to get my head in order and regain my nerves before putting myself in charge of a couple of tons of machinery.

Part of it I expected. Part of it I should have expected, really. Part of it…

Okay, set that aside. First things first—immediate danger. Max went a little off the deep end when he learned about the trove. That's… not great. But at least it's something that's only going to happen once. And him learning about it when in a weird mind-melded state with a dead guy probably wasn't ideal.

The good news is, I still have my amulet, and it worked. I still have my wards, and if they work, they should absolutely protect against Max, especially now. Wanting to steal from me and wipe my mind *has* to count as the intention to do harm, right? But the intention to do harm from whose perspective? His or mine? And technically I haven't tested that they protect against harm, just that they hide magic. I saw them doing one of the things they were supposed to do, and I have just been assuming the other.

Maybe I should have had Gigi steal that tiger. She probably would have enjoyed it.

I near the convenience store, and there are people milling about. If they notice the dirt on my yellow jacket and jeans, they don't mention it. Hopefully they're not putting it together with the late hour and the proximity to a graveyard.

Okay, second thing—Dad and the vampiric spirit. So that was real. And Dad voluntarily took the vampiric spirit into his body, and he must have been the one to bind it to the field he bought—the field I shouldn't have sold.

I have to smile, even in spite of everything. My father, the crazy man. My father, the write-off. My father, the hero. Sacrificing himself to save someone else. It's been a long time since I've felt proud of my father. It feels good.

I reach my car and calm down enough to sit inside. I fight off the pang of guilt for leaving Max in the graveyard. He said he'd be exhausted after the spell, sure, but if he really needed help, he shouldn't have threatened me. At least that means he probably won't be able to come after me tonight.

I call the engine up to life. I've been sitting in such fancy cars over the past few days, it sounds and feels reassuringly normal. Then I head for home, which also feels reassuringly normal.

Of course, Dad-the-hero also meant Dad-the-man-in-control-of-his-choices-who-voluntarily-abandoned-us. That doesn't *not* hurt. Would he have done it if we had been younger? Did he decide both his kids were old enough he could abandon us, tell the biggest lie by omission I'd ever heard of, and step out of our lives?

And then there was Mom. I'd taken for granted that Dad losing his mind had destroyed her—that that was why she is the way she is now. But what if it isn't true? She was always so different, growing up. If Dad didn't lose his mind, then maybe it was true that Mom didn't lose her heart. Maybe it got taken, somehow.

What did vampiric spirits *do*, exactly? They might not be vampires, but that name still sounds ominous. I need that sheet from Wilhelm's **Big Book of Monsters**. And I need more answers about what happened eight years ago.

I park in my driveway. Instead of walking to my own door, I head across the street. It's late, but Mr. Thompson doesn't have the right to complain about me waking him up in the middle of the night. He owes me. Plus, he'll be safer in my house than in his until we figure everything out.

Assuming he can enter.

Mr. Thompson has a doorbell, but I don't use it. I like the idea of pounding on the door with my fist. It releases a tiny bit of the coiled tension in me, and I'll take all the help with that I can get.

It takes a bit before Mr. Thompson comes to the door. When he opens it, I figure he must have been getting dressed, because he's wearing the same jeans and flannel shirt he always does. He looks at me, framed as I must be in the glow of his porch light, standing out against the dark of the night. Smudged, and exhausted, and furious.

"I know," I say. He doesn't give or lose any ground. He just nods with what looks like a mixture of sadness and relief.

"How much?"

"Not enough. I have questions. Do you have the page?"

He shoots me a confused look, but I don't supply an answer. He can figure it out himself. He does. "I do."

"Go get it," I say. Anger confers authority. There's something I've learned. Mr. Thompson—Henry—disappears into the depths of the house. True to form, he must know exactly where the page is, because he returns seconds later with it in hand.

"Grab your coat, we're going to my place," I say. I'm not mad at him—not entirely. Although he did keep a pretty fucking big secret from me for eight years, I'm sure he was just following my dad's instructions. But Dad isn't here to be mad at, so I guess Henry drew the short straw.

I head toward my house, and he follows not far behind. When we get to the front door, he follows me inside like nothing is there. Which either means nothing *is* there, or he means me no harm. Which, I mean, he *shouldn't*, but always good to know.

We sit down at the kitchen table, and I take the old man in. Well, not *old*. He'd been one of the younger teachers in school back when I'd had him—which made him the target for all the girls who were prone to authority-induced crushes. But he looks so tired right now, it's hard not to think of him as older than he is.

Eight years is a long time to let someone suffer for saving you. Eight years is a long time to want to tell people about things you know they won't believe. Eight years is a long time to apologize for.

I'd had two supernatural beings at this table, and I'd fed them. It feels too much like an interrogation without sharing something between us.

"Do you want a drink? Tea? Coffee?"

He breathes out in an almost-laugh, and I feel a bit of his steady, gentle aura return. "Tea would be nice, Elizabeth."

I leave him sitting at the table, fill up the kettle, and put it on the stove. It's weird to be wearing my leather jacket inside, so I shrug it off and hang it by the door. I look over while I do and note that Henry is looking at the torn bits of Wilhelm's Big Book of Monsters like he's examining the face of an old friend he hasn't seen in a while.

There's a certain amount of affection that comes with familiarity, even when the thing you're familiar with has ruined your life. I wonder if this is the way I used to look at the front entrance of my dad's institution.

I take off my shoes, too, and everything starts feeling a little more normal. Henry, taking his cue from me, takes his jacket off and lets it rest over the back of his chair. He wore house shoes for the trip across the street, and he keeps them on.

It feels more like early morning than late night now, even though it's not. There's a closeness to early mornings —a shared sense of being in a separate world from the one when the sun comes up—and I feel that closeness now.

I go to the kitchen and start sorting things out. I bring out two mugs—big chunky things that Olivia's girls made at school. I'd always figured they must have gotten a lot of help from the teacher, because they're pretty nice and the girls are pretty young. Then I dig out the tea box and start going through the options.

I choose a chai-flavored one for me and read off the list to Henry.

He's an internally consistent man, even now, and he brings the same sort of steady consideration that I know he applies to projects even to things like choice of tea. He selects a lemon-mint combo that's one of my favorites.

I stare at the kettle on the stove rather than head back to the table. I've kind of thought things through, but it hasn't all settled down yet. It won't for a while, I don't think. Maybe not for a long while. My cheeks feel hot, and I lean my elbows on the kitchen counter and rest my head in my still-chilled hands to cool them down.

Henry doesn't rush me. He sits at the table like a reassuring statue. And when the water has finished boiling, and I bring the hot mugs over to rest in front of us, I see him looking out over the messy living room.

He was Dad's friend. Mom's, too. I was too young to think about the age difference back then, but there must have been as much of a gap between him and his wife and Mom and Dad as there is between me and him. A couple of years more, actually. And I still don't know the details of what happened, but Dad saved him. There's that.

We each sip our tea. Mine burns the roof of my mouth. How do I upgrade the amulet to save me from the foreseeable consequences of my own actions? That's what I really need.

"So," Henry says at last, breaking the silence that I can't, "how much do you know?"

I mull it over, trying to put it in the right order for him. How much does *he* know?

"There's a thing called a vampiric spirit. It was in you eight years ago. Dad got it out with"—I frown—"a hula hoop. Somehow. And he took it into himself, but also bound it to a field so if it's not in a body, it gets pulled back there. I think he meant it as a failsafe, so if he couldn't keep it contained, it would be somewhere people would be unlikely to go so it couldn't ride them out and come looking for you. But it's now a shopping mall, so it didn't work out that way."

Henry's eyes widen.

"We sold it a few years ago," I say, trying not to let the guilt I feel seep into my voice. "We didn't know not to."

Henry shakes his head. "I didn't remember where the field was. That day is… hard to remember clearly."

I keep going. It feels good to be able to share everything with someone and not worry if I'm telling them things I shouldn't, or if their motivations don't align with mine.

"Dad has a trove of information about magic. Which is real. And terrifying. And fun."

He raises his eyebrows at fun, but it's true. It *is* fun, whatever else it may also be. Maybe it's not polite to say that in front of him, all things considered, but too late now.

"I don't know how Dad got it, but he did a lot of reading and translating, and he made this"—I pull my amulet up from under my shirt and hold it toward him—"and these." I touch my glasses. "And also a lantern."

Henry nods. "I know the lantern. Your dad was proud of it. He should have been. Very detailed. Very delicate. Your dad wanted me to reinforce the joints on it with some small welds. So he gave it to me, and I brought it to school, where I keep the welder."

His raw voice cracks. I feel like when you uncork a very old bottle of wine, and you briefly feel connected to when it was bottled.

"He told me to be careful with it, and I was. I reinforced the joints so it would be strong enough to go in a bag, but I still kept it out on the seat next to me on my way home instead of putting it away. Why did I not just put it in a fucking bag?"

His anger and regret come rolling off him like waves of heat. He boxes them away in an instant and continues.

"I stopped to get gas on the way home, and there was a man at the pump. I spend a lot of time thinking about what would have happened if he hadn't been there. He was plain-looking. I didn't think anything of him. Brown suit. And those kind of speckled…"

He searches for the word, and I hand it to him, my blood running cold. "Tortoiseshell."

He snaps his fingers and points at me. "Tortoiseshell glasses. He saw the lantern, and it pissed him off. He told me…" Henry's face crumples up. Not like he's trying to remember, but like he still doesn't understand, like he's tried to for years. "He told me I cheated. That I'm the cheater he's been looking for, and I'm not going to do it anymore."

I snap back to the great fighting hall at the Casino of Lost Souls—to the face of the man in the glasses. It wasn't fear he was feeling. It wasn't desperation. I see it clearer now. It was anger.

"*She's cheating*" hadn't been a cry for help. It had been an accusation.

Order, rules, permission… A non-wizard doing magic is against the rules, according to the treaty. We don't have permission.

Henry sees something in my face, but he doesn't push me for it. He owes me an explanation, not the other way around. He continues.

"He pointed at me. And… things get a little hard to remember after that. I remember wanting. And *needing*. I remember fighting. I wanted to reach out and *take* from people. From everyone. And I knew there was some core, some 'me,' but it was hard to separate it. It felt like I was the one who wanted it. It felt like *I* wanted to hurt people. To steal from them.

"I remember I went home and got my gun. I didn't want to die, but I didn't want to be a threat to anyone anymore. But I was fighting my own desire to stay alive and the thing's desire to stay alive. So it was two against one.

"Your dad came over when he saw my truck in the driveway. I guess to get the lantern. But he found me. I tried to take from him, but I couldn't. He looked at me— he looked in my eyes. He was wearing those glasses you have now. And then he brought me home with him, and went up into the attic, and told me just to sit still…"

Henry trails off. He's not done, but he's struggling to say what comes next. A sense of dread fills me, starting at my head and flowing down through me like water filling a pitcher of ice. His voice cracks, and tears form in his eyes when he finally gets the next part out.

"And then your mom came home. And I took from her."

Henry has always struck me as a mountain. It feels hard and strange to see a mountain cry. I don't know what to do with it. I just sit, and watch, and turn over my own anger and despair. I try to figure out where to point it. I can't point it at the broken man in front of me. I don't ask what he took from her. I know. I've felt it gone for the last eight years.

I'm crying, too, but not shaking and sobbing into my hands the way he is. The tears just roll onto my cheeks as I sit, still and solid as Gigi. I sip my tea and burn my mouth some more, with automatic motion.

It's a long time, but probably not long enough, before Henry shoves it down and shakes his head and wipes the tears from his eyes to continue.

"Your dad saw. He locked me in the basement for a while where I couldn't hurt anyone. I don't know how he got you and your mom out of the house, but I know it took a few days for him to get everything ready. He let me up into the house sometimes, but… I don't remember a lot.

Everything around that time is hard to remember. The thing in me was angry. Frustrated. And I was so weak.

"But then he took me out to the field, and he stood up this… Well, I guess you know about the hula hoop. He set it up at the edge of the field, and then told me to walk through it. I didn't know what was going on. I could feel the thing… fighting. I guess that's all I can call it. It seemed confused, too. But then your dad kind of threw it down over me, and grabbed me and pulled me forward, out of it. And then… it was gone."

He's waiting for me to tell him it sounds stupid. And honestly, it kind of does. But my dad sometimes did stupid-sounding things for good reasons. I bring the amulet out from under my shirt and get him to confirm it's the same one he saw my dad wearing, mostly to reassure him that I believe him.

"He put it around my neck and told me to put it up in the attic on top of a note on the train set when we were done. He gave me that page and told me to hold on to it. I asked him why he couldn't do all that himself, and he told me that I would need to take him to the mental hospital afterward. And then he told me I could never tell anyone. That he would hold it as long as he could, and that when he was gone, it would come back to the field. He said it was trapped in there, and it could only get out in a person, and hopefully no one would wander by for it to get into.

"I tried to argue with him, but he stepped into the field, and he was different. So I did what he told me to. We went with his plan."

I nod. I revisit the scene from Dad's memories, remembering how broken he was. It makes more sense now, knowing about Mom. And it might be inconvenient, but I'm glad Max lost his shit and lost control of the spell before I got far enough back to experience seeing Henry "take" from Mom from my dad's perspective.

"But that didn't work out, you said," Henry says. It's the first time I've ever heard anything like bitterness in Henry's voice.

I nod my head.

"So, what's happening?" He's laid aside his bitterness, but it's replaced with a gruffness—the voice some men use when they want to cry but don't think they're allowed. I guess he's exhausted his quota.

I could lie to him, but he wouldn't want that. And he doesn't deserve it. "When Dad died, it got pulled back to the field. The shopping mall, now. It jumped into someone who was there and used that body to go looking for you. Walking, mostly. Then after three days, it gave up, and…" I study his face, willing myself to continue. After the longest two seconds of my life, I do. "It makes them kill themselves, gets sucked back to the shopping mall, jumps into someone else, and tries again."

He lays his head in his hands. I take a big breath in, looking for words to say to comfort him. I don't find any, but I open my mouth to say something—anything. He stays my words with an outstretched palm, and I obey his wishes.

When he's finished absorbing this, and he's pulled himself back together again, he looks at me expectantly for a long moment, like he's waiting for questions. I don't have any for him. I don't even have many for my dad, really. Even if I could ask him. Most of them have answers, just not answers I like.

Except one. Henry probably won't know, but I ask him anyway. He's here, and Dad's not.

"What about the lantern? Didn't he use the lantern to try to find someone who could help?"

Henry shifts his gaze back at me, away from where it had rested on the napkin holder on the table. "I don't know. He didn't tell me anything about that."

Okay, Max, couldn't you have held on to your self-control just a *little bit* longer?

If he'd followed the lantern, he should have been able to link into the supernatural community. But Gigi didn't mention him tracking her down.

Gigi. Now there's a thought.

I get out my phone, give the Emporium a quick google, and call the listed number. I'm surprised it's open so late, but the business listing says it is. An unfamiliar voice answers me, and informs me that Gigi's out tonight, and that, no, they don't have any way of reaching her that they are at liberty to disclose.

What's the point of shiny new supernatural friends if you can't reach them? I didn't think to get Wilbur's number, either, come to that.

Maybe "friends" is the wrong word.

I make a note to get out the lantern to track Gigi down after I've sent Henry to bed. I don't want to make him look at it again.

"Is there anything else you can tell me?" I ask Henry, whose gaze has settled onto an empty place in the living room while I talked with the unhelpful shop assistant. "Anything else you remember?"

He looks back at me, and I let him search around for the answer to be sure of it. Back in high school, when Henry told us to measure twice, he said it like a mantra he lived by. He shakes his head, certain at last.

"You should stay here tonight. The vampiric spirit is looking for you. I've got wards around the house." I don't stand, and neither does he. My voice is businesslike, chan-neling Olivia. "There's an empty room at the end of the hallway. There's an air mattress in the closet, and some spare blankets and things."

He takes the instructions for the orders they are and begins toward the hall.

"Henry," I say, just as he reaches the edge of the room. My voice is more me again and less Olivia-under-stress. "A bag wouldn't have helped. He would have seen the lantern anyway, through the bag."

I swear I can almost literally see the weight lift from his broad shoulders. I look into the last face my mother saw as her whole self—a face I know she trusted.

"You did nothing wrong."

TWENTY-ONE

An Education

I let Henry get settled, waiting until I no longer hear any sounds of movement from down the hall. I try to absorb what he said. It doesn't sink in—not fully. I've spent eight years accepting that my father had a disease. That it was just bad luck. I've got all of these pieces fitted together inside myself, and by now I'm really good at putting them back where they belong when they fall out.

But the pieces don't fit right anymore. Some have shrunk and some have grown, and I don't have the space, time, or emotional bandwidth to figure this out right now.

When Henry's settled, I head up to the attic to grab the lantern and track down Gigi. She was the one who told me about the graveling at the casino—what he was, what mattered to him. If anyone can help me come up with a plan, it'll be her. I pull the trove out from under the table, hoping it doesn't bother Henry too much.

I open up the cabinet and retrieve the lantern from inside. I flip my glasses down to see which direction the flame is leaning in, to get a read on whether I'll be following it to the Emporium or somewhere else.

Through the glasses, the lantern looks exactly as it does without them. The once-enchanted object is now entirely mundane.

I swallow hard, my heart racing. I flash back to Gigi's hands resting innocently on the lantern. She's the only one other than me who's touched it, and I haven't looked at the lantern through the glasses since she did.

I stifle the urge to throw the lantern across the room. My lifeline to help—gone. I want to know why, but I also just don't fucking care why. I was right to be angry she'd handled my trove. She can't be trusted. Why didn't I realize that sooner? What difference would it have made if I had?

I channel my anger into finding the answers I have access to in Gigi's absence. I head down to the office and grab my laptop, a pen and paper, and a stack of multicolored sticky notes. I need the power of Google and office supplies for this one. I could go back out to the living room and bring the page back into the office and work there, but it's right next to the room Henry is set up in, and I feel the need for a little more breathing room. I don't think he's sleeping, but I should let him try.

A collection of sites on the internet is helpful for translation, but they have trouble with some of Wilhelm's antiquated terms. It's possible he made some of them up, anyway, or they're wizard words—on top of being ancient. I'm not sure how to enter some of the characters, either. If I had more time, and if I felt comfortable leaving the safety of the wards right now with the way Max looked at me, I would drive out to Skyway Park and ask Wilbur if he knew someone who would help me translate. I've got a hunch that's a connection he could make.

But as it is, I muddle along with my good-enough

translation, cobbled together with a surface-level understanding of the language and concepts involved, and run away with the conclusions. That's the best I've got to go on. College was good for something. The concentration and the distraction help dampen my anger at Gigi, but they don't extinguish it. She and I will talk. Later.

So. Vampiric spirits. Bad. A weapon. Do what they say on the tin. Often a punishment, sometimes ironic. Bound to their target and will dissipate upon his or her death. Not detectable by any magic trace, looks like a cloud of smoke when disembodied, visible in the victim's eyes when in possession. Steals…. Time? Or goodness? Both, somehow?

None of this helps. Until—some vampiric spirits are tied to the caster and perish if they do.

Jesus fucking Christ. I could have just kept my mouth shut at the casino, and all of this might have been over. Saving the man in the brown suit felt like the right thing to do at the time. But when I did it, I sentenced someone I had never met to death.

Unintended consequences are not my fault.

No. Unintended, *unforeseeable* consequences are not my fault. I couldn't have known. And no one else was helping.

I couldn't have known.

I couldn't have known.

I couldn't have known.

It doesn't help. I move on. That helps.

This is a way out. Maybe. *If* it turns out that the graveling is one of the casters who are tied to the spirits it casts. Then all we have to do is draw it out and kill it.

I see the graveling—the man in the brown suit, terrified behind his glasses. I know what he was, sort of. At least, I know what he did. I think of the Valkyrie standing in the ring with her knife in hand about to kill him, and I still feel anger. I picture myself as the Valkyrie, executing him, and I feel sick.

But not as sick as I'd feel if the next victim—whoever the vampiric spirit is walking in now, using them to try and find Henry—dies because I wasn't willing to try.

I've never had to think about whether or not I would be willing to murder someone. It's a question asked and answered—of course I wouldn't. Normal, good, acceptable people don't murder.

I want to scream, but I'm too tired. I don't want to put another body in a grave like the one I've dug up and reburied. I don't want any more bodies in any more graves. Why are there no solutions with no bodies in graves?

I could talk to the graveling. Convince him to pull the vampiric spirit back somehow. Lie? Say I won't do magic anymore, and I'll stick to the role of ignorance and helplessness the treaty proscribes for me? If he asks for the amulet, what then? I give it to him. I don't tell him about the trove, but I tell him *enough* to believe I'm going to go through with it, and I sort out what I'm going to do about Max later. Stay behind the wards as long as I need to. It could work. Maybe.

I don't believe myself when I say this is possible. But it lets me set aside the existential crisis long enough to plan what I'm going to do.

When the graveling ran into Henry at the gas station, he said that he was searching for a cheater. He must have sensed my dad doing magic. He's still in town or nearby—I know that because he showed up at the casino. I don't know if he sensed it when I accidentally interacted with the voodoo train. But if he did, he didn't sense it clearly enough to come looking for me. So if I want to draw him out with my uncondoned magic, I'll need to do something brighter and showier and longer-lasting than my moment with the train.

I know exactly one spell.

I need to science this a little. Faisal could help with that, but he's not here. Henry will have to do. I've got to determine if there's a way to make the one spell I know bigger and smellier and longer-lasting than the thing with the train. Is the magic visible when I snap my fingers? On my fingers, or on me, or on the fire? Or even on the medium the fire consumes? Does it stay for as long as the fire does? Does it make a difference what medium I start the fire on? Does size matter (har har har)?

My eyes flick up to the attic, where I know the rest of the trove sits, waiting patiently. Maybe I should look through there and try to find something else that I could do with a larger impact?

But no—the wizard Stuart knew all the spells I have access to, and this one was the one he thought a beginner could do. And even this one had still taken me a while to figure out. If it turned out tomorrow that the fire spell wouldn't work, I could start looking at the wizard Stuart's other beginner spells.

I've already begun to accept that I can't figure this out tonight. I need Henry's help to do it properly, both because I'll need his expertise to cut perfect squares out of different materials and because I could use an extra observer wearing the glasses to be ready to note how much magic he sees for how long, so that I can focus on getting my Right Mind correct.

And I'm not rousing Henry now. Maybe he's managed to get to sleep. I definitely need some sleep if I'm going to face what I need to do tomorrow. It's going to be hard to drift off, everything in turmoil as it is, but I've got to try.

Especially because of one inescapable fact: For whatever magic I can pull off to be enough to summon the man in the brown suit, it's going to be big enough that it might summon any of the supernatural beings I made enemies of in the casino. Max, too. And the last time I saw Max, he was willing to kill me for my trove. And I left him there in the graveyard, after he told me not to.

Fantastic.

TWENTY-TWO

A Trap

Henry wakes before I do. It's nice having him here. It's nice to come out and share the intimate togetherness of a quiet morning hemmed in a protected space, with traces of frost on the windows from an unexpected cold turn sometime last night.

He's figured out the coffee maker and found the coffee —neither of which are feats that should be underestimated —and the cup of coffee he hands me is somehow better than what I would have made. I sit at the kitchen table, looking out the slider into the backyard, sipping and wondering how that's possible. Same beans, same tools, same everything. But his tastes better.

"It's about the temperature of the water," Henry answers my unasked question as he settles into the chair across the table from me. "You've got to get the water right. And I used that pour-over dripper you've got up on the shelf instead of the automatic thing."

He doesn't say the words "automatic thing" with outright disgust, but I feel it hiding under there, anyway.

Do it carefully. Do it once. Do it right. How many times had he said those words in that one semester of shop class? So few of us had listened, but he just kept on saying them anyway.

Henry would probably be a hell of a magician. The trove should have gone to him to begin with, if there was any justice in the world.

"It's good," I say between sips.

"You buy good coffee," he says.

"Faisal read a review."

I wish he were here.

We don't start by talking about what we talked about last night. He asks me where Faisal is, and I tell him about his job, and about his trips in general. I don't think I sound frustrated by it, and I shouldn't—usually, I'm not. Usually, I'm not dealing with stuff like this while he's gone. Just normal life stuff. I can handle normal life stuff.

When we've both eased our way into the day, and the mental glow of the dawn starts to fade into the hum of activity of the morning, there's no more avoiding it.

"So, I think I have a solution. To the vampiric spirit issue, I mean. According to the page, some of them dissipate when the caster dies. So if worse comes to worst, we kill the caster. But I'm going to try to talk to him first and convince him to just undo the curse. He's called a graveling. I actually saved his life the other day. Didn't know then what he'd done, but he was in trouble, and I helped him. He kind of owes me."

Henry studies my face. "Do you think you should kill him?" he asks, forcing me to the question I'm avoiding. He doesn't even touch the talk-it-out idea, and I guess that's right. Henry has never struck me as the kind of guy good at hiding in justifications. That must have been hell the last eight years.

"It could work. And more people will die if I don't."

"Are we sure there's no other option? Is there anyone else we could ask?"

I look at my phone on the table but make no move to reach for it. If Gigi wanted to be found, she wouldn't have extinguished my lantern. She said she had a business to run, but she wasn't there last night.

"You'll regret it if you don't," Henry says. I hate that he's right.

So I call the Emporium anyway. A different employee, who is similarly unhelpful, tells me that Gigi isn't expected in. I do some quick googling while Henry patiently sips his coffee, fixing me with a soft look of not-unkind interest. I come up with nothing for Gigi. Not even a last name.

Figures. I've run out of leads I can follow from the dining room table, and I've run out of coffee.

"I've got to run out for a bit," I tell Henry, who nods, not looking up from his newspaper.

I don't tell him to stay put, but he's not an idiot.

I drive out to Skyway Park and get a little twinge of disappointment that I'm out and about in the world during the time people are on their work commutes, but I'm not headed to my job. I'd kill to be able to just go back to work and have a normal day in my life.

Maybe that's not great phrasing right now.

Skyway Park isn't great for joggers. It wasn't designed to be. And there aren't any other people here on this particular morning. That's nice, I guess. Means I'll have some privacy talking to Wilbur. But no matter how many times I call his name over the edge of different parts of the bridge, Wilbur doesn't respond.

I stand, looking out over the valley below. Still a gorgeous view. We did good making this park. As I stand there, a couple members of the public show up. They're an elderly couple. I don't stare, but I can't help but notice the way they talk to one another. That kind of gently chiding, comfortable relationship.

My parents should have that coming. Mom shouldn't have had part of her mind stolen. Dad shouldn't have gotten killed.

Gotten himself killed?

I leave that thought on the bridge and head to Max's house. It's still there, still gorgeous. His electric-blue car is in the driveway, so he must have gotten back from the graveyard in one piece. I get some you-don't-belong-here looks from people out on the street in expensive exercise wear as I pound on Max's door for a full minute.

I give up, mostly relieved I don't have to face him right now. He's sleeping it off, I guess. I'm not sure if I hope he's better or hope he's not by the time I'm ready to lure the man in the brown suit out into the open. On the one hand, he could do the killing instead of me. He's a wizard. I'm pretty sure they do that kind of thing. The Fae and gods could testify to that, according to Wilbur.

On the other hand, shunting the responsibility for what I know has to be done onto someone else doesn't make me feel any better. And Max might not give me the chance to talk him down. He might go straight for the shooting. Or killing—however wizards get that done.

I head home.

I look around for Henry when I get in the door, but I don't see him. I do, though, see a dining room chair in the hallway and the hatch to the attic pulled down. I catch my breath. I guess he should know. I guess he has a right to.

I note he doesn't seem to have touched the train set, as far as I can tell. But he has found the cabinet and the scanner. He's started up where Gigi and I left off, scanning in the trove. Careful. Methodical. Helpful. He gives me a weak, expectant smile as I settle down onto the floor beside him. I'm not angry at him for touching the trove the way I was at Gigi. And I wasn't as angry at her at the time, as it turns out I should have been.

"We're on our own," I say. He nods. And then he replaces the sticky notes on a page, turns to the next one, and hits the button. His movements feel like a part of a dance—a little ritual of monotonous, repetitive actions that he's settled into. I don't pull him out of it right away.

"Do you have any ideas for flushing out the graveling?" he asks, not stopping his movements.

"I have *an* idea," I say. "But I need your help testing it."

His hands halt, and he looks at me. "Tell me what you need."

We start doing experiments. I can tell Henry likes the glasses and likes wearing them. He's relishing his role as an assistant, and he falls easily into a kind of teacher-y vibe when we have to go over to his house to use the shop in his garage to make perfectly straight, square cuts in some of his scrap plywood, of which he has a truly impressive amount and variety. We don't spend long over there, though. I feel better with amulet-lacking Henry behind the safety of the wards as much as possible, regardless of the lack of an immediate threat that I can see coming. The threats you can see coming aren't the ones you have to worry about.

After a long morning, a lunch break, and the beginnings of an afternoon, we've wrested some answers from the sea of mystery.

Yes, size matters. The bigger the material we set the fire on, the more magic jumps out, looking like crimson smoke arising from flames but not bound to the movement of the air around it. We can use noncombustible materials, but the fire on them doesn't last long—it's basically just a flash in the pan and then it's out. I've gotten pretty good at cutting, transferring, and positioning vinyl cut on the Cricut cutter, which seems to be reliable. Printed paper with the symbol will only ever immolate the paper, no matter how we affix it to the object.

The longer the fire lasts, the bigger the plume of magic smoke gets. When I go to the attic, the crimson smoke doesn't seem deterred at all by the floor in between. In a moment of panic, I go outside and check to make sure that the smoke isn't escaping out above the house. It's occurred to me that the barrier the wards make might be vertical only. But I see nothing escaping the house. Good to know.

I'm satisfied that this spell will work for our purposes. It doesn't, unfortunately, spread to other objects if the fire does. The magic only flares up with the flames, so I can't just burn a building down and call it a day. I just have to set a lot of fires *inside* a building. And hey, what happens, happens.

And I know the perfect place.

It might not be good for me to admit publicly to wanting to burn a building down. Something, something, civil servant. But there's a perfectly good area on the north side that used to be a mixed light industrial and low-income residential area, and it now has been trying to become a better place to live. There's this one frustratingly stubborn guy, Mr. Elison, who owns a building that builds nothing, sells nothing, makes nothing. City Hall may not get involved directly in real estate deals unless it's something we can buy, but that doesn't mean there aren't things we wish would happen.

Besides, I'm pretty sure Elison has criminal reasons for not accepting perfectly reasonable offers from developers with surprisingly good plans. Probably. I'm guessing. Either that, or he's hoping someone does what I might do today, and he gets to collect on the insurance, and *then* sell the building to someone who would have had to knock it down anyway.

It takes us a few hours to get materials together. I stay with Henry in his workshop, assisting as I can. We figure out the largest board I can easily carry, thirty-eight-by-thirty-eight inches, and Henry sets to work making them. I mark their exact centers, which is a task I'm suitable for. And I've got plenty of time to cut out enough of the symbols on the Cricut cutter.

Henry runs through his wood supply—a feat I thought impossible—and I make a quick run to the hardware store to get the cheapest boards I can find. I'm relieved when I return and don't see Max's car parked out front and Henry's dead body in his garage.

I stop us at one-thirty. I leave enough time to get everything set up and underway before school lets out, kids being kids and a creepy abandoned building being a creepy abandoned building. We have twenty-nine boards, complete with vinyl stickers. In our experiments, I couldn't detect a difference between the process of setting one on fire and setting several on fire at the same time. I'm kind of curious if I'll be able to manage all of them at once or not. I guess we'll see.

I try to convince Henry that he needs to stay home—that given everything, it's best for him to stay behind the wards—but he points out the time crunch and won't hear of it. I think it'll make him feel better, and it's not like I have rank to pull, so I accept his help. Besides, it's his truck.

I'm grateful he's there as we unload, and as it finally occurs to me that leaving his recognizable truck sitting outside what may soon be a burning building would be a bad idea. And I'm grateful he brought the hand truck from his garage. I wouldn't have thought of it. Between loading, driving, and unloading the boards throughout all three levels of the building, it's around two-thirty when it comes time for me to wave him goodbye.

Before he goes, he pulls something from his jacket, wrapped in cloth. I know what it is before I feel the hard weight of it in my hand.

I didn't ask for his gun. I'd heard him say he had it. I'd even thought I might need to use it. But every time my thoughts got close to what I'd use it for and how I should ask him if I could borrow it, I had started running after some shiny new thought like a magpie.

He gives my hand a squeeze when he's transferred it to me.

"I'll text when I'm back behind the wards," he says.

He doesn't say anything else. What is there to say?

Good luck. Maybe he could have wished me good luck. I don't think Henry believes in luck, but I do.

I watch him drive away and keep myself busy to stop myself from staring at my phone, waiting for the text. I check and make sure that the fire suppression system is nonfunctional. I'm not an expert in such things, but it doesn't take one to recognize that it's been disconnected in a way that can only be intentional.

I'm almost sorry to be helping this guy out. But that doesn't matter. The end goal matters. Whatever happens— even if I end up dying in this building, or if my plan doesn't work—this neighborhood *will* get better. I feel good about that. Almost good enough to cover over my nerves.

My phone dings.

Safe, the text from Henry reads.

I head up to the third floor. None of the boards are close to the stairwells, and I have a clear path out. I figure I can set them off, then run a route that takes me to the bottom floor, checking that everything got set off on my way.

When I get to my starting point, I breathe in, and then I breathe out. And then I focus on Elison. I don't know if the target of my rage being connected to the outcome is going to have any effect on the spell. The wizard Stuart didn't mention it, but hey, it can't hurt.

I think about his stubborn refusals to get out of the way and let the neighborhood evolve. I think about the three times I've met the man, all at council meetings. I think about the parents of the children who live nearby, and what they told him about his "attractive nuisance," and the way they wielded those words like they were forged weapons they couldn't afford, given to them by a lawyer they must have banded together to hire.

And Elison just stood there in his navy-blue pinstripe suit. His platinum bleached-blond hair. A serene look on his face. His shoes with their mirror finish. The way he leaned back on the elementary school-sized plastic chairs, stretching his arm out just so, displaying a watch that easily matched the positive net worth of everyone else in the room that he hadn't brought with him. Probably including me at the time, considering my student loans, and that this was before I got my part of Dad's inheritance.

He didn't even have to be at the meeting. Whatever publicist he had must have warned him not to attend. Something about the man struck me as enjoying their pain —struck me as the kind of person who would enjoy other people's suffering.

You know the crack of a fire when the logs release some trapped air or moisture? You know how it's always louder than you expect?

I get that in surround sound, at the exact same moment

as I snap my fingers, carrying like thunder through the paper-like walls of the building.

Something in the back of my chest opens and trembles. It feels good. It feels really fucking good.

I give a cursory glance through doorways as I walk in a calm, orderly, swift fashion down the halls along my planned exit route. It doesn't take a lot of investigation to see that I got all twenty-nine.

Okay, twenty-seven. There were two of them that didn't catch. Either the vinyl wasn't cut quite right, or it wasn't attached in the perfect center, or—less likely— Henry hadn't cut it straight. But ninety-three percent is an A-minus. I'll take it.

At the back of the building, there's a large room that I assume was where some of the work actually got done, as opposed to the offices that had been skillessly carved out of all the other interior spaces. It has the advantage of being double height, not under any of the fires I'd set, and protected by a heavy set of fire doors that just might be the only thing in the building that still functions.

There are various types of machinery in here. Some of it is under covers, and I can't identify it. I do recognize broken sewing machine parts lined up along the side wall.

I sit down on the ground and wait, my fingers reaching up to feel my amulet underneath my shirt. It's amazing how fast you get used to something. Already in the moments I feel unsure or afraid, I'm reaching for it before I realize I am. It's calming. I let the feeling of it there steady me, solid and always just a little bit cool on my skin, as I wait for whatever it is I've ended up calling.

TWENTY-THREE

A Killing

At what point does dust become dirt?

A puff of ash comes flying out of one of the second-floor windows that look out over the space. It's beautiful.

I'm calmer right now than I think I have been in a long time. Which makes no sense, but there it is. Everything that matters normally doesn't right now. I feel disconnected from all of it in a pleasant way, like all of that was just who I was in all of the parts that make up my life, and who I am now, in this moment, is who I really am. I think I finally understand the feeling Faisal gets when he's traveling that he's tried to describe, and I always have to struggle not to take personally.

I don't know how long it takes the man in the brown suit with tortoiseshell glasses to appear at the door, right where I'm looking. Right where I expect him. I only know that my legs have stiffened from the waiting as I stand to greet him.

The set of his face projects confidence. He's steadier on

his feet than I've ever been. He looks bigger to me now than he did at the casino.

I wrote a speech in my head. I've been getting better at speechwriting from supervising the speechwriters, but it's not my milieu. I've got the words on the tip of my tongue.

I don't say them.

"Hello?" I hear my own voice say. It's shaky and uncertain. It has no effect.

"Can we talk?" I ask. He takes two more paces toward me, unhearing and undaunted.

Fragile. Gigi said that gravelings are fragile by supernatural standards, and Gigi tells the truth. He won't talk? Fine. I have a gun.

I bring it up in front of me, trying to remember everything I've ever heard about gun handling and gun safety. Grip firm but flexible. Two hands on the base. Don't put my finger on the trigger until I'm ready to take the shot.

I shoot at him. I hit. Blood—dirt, I know—hits the floor.

I expected the gun to kick back, but the kickback is stronger than I thought it would be, and I have to recenter after the first shot and aim again. The second shot is easier. He's a bigger target. He's coming closer, pulling out—I shit you not—a gleaming silver spear that seems to emerge from the side of his body like it was a part of him. Even the powerful wizard illusion can't make *that* look entirely normal.

My glasses are on my head, but I don't bring them down. It would shake me. He can't hurt me through my amulet, but the trail of what looks like blood tells me that I can hurt him. That's good enough.

I stand firm as he closes the distance. I keep shooting until the gun is empty.

I've heard that people don't understand how loud guns

really are until they are close to one. That's right. I can't hear anything but a high-pitched whine. I should have accepted Henry's offer of sound-isolating headphones.

Still, the man in the brown suit steps toward me.

How? I don't understand. I've hit him so many times. Shit. I should have brought more bullets. How was I supposed to know how many bullets it was going to take?

Shit.

I need to see what I was shooting. I should have to begin with. I thought it would be easier for me to keep my nerve if I didn't. And, besides, I thought he would at least talk to me.

I have a lot of excuses. They don't hold much water. I was afraid, and I made a dumb decision because people make dumb decisions when they're afraid. And I'm not experienced with this kind of fear. With any kind of fear, really.

I pull my glasses down over my eyes, now. Better late than never.

I see my mistake.

All of the shots I thought were hitting him in center mass ended up, at best, in his thighs. He's easily twelve feet tall and made chiefly of a roiling mass of roots. Not friendly, Groot-like roots. More sickened, black, and snake-like. The dirt they coil around and over and through is almost like a vapor. No—like rich silt suspended in water. Impossible to predict but entrancing to watch. It's silky, in a way. It's impossible not to think of how it would feel to be drawn down into it. It's impossible not to imagine it filling my lungs and encasing my body. I wouldn't be anything then. I wouldn't have to worry about anything. It would be right.

His spear is made of that vapor, and a part of me that terrifies my rational brain wants to kneel down in front of it and let what must always happen, happen now. To be where I belong. Where all of us belong.

I'm frozen when he stops barely ten feet from me. He's close enough that his outstretched spear nearly touches my chest, which jerks unevenly as I fight to draw ragged, horrified breaths.

From the tip on his spear, the movement of smoke draws my attention. With a sickening, sinking feeling, I recognize it. A new vampiric spirit made just for me. It curls around me—shifting black, gray, and white smoke. It encases me, trying to find a way in.

I have an amulet of invincibility.

He can't hurt me.

He can't.

I know that. I *know.*

My legs, however, aren't as well informed.

All humans are afraid of the violent embrace of fire. But that's only a secondary fear. All humans are *more* afraid of what comes after the fire, and I am no exception. I throw myself into the heavy steel fire doors, tossing them back with everything I have in me.

I set no fires in the hallways, but that doesn't matter. If my brain were a useful organ at the moment, it would remember that the real hazard of the fire isn't the heat or the flames—it's the smoke. I pull my shirt up to cover my nose and mouth, coughing as I lurch forward. I should have run to the side. I should have tried to dart around him and break for the door he entered. I should have been *thinking.* I should have led a life that would have prepared me for this. I'm fine under the kind of pressure I usually face. I'm shit under this kind.

Can't go back now. The creature fills the hallway behind me. I guess the rodent in me had hoped that by heading into the smaller space of the hallway, he wouldn't be able to follow. But the twisted, writhing roots that give his mass structure have altered to fit the dimensions of the hallway, and he strides forward, unhurried. Unworried.

I stumble over something—I don't know what. I rise. I stumble again. He gains more ground. I turn onto my back to look back, scrambling away, pushing my legs as much to feel like I'm kicking against him as I am trying to move myself forward. I'm every idiot blonde that gets murdered first in a horror movie. And I never even got to be promiscuous first.

My thoughts, my legs, and my will all stop moving when I see his eyes. Not human eyes, but a sense of that same vibrant brown that I'd seen looking so fearful at the casino. That same warmth.

Eyes don't really tell us anything. It's the muscles and face around them that do. I look into the creature's eyes and the featureless mass of writhing, seeping movement around it, and I see nothing. I know nothing of what he is. I never did.

Wizards made the world as it is more palatable so humans wouldn't see it for what it was. I'd focused so much on the truth the lie told. I should have remembered the lie part. There's nothing in this thing for me to relate to. My hand goes to my amulet. This time, I pull it out from under my shirt, gripping it in my fist like a grandmother who's been to too many funerals grips a rosary.

It's not going to save me. I set the fires myself. The smoke fills my lungs. It could only have been seconds. I'm going to have been killed in seconds. The thing isn't moving.

If it happened any other way, I would have died. But splinters and force erupt from one side of the hallway, and I'm dimly aware of the feeling of movement.

But moments after it happens, another sensation grips me.

One February, when I couldn't have been more than six, the bus didn't come. I decided to walk home. I thought it was going to be an adventure. It wasn't.

They found me four hours later in an unfamiliar neighborhood. I never recovered firm, orderly memories of the walk that led me there.

I don't know why I didn't ask for help from any of the houses. The running theory was that stranger-danger was a little too impressed upon me. What bothers me more is why none of the people in the houses helped me. But all that is later—rationalizing after the fact. All I remember from that day is the cold and the fear, and how they filled me. They felt bigger than me then. And they feel bigger than me now.

There's one other thing I wanted that day, that I remember so clearly. I remember wanting my mom to find me. To lift me up. To make it better and give me the things that I needed. She would take them away—the cold and the fear. I've never known a longing like that.

I know it again now. I need people. They'll help me. Just any people. They'll make it better. They'll take it away. They'll get me warm again.

I struggle, and I'm aware that I'm pinned, and the fire is louder now. Those same crackling, settling noises that made me feel so strong are going to consume me.

I'm still coughing. I still can't see well. But when a current of air draws away the smoke for a moment, I can see that the creature's roots aren't moving as much anymore. They're barely moving at all now.

I'm still cold and afraid, and I want to see people so, so much. My amulet is gone. I can't feel it in my hand. My grip must have broken the flimsy string my father had put it on when the explosion threw me to the side.

Of all the stupid, fucking ways to die, running into a fire *you created* and pulling off your invulnerability amulet *yourself* has to be up there.

But…

But….

If the thing stops moving, the vampiric spirit fades— maybe. And people get rescued from burning buildings all the time.

It looks really fucking bad right now—and it *hurts* really fucking bad. But maybe this is winning?

And if it is…

Nothing touches the cold. Nothing touches the fear. But a new fear piles on top of it like carpet over hardwood.

Max.

He's going to come. He's going to take my mind.

I feel around for my amulet. It can't keep me from the vampiric spirit already inside of me, but it can save me from Max.

Another burst of clear air and I can see the amulet, maybe a foot out of my reach down the broken hallway. I reach for it. The smoke blocks my view again, but I keep reaching for it.

There's a sharp sensation on my sternum. A bit of broken building is there, pinning me, holding me in place. The more I struggle, the more it digs in.

It doesn't matter. Max is going to take my mind. But no matter how much I struggle, I can't force myself forward toward the amulet.

The smoke clears again, and I see that the roots of the creature have stopped moving.

I can't tell very well what happens next. I only know there are more roots, and then everything's moving again.

The building foundations are bucking beneath me, and that frees me just enough to surge forward and snap up my amulet with only a searing pain in my torso to show for it. I shove the amulet deep into the pocket of my jeans, not trusting my own hands.

And then, in the shifting, I'm free. Sort of. I scramble toward what I think is up. Toward what I think is out. But I'm bloody, and coughing, and fading.

There's the sensation of arms pulling at me, and then fresh air.

The ringing in my ears never stopped. I can't hear Max talking. I try to make out what his lips are saying.

Eyes, maybe? He's saying something about eyes? He wants something from me. He wants to *know* something from me.

I want something from him. He will warm me. There is enough there. I just need to take it.

I reach my hands up toward his face, and he takes one of them in his own hand, as if by reflex.

And then he catches my eyes, and fear shoots through him.

No, not that. Fear isn't what I want. Fear won't warm me.

He shoves me back—no. He shoves me away from him, his face stricken with horror and disbelief. And then he jerks his head up, looking around like he's heard something.

Then I feel only the cold and the fear, and I see nothing.

TWENTY-FOUR

A Betrayal

I hear the beeping before I open my eyes. The cold and the fear are still there. They are most of me now. I'm lying on something soft, but I'm still so, so cold.

It's wrong. This is all wrong. My eyes shoot open, and I see the institutional tones of the room around me. I'm an engine that has seized. Contrary motion, conflicting drives. My muscles are tense, and my breaths come in ragged bursts.

"It's okay, it's okay, it's okay," Olivia breathes. She waves aside a hovering black fly and touches my shoulder, concern written on her face.

She thinks I'm in pain. The realization lands dully. She's right—there is pain somewhere in here. Buried under everything that matters more. A gash splits my torso at an angle. Bandages hold me together.

But all that matters is Olivia's hand, resting on top of the hospital gown on my shoulder.

Olivia! So much sweetness in her past. So much sweetness in her future. It will warm me. It will bring me back. It will take everything harsh and hard inside me away. I can trust Olivia. She will save me. She would *want* to save me. She loves me.

Oh, fuck. Oh fuck, no.

My hand begins raising, and I try to keep it down. I think whatever drugs they have me on must be helping. Everything feels just muddled enough. Everything feels separate, just enough. I've got to keep it that way.

And then it doesn't feel separate anymore. I'm remembering Olivia, sitting with me in a tree house at our friend's house, telling me the way the world worked from her older, wiser, thirteen-year-old perspective. Drawing a henna tattoo on me and promising me that I've always got her.

It's so sweet. I want to climb into that memory. I want to feel it again. I want to make it mine. To take it. To turn it into warmth.

My hand creeps up. Why is it only creeping? Why isn't it flying to touch her skin? It's trembling. I fight through the trembling to take what my sister offers me. What she's always offered me. She would want to help. She always wants to help.

My hand lays on hers.

And nothing happens. I don't get what I need from her. I grip her hand.

"Beth, are you all right?"

My sister's voice trembles with worry. I'm squeezing too hard.

Why isn't this working? Why is she holding back her help from me? Why isn't she saving me? She'd always be there. She told me she'd always be there for me. She *promised.*

My eyes cloud with anger. "The necklace," my voice croaks. "Give me the necklace."

Olivia's eyes widen. She takes an object from her pocket. The amulet.

"You mean the thing they found you with?" Olivia asks. "Is it… some kind of watch?"

Olivia loves a mystery. Even with me hurt, in the hospital and acting strangely, she's going to seek out more knowledge—indulge her curiosity. There's a sweetness in that, too. A sweetness I want. A sweetness that will warm me.

Weakly, I hold up my left hand—the one with the IV line in it.

"Put it in my hand," I say, like I'm talking to a child holding a gun.

She leans over me, and I feel the warmth of her. The strength of her love. The steadfastness of her character. She's strong enough. She's good enough. She will be enough.

My left hand grips the amulet with a strength I didn't know I had.

Finally. My right hand reaches to hers, and I take a deep, sharp, anticipatory breath.

Nothing. Fucking. Happens.

Anger at the amulet flashes through me. That's what's wrong. It has to be.

I try to release the amulet, but my hand doesn't respond.

"Get away from me," I breathe.

Why did I say that? I don't mean that. I mean the opposite of that.

"Beth, what's wrong?" Concern drips from her lips.

"Get away from me!" I scream.

I want to stop myself, but I can't. I don't want to hurt her. I recoil in horror at my words and the stricken look on my poor sister's face. She draws back from me a little but doesn't stray too far away. She's still leaning over me, still worried.

My left hand, the one with the amulet in its viselike grip, flies out and hits her across her cheek.

I've never hit anyone. I never thought I would need to. And to hit my sister… it feels so wrong. But I put real force behind the strike, and I feel the sickening certainty of a firm connection.

I want to apologize. I don't know why this is happening. I don't know why my hand is hurting her. But instead, I hear my own voice again, rasping, "Stay away from me!"

And then I'm up out of bed, barely covered by a hospital gown that's blessedly designed for someone a lot bigger around than I am. I yank my arm away, the motion ripping out the IV. My wrist bleeds, but I don't care.

I need to get home.

Yes, home will work. Henry is at home. Henry will help—Henry likes helping.

Olivia shrinks away from me now. I must have hit her harder than it felt like. Her fingers rest gently against her cheek, as though she could heal the bruise I think I can already see forming there. Or maybe that's just my guilt.

I'm sorry, I want to say. *I'm so, so sorry. I don't know why I did that. I'd never want to hurt you. Come here. Come, let me wrap my arms around you.*

But I don't say any of that, and the loss of control over my own mouth terrifies me.

I stalk into the hallway, feet bare, fingers still clutching my amulet. The nurses aren't paying attention to me. There's a flurry of activity drawing them elsewhere.

Good. I can get home to Henry, so he can help. I slip down the hall toward some glass doors that lead to a metal industrial stairway. It feels good to do something my body will let me do. Something it doesn't fight me on.

It doesn't fight me as I silently make my way down the stairs, finding a door marked "fire exit" after two flights.

This gives me a moment of pause—don't want to set off an alarm—but it's propped open with a rock. God bless the casual flouting of rules for the sake of convenience. One of life's few constants.

I slip out the door and see a pair of smokers laughing and joking with each other, too wrapped up in each other to notice me. They look happy together. Maybe they would help me? They work at a hospital. Does that mean they're the kind of people who like to help others? The warmth of their friendship is promising—enticing. But my fingers tighten around the amulet, and I know it won't work. I have to figure out how to get my hand to obey me again before anyone can help me, and they're not going to be able to assist me in that. Henry's my best hope.

The crisp air and muted light indicate that it's early morning. The dirty cement is cold on my bare feet, but it barely registers. It's nothing against the cold that runs through me.

I move quickly, with purpose, cutting the opposite direction so the smokers don't see me. Home is within walking distance of the hospital—barely—but I'm motivated. I let the promise of relief propel me forward.

I have to hide from people who seem to be looking for someone—me, I'm guessing—twice. But that's easy enough to do. I luck out with a well-placed dumpster and an unlocked back entrance to a building. I avoid people as much as I can. I take alleys and back streets. It works.

It takes something like ninety minutes to reach my front porch. I stare down at my feet. A trail of bloody footprints stands out starkly on the white steps and white porch floorboards. How much more blood did I lose on the walk here? I didn't even notice. My body feels weak.

"There you are." Henry's voice is a mixture of relief

and worry. He stands in the doorway, face crumpled in confusion and horror.

My chest tightens, though I don't know why. I'm relieved to see him, too.

"You can help me," I let out. I can hear the desperation and relief mingled in my own voice.

He nods his head slowly, looking me up and down. Examining.

"Why don't you come inside?" he asks, and I want to scream at him. Why isn't he helping?

"You need to help me," I say. This all feels wrong. My leg takes a step forward.

No. No, no, no. I should have known why my body let me come here. The wards. Something's wrong with the wards. They're going to rip me apart. Anger wells up in me, and I stop my legs from pulling me any further forward.

"I need you," I say to Henry. "Please. I *need* you."

I hold out my hand, gripped around the amulet. He has to understand. If he will just understand, he'll help me.

After a moment, thank god, his face clears. He understands. He's made up his mind. He nods slowly, steps out of the door, and wraps his arms around me.

I bury my face in his neck. Henry has always struck me as kind of sad in his own way, but there's still so much sweetness in him that was and that will be. It will be enough. It's got to be enough. If he will just take the amulet from my hand. I know he will. He's too good to abandon me. Too kind.

But then, with a surge of panic, I feel him dragging my body toward the doorway. He's holding me tightly, and I'm too off-balance and weak to stop him.

We cross through the doorway, and the threshold rips me to pieces.

TWENTY-FIVE

A Corner

I can't tell if I can't breathe or if I'm breathing too much. The mechanical feeling of air-in-air-out takes over everything for a while. A long while, maybe.

My eyes are close to the hardwood floors. They fill most of my field of vision. They get darker—the door closed.

I count my breaths. One in, two out, three in… up to ten, then I start over.

I'm on my fifth—maybe sixth—round when something new drops into my line of sight. The weird warping of the grain of the wood through water and glass.

I corral my errant pieces and parts up into a sitting position. Everything hurts—my torso and feet most of all —but I snap up the glass and start pouring it down my throat. I get most of it in my mouth, but I'm too eager. Streams leak out the sides and run down onto the thin fabric of my hospital gown.

God, it feels good. My temperature is all out of whack after… that. I have a sense of being overheated, but I can tell from the numbness in my legs that my body hasn't caught up to my mind yet.

When the water is gone, I close my eyes and focus on the movement of the water in my body. I set the glass down on the floor, and the clattering sound when it settles tells me that my hands are shaking. Were they before? Have I been shaking this whole time?

Sorting out the sensations and reactions and filing them all away in the right places takes time.

I've just about got a sense of self reconstituted—weak though it may be—when movement beside me calls my eyes open.

Henry's there. He doesn't look scared. He doesn't look much of anything. He's just watching. Waiting.

I pick up the glass, proud of how much less I'm shaking now. It barely hits against the floor as I summon the strength to bring it up.

"No." Henry's voice is gentle. "You'll throw up if you drink as much water as you want right now. Ask me how I know."

We're in an exclusive club, Henry and I. How many of us are there? Can't be many.

Henry's eyes go to my battered, bleeding feet. "Do you want help with those?"

At the word help, I shiver. The shiver can't be easy to distinguish from my base trembling at the moment, but Henry does and takes it as an answer.

"Okay."

He doesn't speak until I do. And I don't speak until three more ten-counts of breaths have brought me back further into myself.

"That was a risk."

The words are loaded with something, but I'm not sure if it's awe or apology. Henry readjusts, bringing his legs up in front of him and wrapping his arms around them.

"Not really. The heater kicked out, and I went down into the basement to sort it out. I saw what the wards looked like, and I recognized them."

I smile.

"The hula hoop," I say, feeling close to my dad in a way I haven't in eight years. It pulls one of the thorns out of me I didn't know I'd been carrying, and that's its own, new kind of pain.

Never let it be said I don't like variety in all things. One kind of pain? Never. I'll take five.

"The hula hoop," Henry confirms with a wistfulness in his voice that matches mine.

"Still," I say, "I could've eaten you."

Eaten isn't the right verb, but whatever. He knows.

He raises his eyebrows and looks away. "I'm stronger than you," he says matter of factly. "And you've lost a lot of blood. You're pale."

"Going for the authentic vampire experience."

We're not ready for jokes yet, but we both wince-smile gamely.

"I mean you wouldn't have… taken… for long before I pulled you through the door. And I've got a lot. I can spare a little."

I breathe out slowly and rest my head in my hands.

He doesn't say what he can spare a little of, but we both know. I want to cry. I want to hug him, but the thought freaks me out, even if I felt coordinated enough to try. Instead, I look around for my amulet. I don't see it, but Henry sees me looking and pulls it out from his pocket.

He hands it over in a smooth, easy motion, and that shouldn't be remarkable. It's mine. But it also makes me very aware of what a valuable object it is.

Or would be, if I didn't keep finding ways to get myself hurt despite its best efforts.

"This stopped it," I say, and tension in Henry that I hadn't noticed uncoils. Fear for me, I realize. "I didn't." I pause. "I don't know whether it's because it would be harming me in some way, and the amulet was protecting me from harm, or if it protects people I touch while I'm wearing it."

I don't know what's more likely, but I know what I'm hoping for. Something else occurs to me. "How did you know I wasn't carrying *your* vampiric spirit? How did you know I had my own?"

Henry shrugs. "I guess I didn't. But how would you have gotten mine? We don't even know where it is. And you were going to draw out the same person who cursed me, so…"

I nod. "If he did it before, he'd do it again."

Henry isn't going to say the next part out loud, but one of us needs to acknowledge my profound failure.

"So instead of getting rid of the one vampiric spirit, now there are two. And one of them isn't bound to the shopping mall."

Henry looks to the porch, and so do I. Neither of us can see it, and my glasses are still back at the hospital. But it's there, probably. Writhing. Trying to get in. I shove the terror I feel at the thought of it away from me.

I need to get cleaned up, but I don't want to track blood through the house on my way to the bathroom.

"I have flip-flops on the floor of my closet," I say. "Last door on the right."

He takes a second to follow the changing subject with me. When he does, for a passing moment I think he's going to try and carry me to the bathroom. I'm glad that moment is brief. He disappears and comes back with the shoes, and I walk carefully to the bathroom. I sit on the toilet lid, dangling my feet into the tub and letting the lukewarm water run over them. It's both too warm for my still-chilled body and too cold for my blazing-hot soul. It feels painful but good, on both counts.

Henry brings me clean towels and a first aid kit he must have hunted down in one of our boxes. Then he mercifully closes the door and leaves me alone to tend to my wounds. The one on my torso is fine, I think. It's still wrapped up and presumably clean. No blood seeping into the bandages, so I guess that means I didn't tear a stitch, which is what action movies have led me to believe happens when you ignore freshly patched wounds.

I get my feet clean, dry, and wrapped up in what is probably too much sterile gauze and tape. Then I head into my room and get dressed in something a little bit more substantive than the hospital gown.

Fuck fashion; I deserve comfort. I go for leggings and a T-shirt. I feel the need to wear shoes, though, to keep the bandages in place and soften the unfortunate experience of walking. I end up in a pair of high-top sneakers with a lot of padding that I feel ridiculous wearing. I think they kind of make the leggings look like they were on purpose, which is… good? I lace them up tight and feel almost like a person again.

I wander out and find Henry in the dining room making sandwiches. Big sandwiches. We may be an exclusive club, the surviving hosts of vampiric spirits, but we know what we need. We eat in silence, and I swallow some painkillers that Henry has fished from wherever they ended up after the move. I try not to look at the sliding glass door. I still can't see it, but in my mind, my vampiric spirit is there, doing its best to get close to me. Staring at me through the window. Roiling just beyond the glass.

How very unfortunate for it.

When one sandwich is gone, another appears. Henry has deigned, in his infinite wisdom, to allow me more water. My mouth is full of a combination of both those things when I hear the doorbell ring.

I panic, not sure what I'm afraid of showing up, but knowing there are plenty of things out there to be afraid of. But I swallow and wince at the pain in my feet as I walk to the door. The painkillers haven't kicked in yet.

My heart drops into my stomach when I open the door and see Olivia there, deep blue bruise on her cheek and yellow jacket in her arms.

"I'm so sorry," I breathe out in a rush. "Olivia, I'm so sorry."

I'm trembling again. Any other day, I'd have hugged her—or at least tried.

"Are you all right?" she asks, in her efficient, problem-solving voice. "No one could find you. And then I get a call from Mr. Thompson that he saw you coming in here. He says you had a bad reaction to the drugs, but you're doing better now. Is that true?"

Politicians are supposed to be good at lying. And I'm not a politician, but I do work for one. Unfortunately, the politician I work for hasn't gotten the easy lie down yet, so I haven't had a chance for it to rub off on me. I feel rotten and wrong when I lie to Olivia.

"I think that's right," I lie to Olivia.

"I think I'm okay now," I lie to Olivia.

"But I'm so, so sorry." I tell the truth.

I don't know if she bought the lies, but I know she buys the truth. She sweeps in through the door, full of her characteristic grace, and hands me my personal effects. The shirt I was wearing at the warehouse isn't there—they must have had to cut it off. The jeans are bloody and have holes in them. But the leather jacket is more or less fine, and I can feel the glasses in one of its pockets. I fish them out and put them on my head. They already feel like a habit—like a uniform.

I join Olivia at the table, where Henry has lured her in with yet more food that I didn't know I had in the fridge. They make small talk. I listen. Neither of them talks about me, and neither of them tries to engage me, which I feel grateful for. The wards in the basement make me safe, but the people at the table make me *feel* safe. Humans are dumb like that.

I'm amazed at how easy the conversation is between Henry and Olivia. I guess Olivia doesn't know what's going on, and Henry's lived with it for a long time already, but still. I don't track the conversation well. I'm exhausted, so it's easier not to focus on that. But I am still watching them, so I notice when Olivia shifts into problem-solving mode.

"Beth," she says, her face and body and voice just as carved from stone as Gigi's, "there's a man looking in your front window."

I follow her gaze and see Max, his hands cupped around his face to block out the glowing light of the morning and allow him to look inside. When he sees me notice him, he waves.

"You know him?" Olivia asks.

I clear my throat. "He's the new guy at work."

"Weird for him to come here."

Weird is one word for it. "Yeah."

I get up on unsteady legs. They say that you know a dog trusts you when it lets itself look injured around you. I try not to connect that concept to the instinct I indulge to walk to the door like it doesn't hurt at all, but it probably applies. The painkillers have kicked in now, so that helps.

The only person here Max can't speak freely in front of is Olivia, and I hope he's not going to try. I'm pretty sure his reaction to "normal human accidentally heard me talking about magic" would be "let me just get in there and clean that up real quick." I don't want Max digging around in my sister's brain.

"Olivia, I think he wants to talk to me about work stuff. Stuff you don't want to hear about."

Olivia raises her eyebrow. My boss, Sharon, plays things pretty straight, and I can see Olivia reforming her opinion of her in real time. Shit. Well, better than the alternative. I think. Probably?

Still, she gathers up her things, puts on her coat and shoes, and lets me gently but firmly usher her to the door.

Just before we open it, Olivia's face lights up with a spark of remembrance.

"Oh," she says, "I forgot to tell you. A few guys from the sheriff's office were at the hospital. Said that they wanted to talk to you about what you saw at the warehouse when you are well enough."

Fantastic. "Thanks. I'll get in touch with them."

When I've sorted this out. A week ago, the idea that the sheriff's office wants to talk to me about anything would have sent me into a tailspin of worry that I would have had to fight down. But now they need to get in line.

Max looks like he wants to introduce himself to Olivia as she passes him on the porch, but my sister is uncharacteristically rude—walking by him like he doesn't exist. He doesn't push through and introduce himself anyway. It's my first indication that something is wrong.

Well, more wrong than it was already. You know what I mean.

I don't walk out onto the porch. I have my amulet in my hand, but better not to risk it.

"Hey, you're alive!" He says it lightly, like a joke. I don't laugh.

"Why don't you come out and talk to me?" he asks.

"No thanks. Why don't you come in?"

He shakes his head. "No, I don't feel like…" His face twists up in confusion. He tries again. "I… don't feel like coming inside."

He says the words like he doesn't understand why they're coming out of his mouth. And then, with dawning realization, he starts to laugh.

"You've been busy," he says finally. "I wouldn't mind getting a look at those things. Where are they?"

He starts looking around the outside of the house. Good—let him look. There's no way he'll be able to see the design from outside, and he means me too much harm to get in.

"That's not what you came here for," I say.

I guess we're having this conversation like this—him on one side of my wards, me on the other. It feels like I'm talking down to him from a castle rampart. Just, you know, much more convenient.

"No," he says, looking around. "I came to tell you…"

His voice trails off as once again he looks confused. He's staring at the empty air of the porch. I pull my glasses on to get a look at what he's seeing.

At first, I don't get it. It's the vampiric spirit, sure. And it freaks me out, sure. I want to scream, sure. But that's to be expected. But then I look a little closer and puzzle it out.

Two of them. There are two of them. That can't be right. One of them is bound to the mall.

"What happened to the binding?"

Max doesn't look at me. "I undid it. I guess Henry's

spirit and your spirit are friends. They must communicate somehow. Good to know."

Max isn't great at forcing levity.

"Why did you undo the binding?" Maybe it's just because I'm looking at the vampiric spirits, but I start feeling a little cold again.

No—that's not why. It's knowing that Henry's spirit was walking around in someone, and that someone must be dead now, if the spirit is free to fly around.

"Because I know how to get rid of them," Max says, sadder than I've ever heard him.

I shift my gaze to the more human-looking monster on the porch. He still doesn't look at me.

"You're going to kill us," I say, no hint of question in my voice.

He nods. "Do the right thing. Set your amulet aside and step out onto the porch."

My blood runs cold. Well, colder.

"That's not going to happen," I say, less sure than I want to be.

Max deflates. He steps back and sits down on the balustrade, the same place he sat just a few days ago, just before we went investigating together. He looks tired. So tired. It makes him look older.

"I don't want it to."

The words don't give me an inkling of hope. He's not saying he won't do it. He's not saying he thinks he has a chance to do it differently. His words have a finality to them.

"This is what happens when humans mess with magic," he says.

The warmth of anger replaces the ice in my veins. "No, this is what happened this time. And it's still happening. It's not over."

He breathes out hard through his nose, like a half-formed spiteful laugh.

"Where do you think you go from here? Okay, you've got those wards. Great. You've got an amulet, so I guess the two of you can take turns leaving the house. How long does that last? These things are pretty dumb, and it might take them a while, but eventually they're going to figure out how to get you to leave."

I don't ask him how they could do that. I know. Hostages. Killing. Leverage. All they have to do is start jumping into humans and killing them in front of the door, and we'll have no choice but to surrender.

"You're really not going to help, are you?" I spit the words at him, and he finally looks at me. I'm not prepared for the intensity in his gaze.

"I *am* going to help you," he says. "I'll make it peaceful—gentle. You'll feel warm, and happy, and loved. You won't regret anything, and you won't be afraid."

I must not be responding the way he wants me to, because he keeps going, more desperately.

"No one gets that. No one gets to die like that. And when you're gone, the people who knew you won't mourn. I'll take care of it, I promise."

His sincerity hits me like a freight train. I clench my jaw. I can't form words to yell at him, can't sort out my anger enough to make him understand the nightmare he's offering me.

"Go away," I grit out through clenched teeth.

His thousand-yard stare looks a thousand yards *into* me.

"All right," he says, after the longest moment of my life. His voice is velvet. "I'll get out of town. Give you a couple of days to come to terms with things. I could use a change of scenery anyway."

He's trying to bring the tone of the conversation up a little. He fails and relents.

"I'm sorry," he says, back on the same level of intensity as my seething anger. "I really am. I should have found a way to shut you down before this. I should have paid more attention. I should have been better. It didn't need to be both of you."

And then he heads to his electric-blue car and drives away. The vampiric spirits churn and roil in the air on my porch.

TWENTY-SIX

An Idea

Henry sees the state I'm in after the conversation. Was he listening in? I don't remember if he was there standing near me the whole time, or if he stayed in the kitchen until Max left. I'd lost track. But he suggests I get some rest when he sees that I'm barely holding it together.

That seems impossible, but he wants me to try, and I want to repay him for his kindness over the last few hours, so I do. I lie in bed, stare at a black fly fumbling around by the ceiling, and seethe.

I think a thousand hateful thoughts. They build on themselves. I imagine what it would feel like—the peace he promised. Thing is, an exit like that *would be* a gift. If it were really hopeless. If there were no other option. If I had terminal cancer and was in pain or something. I wonder if Henry thought about his wife when Max was talking, if he *was* listening in to our conversation. I hope he wasn't.

Anyway, I'm not ready to accept that.

I grab my phone up off the nightstand like a weapon

and try The Emporium again, harassing yet another unhelpful employee. I consider going to Skyway Park to try and find Wilbur. But even if he were there, I doubt it would be helpful. His thing seems to be more connecting people to things. And what I really need now is to be *less* connected to something.

But is that true?

My hazy brain thinks there's something there, but I'm not sure what it is. I alternately seethe and try more seriously to sleep for a long time. I hover in a state of fitful half sleep. My anger and turning the problem around in my mind like a puzzle blends into dreaming until I'm not sure how in charge of my own thought process I am.

It's only been about an hour and a half, but it feels like much longer when I pull up my phone and start scrolling through my contacts. I've got half a plan in my head, and I'm trying to pull together the details, but I start putting it into motion regardless. Probably not wise, but I'm going to keep feeling like I'm in freefall until I *do* something.

I find the number for Sheriff's Deputy Andy Royals. A nice guy. Went to high school with me. Kind of a weird kid back then in some ways, but he turned out all right.

"Hey, Elizabeth," he says when he answers. "How are you doing?"

Is he asking out of reflexive politeness, or because he heard my dad died, or because he heard I was in the hospital following being in a burning building when it collapsed?

There are so many reasons to fear for my well-being. I decide it's probably the third option, with just a tinge of option two. The sheriff's department isn't a big place, and the owner of the building that burnt down is likely to make the fire a bigger deal than it otherwise would already have been.

"I'm doing better. Lost a lot of blood, they tell me, and I had a weird reaction to the drugs. But I've steadied out now." I don't know a lot about lying, but telling the same one to multiple people seems like a good plan. "Olivia told me you guys want to talk to me?"

Andy hesitates. "We did," he says. "We… do."

I don't understand his weird hesitation. Until I put it together, and I laugh.

"You've been told that investigating this isn't a priority," I say. "Because Elison doesn't want you to figure out why his building that was just on fire and wasn't zoned for hazardous materials storage, exploded. Is that right?"

"And collapsed like that," he adds, which sends a chill down my spine. Elison doesn't strike me as the kind to let sleeping dogs lie and ignore that. While he has an explanation for the explosion, he doesn't have an explanation for the way the foundations of the building then spontaneously collapsed in on themselves. Hell, I don't have a good explanation for that, either, unless you count "supernatural creatures have unique burial practices," which I don't think you should.

"All right, well, if you want a statement, let me know." I've got the amulet. I can go down there, ignoring the vampiric spirit swirling around me. Although getting through the metal detectors might be interesting. Something to figure out later if I need to.

"I'll let you know," Andy says, in a voice that makes me think I probably won't have to figure it out after all. "I'm glad you're feeling better."

The words have a finality to them, and I have to speak quickly to interrupt him before he starts saying goodbye.

"Actually, that's not why I'm calling."

More hesitation, then, "Oh?"

"Yeah," I say. "I need a favor."

I let the words hang in the airwaves between us for a moment, and so does he. "What is it?" he asks at last, noncommittally.

More lying. But at least this isn't to Olivia. That makes it easier. Should it?

"I have a personal issue. And I think some friends of a guy I know could help me out with it. Problem is, he isn't going to help me or put me in touch with them." I let my voice drop. He's going to make some assumptions about what I'm about to say that aren't technically true, but hell, they probably aren't that far off. "Not unless I let him do something to me that I really don't want to."

Those words hang in the airwaves, too.

"I can help," he says, and I wince. Should have expected that. Maybe I shouldn't try and move forward with plans before I think through them all the way. I thought I was calling to get some information, but of course Andy is going to want to rush in and save the girl he knew way back when from her clear and present danger. I'm feeling cast as something I'm not.

Except that, yes, I *do* need some help. Shit. I'll have to sort out how to extricate him from all this later. That'll be easier to do when I don't have the threat of being possessed by a vampiric spirit and murdered by a well-meaning-but-nonetheless-terrifying wizard hanging over my head.

"You can," I confirm. "You can look up their number, so I can ask them for help. I don't know their names, but I know they called the guy I know two days ago. I think on his landline. I'm guessing, but I think so."

Max's masters seemed old-fashioned. And, to be honest, I doubt Max would have voluntarily given them his cell number. I don't remember it ringing when we were out investigating, and he seemed to want to distance himself from them enough that he wouldn't want them able to contact him at any time, wherever he was.

"What's the problem? Whatever it is, it probably isn't as bad as you think. I can probably help."

I haven't talked to Andy that many times in his official capacity, but I'm impressed at the way he has the "helpful, trustworthy authority figure" tone of voice nailed down. Hell, I almost think for a second I *should* tell him.

But no, obviously not.

"It's personal." That's the truth. Sort of.

"I'm not really supposed to do that kind of thing. We're supposed to get warrants, and…"

Yeah, but I bet he can get it nailed down without going through the paperwork. That's the thing about systems: they work, but there are always paths around them.

"I'd owe you a favor."

I don't emphasize that I work for the mayor. He knows. And this conversation feels slimy enough with just the implication hanging there. For a second, all the sandwiches that I wolfed down feel like they might be coming back to haunt me.

"I'll see what I can do," Andy says in a harsh tone that breaks my heart a little bit. "What's your friend's number?"

I'm *less* to him now. I give him Max's address, and the line goes dead.

▭

I tell Henry what I'm planning to do, and he insists we test to make sure that the amulet will protect both of us first, before we go any further. We do so, stepping out onto the back porch holding hands. I'm ready to lineman-tackle him back into the house if the thing gets into him. I keep my glasses on, my eyes on the spirits.

They swirl around us, blocking my vision, but they can't get in. As long as one of us has the amulet and we're in physical contact, we should be safe from the threat of possession.

So hey! One tiny win for the home team!

I head to the bedroom to dig out my jewelry box, which only requires unpacking three different cardboard boxes and leaving their contents strewn about the bedroom floor. Sorry, Faisal. I find three necklaces with strong chains that sit at about the same place on me. I pick shorter ones that I know won't be able to be pulled over my head. Then I remove the extraneous pendants and use all three to string the amulet back around my neck. One of the necklaces is silver, and the tone of the gold on the other two don't match, but that's not the point. It might look odd if someone notices, but we're a bit beyond that now.

The amulet feels firmer around my neck when I put it on. It feels like something clicking into place. It's funny how losing something valuable makes it really feel like yours when you get it back.

By the time I get a text from Andy—just a phone number, no words—we're ready to go. I keep my glasses up on my head. I wouldn't be able to see anything if I kept them on—not with the vampiric spirits swirling around us, trying like hell to get inside. Even just maneuvering our way into the car is tricky and awkward enough. Plus, I have to drive one-handed, keeping Henry's hand in mine. I hope we don't get pulled over. That would both look odd and potentially go very badly, very quickly.

We don't. We make it to Max's overblown, expensive Victorian without incident, other than those same old harsh looks from Max's neighbors that I let bounce off of me. His electric-blue car isn't out front, and it occurs to me for the first time that he's probably locked the door, and I won't know how to get inside.

We go around back, climbing another set of exquisite stone steps and making our way through an intricate, half-height wrought iron gate. It's hard to maneuver with one hand, but we're getting the hang of things. We've got two hands between us, and it's easy to communicate without speaking when you have a shared goal.

In the backyard—which is, of course, a perfectly manicured garden full of carefully designed plantings surrounding a lush patch of close-trimmed green grass—we're safer from prying eyes. No one sees me break a pane of glass in the back door and reach my hand through to get inside. I take on the breaking and entering myself. I'm already on Max's radar as a pain in the ass. It's good to be consistent when managing other people's expectations.

I haven't been in this part of Max's house, and the clarity of the floor plan leaves a lot to be desired. But we wind our way down a couple of claustrophobic hallways until we find ourselves in the living room.

It looks sterile and lifeless without Max in it. When I was here before, I thought it suited him, but now the furnishings just feel mismatched, and the whole place feels like it's trying too hard. I find the ornate phone I noticed last time I was here, and set my own phone, open to the text from Andy, on the side table next to it.

From here on out, our success is based on a series of seven assumptions, some of them further reaches than others. Henry knows this, and he came along for the ride. He didn't really have a choice, though. We couldn't think of anything better. I nod to him, and we lean hard into…

TWENTY-SEVEN

An
Assumption

Assumption 1: The number Andy gave us is the right one.

Henry picks up the phone and holds it to my ear. I dial the number. One ring. Two rings. Three rings. Then—

"Muppet!" a female voice coos. She doesn't sound like I'd expect. Her voice is warmer. *All the better to eat you with, my dear*, I guess.

I nod to Henry, and he sets the phone down on the receiver. I nod again, and he picks it back up. I redial.

"This isn't funny," the female voice says, and this time I believe that this voice came out of the body I saw here the other day. It's got an edge to it underneath the velvet. I nod to Henry, and he hangs up the phone. We wait. The phone rings. Which brings us to…

Assumption 2: Max's masters will respond to a cryptic signal from Max the way Gigi responded to me blinking the lantern on and off, and they'll come to see what the problem is.

I know that wizards don't use the crossroads, but I still figure they've got some way of avoiding the perpetual disaster that is normal travel. I'm also not sure how long it'll take them. I flip down my glasses and verify that, yes, our not-so-friendly companion spirits are still here, trying to get into us.

I don't know how observant these things are, but I do my best not to look at the coffee table. The less it's on their radar, the better.

Time stretches on. My adrenaline doesn't care at first. A minute. Two minutes. Five minutes. Standing here by the phone starts feeling weird.

"How long will it take them, do you think?" Henry asks, more to break up the uninterrupted span of time than anything.

"I don't know."

"And if it takes them all day?"

"Then I sure hope you like holding my hand."

He laughs, and my adrenaline takes it as a cue to take a break. Slacker.

We maneuver our connected mass down onto the couch. Now would be the time to break out a deck of cards, but we don't have one. I'm not going to go looking for one, and playing one-handed would suck the joy out of it for both of us anyway. Instead, we make light conversation. It's neither of us at our best. It's mostly stories, but no sad ones. I learn about Montana, where he's from. He learns about the surprisingly petty world of local politics. He doesn't seem surprised by it.

Neither of us devotes too much thought or effort to the conversation. We're both sectioning off the larger portions of our minds, waiting for the cue that will tell us whether I was right to think that…

Assumption 3: Max's go-see-what's-out-there wards will affect the vampiric spirits the same way they affected me.

I can tell Henry feels the wards when they trigger by his intense, questioning look. I pop down the glasses and breathe a sigh of relief. This was probably one of my bigger reaches, but they've left the room, careening out to the windows. Which means that we don't have much time to find out about…

Assumption 4: I can open Max's magic box and get us inside it before the vampiric spirits get back.

We move fast, my hand flying to the edge of the table, as close to perfectly where he put his hand. I use my right hand, which he did as well. I've had a lot of time to think about what the Right Mind was for opening the spell, and I think I've got it: defiance. That comes easy to me at the moment.

Either I guessed right, or this thing didn't need Right Mind at all to open. Either way, there's no time to be relieved.

Henry and I throw ourselves into the box, momentarily losing contact. That feels risky, but we'd talked about it beforehand and agreed that it was our best chance to accept that risk to avoid bigger risks. The lid comes down on top of us, and I feel like I can finally breathe.

Okay, breathing in a tiny box that is nowhere *near* as roomy when I'm sharing it with another fully grown human being. It's a claustrophobic sense of relief, but it's relief, nonetheless. And hey, at least in here we don't have to worry about keeping ourselves in contact. We don't really have a choice in this space. A black fly sits on the glass of the coffee table just above my chest.

My heart pounds as the vampiric spirits come back in through the window. Time to test…

Assumption 5: The vampiric spirits won't be able to see into the box.

Five for five. Is it still *schadenfreude* if the thing whose despair you delight in is an evil spirit bent on your destruction? Unclear.

They circle around themselves before shooting out and searching the house. They'll… they'll come back, right? This whole thing kind of hinges on them hanging around where they last saw us. That wasn't even an assumption I was keeping track of. That wasn't even something I thought about going wrong.

And neither is what happens next. I'm half dazzled by the couple's beauty when they enter, even having seen them before. They're more casual this time, presumably since this was an impromptu trip. The woman looks just as stunning in loose-fitting jeans and a button-down shirt as she did in that the bodycon dress getup. Her hair is piled up on top of her head, and I'm not sure if she's wearing makeup. I'd like to think she is, but I could be wrong. There's no definite proof to my eye. The man is in jeans, too. Black and a little bit tighter, but still. I'm struck again by how crisp and put together he looks. His black and gray sweater is probably part of it, as are his hawkish symmetrical features.

I'm watching their faces—still gorgeous even perturbed and picking at one another with unheard words—when their heads almost simultaneously slam to the side. The man's hand has time to come up to his neck, where I see something glittering. The woman just falls. They convulse a few times, slowly.

Fuck. Fuck, fuck, fuck, fuck, fuck. I should have known to expect something. I should have checked behind the TV. I've never been so jealous of a wizard's memory. So many things happened the day I met these people that I'd forgotten what Max did just before they came in.

And, too, I must have underestimated how much he

hated them. Booby trapping your house against them specifically is a new dimension in hot—under the collar—for teacher.

Or would it have triggered for any wizard? What about magical creatures? Are only humans safe?

I'm so distracted by these questions that I barely catch a strange movement of the woman's hands before both bodies on the floor are gone.

I catch my breath. The vampiric spirits are back, swirling around as they did before, but the people I'd pinned all my hopes to are gone.

Teleported to safety? Somewhere they can heal themselves? A nice trick to have in your back pocket. Gotta get me that one.

But then the vampiric spirits head off to go search the house.

What?

I can't be certain, but they seem like they disappeared in the same way.

"The clock," I hear Henry say. His voice is quiet—barely a trace of a whisper. But the tiny space we share makes it fill my ears. I look at Max's stylish modern clock.

Ten Oh Five.

I check my phone: 10:06 p.m. I'd spent some of our time earlier enamored of Max's, and I didn't remember it being ahead of my phone. I think I would have noticed.

It's thin evidence, but it becomes a whole lot more substantial when the wizards reenter the room.

I take it back—I gotta get me *that* one.

The man looks exactly the same. He's talking in the same way, gesturing in the same way—everything. But the woman has a slight smile on her face as her eyes search the room.

She holds up a single finger at the man, and he falls

silent. If I had to bet, I'd put money on it that this is a regular occurrence.

The woman's lips move, and she forms a sphere out of her outstretched fingers. Inside her hands, I see a hollow globe of violent sparks. Making as little noise as I can and trying not to kick Henry, I maneuver my hand up to momentarily move the glasses off my eyes. Nope, nothing there. I settle the glasses back down and watch the fireworks. The globe reminds me of nothing so much as sparklers on New Year's Eve. It's impossible not to fill with a grief-stricken nostalgia, no matter how inappropriate to the moment.

I'm watching carefully this time, so I see a couple of blazes of light, maybe about the size of june bugs, soar out from behind the TV. They're heading for where they struck last time—the wizards' necks. But this time, they arc as if attracted to the sparkleball.

Yes, sparkleball. It's a stressful day; I'm taking entertainment where I can get it.

When the booby traps are in the sparkleball, the woman drops her hands. The sphere collapses, and a few lumps of charcoal fall to the floor.

The man says something. The woman responds. The man laughs. The woman smirks. And the vampiric spirits finally decide to grace us with their presence again, so we finally get to find out if...

Assumption 6: The badass wizards are better at wizarding than Max is.

This is a resounding success. There's a little of what looks like playful banter between them, and the woman eventually favors the man with an overly gracious "go ahead" gesture.

The man makes very similar motions as the woman did before, and he presumably says the same words, although I can't hear them. His sparkleball, however, is much bigger. It fills his outstretched arms.

The vampiric spirits fight against it. They form sort of white heads of smoke with trails of gray and black smoke being pulled toward the sparkleball.

In the confined space of the box, I hear Henry's breathing quicken. It's hard to pull my eyes away from Max's master's magic trick, but I force myself.

Henry is enraptured. He can't see the sparkleball, sure, but he should be able to tell more or less what's happening.

He deserves to see this in full detail more than I do. He's carried a heavier weight. I maneuver my hand back up to my eyes so that I can pull the glasses off my eyes. It's tricky to get them over to where Henry can take them and put them on, but I manage it.

I watch his face rather than the wizards. I'm sure what they do won't look that impressive without the glasses anyway. His jaw clenches as his eyes come into focus through the glasses. The first time he's seen the burden that's been riding around on his memory for all these years. I can't imagine. I didn't hurt Olivia. If I had…

And then, in sync with a broad motion of the wizard's arms that I catch in my peripheral vision, I see, hear, and feel Henry let out a hard, harsh exhalation. His shoulders loosen and then jerk with a few tearless sobs as the tension and weight leaves him. His face is stuck in a contorted mask of horror as he sorts through his own reaction. It takes him a full several seconds to set it aside. Finally, his face loosens. He shifts his gaze to me and gives me the saddest smile I've ever seen. He looks grateful and regretful in equal measure. Warmth rushes through me, starting at the knot in my chest and spreading outward.

I look back at the wizards, more to break away from the intensity of Henry's smile than anything. They're laughing and smiling at each other. On the floor, not far from the charcoal lumps that are all that remain of Max's booby trap, I see a fine layer of gray ash.

That's it. They're done. It's over. I try to connect the fine layer of ash to the weight of the human heartbreak and grief it has caused. How many dead? Counting my father, it's what, six? The pain of all those that mourned them—or that would have been mourning them if Max hadn't stolen their grief. And then there's eight years of my father's suffering. I can still feel it, so real from the memories I experienced from Max's ritual. And my mother... her loss. How do you even quantify that?

It's too much for that fine layer of ash to bear. It's not equal. It's not fair.

Max's masters stand around talking for a little longer than I would like. Come on, guys. You've been together for centuries. You can't possibly have this much left to say to one another. But eventually they leave, arm in arm. I don't think they'll drop the issue. I'm sure they'll have something to say about it later. But that's Max's problem to deal with. If he didn't want to have to clean up a little bit of my mess, he shouldn't have threatened to kill me.

I give it a couple of minutes before I test my final assumption...

Assumption 7: We'll be able to get out of the box from inside.

Well, fuck.

TWENTY-EIGHT

An Infinity

This is fine. This is all fine. I planned for this. Sort of.

I try not to freak out. We're in an enclosed space, and it's only a matter of time before we run out of air. Or—more accurately—poison ourselves with carbon dioxide. What does dying from carbon dioxide feel like? Is it peaceful? Like carbon monoxide? Would we just go to sleep? Or is it horrifying? Breathing deeply, over and over, but unable to get enough oxygen?

Yeah, this isn't helping with the not freaking out part. A glance at Henry's face, with his clenched jaw and perfectly even breaths that seem timed, tells me that he's fighting the same battle.

Plan A for this scenario was to call someone. Olivia, probably. It would take some explaining to get her to understand what she needed to do to get us out of here, but it would save us. That's what matters.

I maneuver my phone into place and see what I expect to: no signal. I guess the cellular network isn't better at getting into this box than the concept of time. What a shock.

God, I want to scream. I want to pound on the glass. Maybe if I were alone, I would. Maybe I would use up all that precious oxygen. But I'm not alone, and I keep myself under something that, from the outside, might resemble control. For him—the guy my dad threw under the bus when he involved him, and that I continued the family legacy with by keeping him involved.

Okay, Plan B. The dead man's switch that I've been trying not to call a dead man's switch. I scheduled an email to go out to Max telling him we're in here. While we were sitting, waiting for Max's masters to show, I kept pushing the schedule out, an hour each time. And now, trapped in here with no way to delay it, it'll send.

When was the last time I delayed it? How long do we have to wait in here? I check my phone.

9:55 p.m.

The clock on Max's wall reads, *Ten Oh Seven*.

Not the best. Not the worst.

"Forty-eight minutes," I say to answer Henry's expectant gaze, when I can get words out without sounding like I'm about to lose it. The sound of my voice confirms that I'm mostly right—you could almost believe that I'm not angry at myself.

"All right," Henry replies, and I do him the courtesy of not looking too hard for the panic in his own voice. "Ever done any meditating?"

It's been suggested to me more than once. Unfortunately, I never listened. "No."

"Try to focus on your breathing. Acknowledge thoughts and let them go. Try not to get too attached to anything."

It's a good strategy, I guess. The lower we get our heart rates, the longer we'll last. The more likely we'll survive the forty-eight minutes until the email gets sent to Max, plus however long it takes him to receive the message—all

I had was his shiny new work-email address—and get back here.

I really, really hope he configured his work email to go to his phone. Most of us at the office do, even if we make attempts not to read it off-hours and sometimes succeed. My life depends on how seriously a man with infinite funds takes a job he took as a cover to keep an eye on someone.

It sinks into my bones what a bad idea that was.

I'd spent some of my time earlier trying to get the internet to tell me how long Henry and I were likely to survive in this box if we couldn't get ourselves out of it. But even when I searched by how long you could survive sealed in a coffin, which was, unfortunately, the closest corollary, the internet was less than helpful.

There were a few sites with calculations of how much oxygen you would have, which were encouraging—right up until the discovery that the issue isn't the lack of oxygen. The issue is the build-up of carbon dioxide that will slowly poison us.

The internet said it could be as little as ten minutes. Maybe an hour. Maybe a hundred minutes. Conclusions varied.

But those estimates were for one person, and there are two of us. This coffee table is bigger than a coffin, sure, but how much bigger? Was it enough to last?

I try to stop the spiral. I try to focus on the present moment and ground myself in my physical surroundings. Here, in the magic, hidden box in the house that everyone I know either doesn't know about or is terrified of.

Cool. Cool, cool, cool.

But I try. Spiraling off into the hopelessness of the situation isn't going to help me or Henry. I've got to try.

So I do. It's hard. I feel like I'm failing. Instead, I start running through the scenarios of the things I could have done—*should* have done—to prevent this. I should have gotten a different email for Max. Or a phone number. Can you schedule texts? I should have found out. What was my rush?

An admonition from a therapist way back when that I should be gentle and forgiving with myself goads me like a hot iron as my heart races with my self-directed anger.

Yeah, this isn't helping. I try to redirect back to what Henry said. I glance at him, and he seems to be having more success. I'm letting the team down with my self-immolation, however much I deserve it.

I refocus and try again. I focus on my breathing. I let the thoughts come and go. Acknowledge and release. Focus on the feel of my body. I loosen my muscles.

It isn't easy. I'm used to *doing*. I'm used to *succeeding*—or at least trying to. I'm not used to marinating in the knowledge of my own failure. But I try to let go.

And I continue to fail.

Fuck this, I need something to occupy myself.

I shift my body weight, and a pang of jealousy runs through me at how little it seems to disturb Henry, who is a mountain of calm. I don't envy whatever made him have to learn how to do this, but I envy the skill.

I find the random objects Max shoved in here. Things he didn't want his masters to know about, I suppose. I nudge Henry and get him to give me back the glasses so that I can look at them.

The objects have a grab bag of different visual effects to them. Some glow. Some look cut-out against the background, like Max and his masters. Some look desaturated or oversaturated.

No idea what most of these do. Even if I could get them to work, the likelihood that they'll make our situation worse is too high to mess with.

All except the flashlight. What harm could a flashlight do? Maybe it would even be able to signal out of the box.

It seems improbable, but it's something to pin my hopes to. It's a puzzle to draw my focus, and that's what I need as a survival strategy right now.

It's intricate the same way my lantern back at home is. It looks similar. When I unscrew the base, where there would normally be a space for batteries, I see more of the tiny, perpetually moving gears like the ones that are in my amulet. I screw the base back on and look at the switch on the handle. I snap it back and forth. It makes a solid, pleasing click.

But even through my glasses, I see nothing.

Okay, it needs Right Mind. Unless Max created it wrong, which I doubt. I start cycling through, whipping myself up with one emotion after another and clicking the switch when I think I've distilled a clear, pure one.

Nothing.

Nothing.

Still nothing.

I try everything I can think of before I'm left drained and emotionally exhausted, searching around for other feelings.

The rambling of my brain, scouring itself for ideas, is the closest to successful meditation that I've managed. I close my eyes.

When I open them next, the clock on the wall tells me that twenty minutes have passed. I let my eyes lie open, looking at the room. I'm calmer now. My head aches, but I can't figure out why. I feel like I should know. I've mostly found a way to let everything lie. As long as nothing changes, I guess I'll stay this way until…

Things I don't need to upset myself with.

Another eight minutes passes with my eyes open.

And then I see movement.

The slow, steady heartbeat that I spent the better part of the last hour cultivating shatters as I watch Max. My eyes and brain, starved for input, devour every detail of him.

He's in dark-wash jeans and a gray T-shirt with a black jacket. The jeans and as much of the T-shirt as I can see cling to his skin just enough to do no favors to my efforts to get my heart rate under control. I don't recognize the brand of his sneakers, but they look both very clean and very expensive. He has a medium-sized duffel bag—full, but not bursting—in one hand. In the other, he has a coffee take-out mug with the logo for the Springfield sheriff's office.

Huh. I guess Andy called him. And I guess Max took care of the ideas I put in Andy's head before taking a souvenir. That seems suitably Max-like in behavior.

But what he's doing right now doesn't. I look up at his face. He looks tired. Still gorgeous, of course, but tired. He throws the duffel bag on the floor and sits down heavily on the couch. He puts his face in his hands, just resting them there for a long moment. Then he rubs his face with his hands and stands.

He disappears into the kitchen area and returns a few seconds later with a bottle of vodka in his hands. I don't know a lot about vodka, but I'm guessing the fact that I've never even heard of the brand means it's in a price range well beyond my means. He sits down on the couch—again, heavily—and breaks the seal on the bottle. He pours way too much of it for a single sitting into the to-go mug from the sheriff's office.

He sets the bottle aside and stares at the mug. I can't tell what he's thinking from his face. I feel like I'm intruding. Technically, I am. With deliberate motions, he takes a long drink, wincing a little in reaction to the strength of the alcohol.

His muscles relax—especially his shoulders—in the aftermath of the drink. He repeats the process twice more, then sets the mug aside and leans back on the sofa.

He stares out the window, then he glances around the room. He looks like he feels as helpless as I am. He looks lost. His eyes roll over everything, stopping nowhere. At one point, it feels like he's looking directly into my eyes, but his complete lack of reaction confirms he can't see me. His chest rises and falls a few times in great big heaves. Sighing, I guess.

There's frustration somewhere in me. A hot, burning fire struggling to get past the heavy blanket of whatever it is that's weighing me down. I should be screaming. I should be railing at Max to notice me. But instead, what cuts through my malaise is an instinctive desire to comfort him. It seems so mind-bendingly unfair, considering he's probably upset about, you know, *deciding he needs to kill me*. But the desire to reach out—to talk to him, to communicate— is a state of Right Mind I haven't tried yet.

My weak hands position the flashlight and point it at him. I try to move my head a little, but even that small shift makes me feel so dizzy I give it up. My dull headache throbs as my heart rate surges.

I center myself around a desire to reach out—a desire to communicate.

The sound of the switch clicking feels like it shatters my bones, and I wince at the golden light that consumes the world around me.

TWENTY-NINE

An Emancipation

A rush of cool, fresh, dry air hits my face. Fingers wrap around mine, and by instinct I try to fight them. But I'm so weak, and Max's fingers are strong, and the sound of the switch flipping back echoes somewhere in the far distance.

A laugh fights its way out of my chest, steamrolling over rounds of coughing and coming out victorious. Henry's low chuckle joins it.

We've done it. We're free. It's done. We're free.

Henry and I spend a long time breathing and laughing and recovering, and Max lets us. Finally, we start moving, untangling our limbs.

"Welcome to my home! Make yourselves comfortable!" I hear Max say, but I'm too busy stretching out my painfully cramped and stiff limbs to exchange whatever witty banter he's expecting.

After I successfully stand up and get past the pins and needles, I beam down at him, crouched beside the box as he is.

"Thanks," I say. I mean it to sound strong, but it's more of a strangled croak instead.

I don't know why that knocks him off balance, but I don't much care. I'm floating in the glow of success and survival, distracted by the pins and needles all over my body. I lay my hand on his shoulder to steady myself as I step out of the box that was almost my coffin. Henry does the same.

"You seem pleased with yourselves," Max says once Henry and I are fully free from the thing. The lid is closed now, and it looks like an unassuming coffee table once more. Max is trying to look stern and critical, and his mouth is doing so successfully, but a smile dances in his eyes.

"I love it when a plan comes together," I say.

"Oh, you planned for me to come back early to clean up the mess you made of my reputation with the sheriff's department?"

I shoot him a wide smile. "Of course."

He looks skeptical, but that same smile is still there under the surface. I make a mental note to recall the email that may or may not have been too late to save our lives.

"And you planned for me to then come back here, figure out you were in the table, and set you free?"

Yeah, there are disconnects there, but I don't feel like arguing the point. I shrug. "It all worked out."

Henry is on the couch with the bottle of vodka in his hand. Going by the slightly glazed look in his eye, he's already taken a pull. He's let his steely reserve down now. He's human after all.

I go to the armchair and sit down, still stretching out my limbs. Max, for his part, sits down next to Henry. I'm not sure I like the way he's looking at him.

"All right," he says. "Vampiric spirits gone. My masters didn't see you. Sounds like it's tied up, then."

He's addressing Henry, but I'm not sure why. Something in my chest sinks.

"How would you like to be free?" The words are for Henry alone.

Henry, still reeling from the emotional ride I'd put him through, doesn't fully focus on Max. "What?"

"Free. I can take the memories away from you. You won't remember about any of this. You won't know magic exists. You won't know what it feels like to have a vampiric spirit in you. Whatever you've been carting around for the last eight years, I can take it off your shoulders." Max reaches forward and removes the vodka from Henry's hands. He sets the bottle on the table. "It will be a lot more effective than this."

Henry, his hands empty and his eyes focused, looks to me. I shrug. My heart is racing, but I try to keep my expression neutral. I'm having my own reactions to this idea, and I'm not sure any of them are impulses I want to own up to or endorse.

"It'll also get you out of danger. And you'll stay out of danger—as long as *she* doesn't pull you back in again."

I take a little bit of offense, but I'm mostly taking a moment to sort through things.

I don't want Henry to accept this. I'm not sure Max is actually going to give him a choice, though, so maybe it'll be better if he *does* accept it? Maybe it'll work easier—go down smoother, as it were—if Max gets consent? Otherwise, why would he bother?

But I feel like I'm about to lose Henry. I feel like I'm about to be a lot more alone

"What about the days I don't remember? Won't I notice the gaps?" Henry asks.

Max smiles. He's sliding into the Right Mind for the spell already. He's building up an affection for Henry that I instinctively code as paternal, though that doesn't make sense with what I judge their ages to be.

"No," he says. "You'll just think of those missing times as days when nothing particularly interesting happened. You'll fill them in with routine actions that can't be confirmed or denied, but you'll never wonder about them. It'll kind of… scab over. You won't miss it. You'll feel *better*, but you won't remember feeling bad."

Henry looks at his own hands, and it feels like a way to avoid looking at either me or Max. Not wanting him to accept Max's offer is a selfish impulse. I'm looking for a reason Henry shouldn't accept—scouring the situation for some kind of justification for me to get to keep him as a well-informed ally—but I can't find one.

This is better for him. My dad got him involved in all this, and it hurt him. I kept him involved, and it almost got him killed. He deserves better. He deserves safety.

If he wants it.

He does. He nods. He breaks my heart.

"Okay," Max says. His voice is gentle—loving. He stands up and takes Henry's hand to pull him up, too. He puts his hands on either side of the base of Henry's skull, cradling him like a lover. I'm uneasy but entranced.

Max leans his forehead onto Henry's. He's got a good five inches on him, height-wise, and the motion makes Henry tilt his head up. Max closes his eyes, and Henry does, too.

They breathe together for a solid ten seconds. Then Max whispers a few words, pulls back just slightly, and places a long, gentle kiss on Henry's forehead.

Max pulls back, and both men blink their eyes open.

"I still remember everything," Henry says, his voice rough, like he's just woken up.

Max nods. "It's better to do it that way. Minds reform easiest when you're asleep. You should walk home from here. It should only take you an hour or so. Wear yourself out. The deeper you sleep, the more naturally the changes will take."

Henry nods slowly. He doesn't speak again. I want to hear his voice. Instead, he comes over to me and hugs me. I feel a moment of panic, post-traumatic-something-or-other from being possessed by the vampiric spirit. But I fight through the fleeting feeling so that I can grip him tightly. He'll be Mr. Thompson tomorrow.

He leaves without another look. I go to the window so that I can watch him walk away down the street. I feel accomplished and proud and sad, all wrapped together.

"It could be just like that with you," Max says. I didn't notice him move, but he's beside me. "Or faster, even."

"Is that a sales pitch or a threat?" I mumble.

A fly lands on my shoulder, and I turn my eyes away from the window to look at it. The motion brings Max's face into my field of vision, and the look of horror there pulls my attention.

"You never answered my question at the warehouse," Max says, his breathing suddenly uneven, his voice harsh.

"What question?" I ask, remembering the way Max's lips had moved against the backdrop of cold and fear and high-pitched ringing.

"Did you take the graveling's eyes when you killed him?"

THIRTY

A Descent

"What?" I blurt out. Max's eyes shift from the fly on my shoulder to meet mine.

"After you killed the graveling, did you take out his eyes?" His voice has an eerie, terrifying control to it.

"No," I say.

"So they know you killed him." His eyes shift back to the fly. "And now they know you slipped your punishment."

Rules. Order. Permission.

Max's come-and-see wards activate again. But this time, instead of drawing my attention out to the street to see someone walking toward the house, my attention is drawn down. Down, down—into the earth below.

"Get out of the house!" Max yells. He grabs my arm, though he can't grip it tightly enough to cause pain. From what I understand of the amulet, if I decide that moving me onward is harm and fight him about it, I'll slide from his grasp. But I don't, and instead, I let his force act on me. I run with him down the hall. The glass from the pane in the back door that I broke earlier crunches beneath our feet as we scramble out to the backyard.

We stop, panting, probably ten feet from the house.

"What now?" I ask, and he looks at me.

"You might want to take those off," he says, gesturing at the glasses perched on top of my head. I oblige, dropping them into one of the inside pockets in my jacket.

"And?" I ask. His face, panicked up until now, turns grim.

"I'm sorry," he says. Not as an apology, but as a condolence. I've learned the difference.

And then the ground underneath my feet isn't steady anymore. I feel two sensations clearly: first of falling, and then of being wrapped up strong and sturdy in something. I'd say tentacles, but I know they're not. They are roots like snakes; I've seen them before.

Falling, sinking into earth that won't hold me up anymore. It's inevitable. Gravity is still gravity, even if magic exists. I don't think of the roots that guide me as harm. I don't want to risk the amulet that's supposed to be keeping me safe leaving me buried alive instead.

Instructions on what to do when you're trapped in an avalanche drift unbidden to my mind. You're supposed to swim. Swimming, strange as it sounds, kind of works. The point isn't to end up not buried. The point is to try to end up buried as close to the surface as possible.

The advice doesn't help me here, but that doesn't stop me from thinking of it, so I've got snow and the might of nature in my thoughts as the roots and the movement of earth pull me down, down, down, and over.

I lose time, I lose track. I'm lost in a sensation of travel and speed for forever. There's air along with us for the ride, though there's so much dust and dirt mingled with it that I catch dirt into my lungs and cough and sputter and hurt.

The wound on my torso announces itself. The stitches must be ripping themselves open now, right? So much for sterile bandages.

And then the quality of the falling, the quality of the movement, is different. There's no resistance at all. Max and I and the dirt that comes with us are surrounded by more open air. I can tell by the sound—and by the feeling of freedom around my twinging limbs just before I land heavily in a mound of soft earth.

I claw at my face, trying to clear my eyes. I cough, and chew, and spit, and wheeze.

"Hell of a way to travel," Max says beside me. In spite of everything, I roll my eyes. I'm not sure how much of my body still works, but that impulse will never die.

When the most immediate needs of my body have been met, I look around me. I taste the iron tinge of dirt and blood in my mouth as I see a small sea of faces around us, lit by some indirect light that I can't find the source of. Just like in the casino, they're dressed all as they want to be, in the illusion I'm forced to see since my glasses are still tucked away safely in my pocket. I even recognize some of the faces from the fight night.

What are the chances that they're the eight people in the crowd that night who *don't* hate me for ruining their bet? Some of the faces are solemn, and some are gleeful. A few are just interested, but neither grim nor happy. Most, I'd say.

I pick out Aloysius, the chance demon. His face is unreadable but intense. And I find Gigi eventually. She's standing surrounded by a group of brown-suited men, who all look very put together and well-trimmed. Next to them is a throne made of nobbled, cobbled roots, upon which sits...

My father.

The recognition pulls me to my feet just as surely as if there were a noose around my neck pulling me up. I step forward, every step sinking a bit into the freshly disturbed earth. This cavern isn't natural, some part of my brain trying to put everything together in the background recognizes.

It's not my father—it's not his soul, I feel certain as I look at his impassive face. My father was a lot of things, but cold was never one of them. It's just the body of my father. His eyes are open but missing. Missing because Max ate them. A memory of the moment he did so flies before my eyes before I shove it away.

The body of my father sits up straighter than he ever did. He's regal and rotting in his best suit. There's a gravitas to him that feels wrong.

"Wha—" I try to speak and erupt into coughing and throat clearing. I let it run its course and try again. "Who are you?"

No sound echoes back from the walls. This place is dead, sonically speaking. It feels like I'm screaming into a closet full of clothes.

"I am order. I am equality." It's my father's voice—air from my father's lungs forced through my father's vocal cords and shaped with my father's mouth. But the intention—the heart and emotion behind it—is all wrong.

That's not a fucking acceptable thing to do to a human body. It's not respectful. No one gave them permission. Aren't they supposed to need permission?

"You are a cryptic motherfucker is what you are. Order and equality aren't proper names. I asked... Who are you?"

I hear a pitiful noise beside me as Max laughs, trying to stifle it and make it sound like coughing instead.

"I am beyond your understanding," my father's body says.

Yep, it's confirmed again. Rolling my eyes still works. "I think you'll find I understand a lot," I say.

"You do not understand enough," my father's body answers.

"I understood how to kill one of your little disciples."

In my peripheral vision, Max winces at my words. Oh, whatever. Not like they didn't know. Not like that isn't why we're here. See? I understand things.

I continue. "Gravelings, I think they're called? See, they have a name. And they're your underlings. What's *your* name?"

My father's body tilts its head. "Wizards call them that. I do not call them that."

Welp, not getting a name. Fear starts reaching up toward my heart, rising through my feet. I fight it back.

"Wizard," my father's voice says. "This human killed one of ours."

Max rises to his feet. "I don't dispute that, sir." The word is respectful, but the air around it is defiant.

"That is not allowed."

"No, sir." That time, the *sir* was a little more polite.

"There must be an answer for this"—my father's body tilts its head the other way as the thing inside it considers its next words, giving me the impression it hasn't talked in a while—"infraction."

Max shoots me a glance. It's not a kind one. I think his eyes are watering, but I'm not sure. "There will be," he says.

"And will it be on the human, or will it be on the wizards? You are the wizard who rules this territory, are you not?"

"I am," Max says. I almost hear humility in that, although I'm pretty sure I'm making it up.

"And do you, as is proper, take responsibility for the actions that you have allowed one of your subjects to carry out? Do you and your kind accept the consequences of allowing the treaty to be broken?"

I'd say you could hear a pin drop, but I doubt it would make a sound on the soft dirt floor. In the endless silence between my father's voice and Max's, I hear my heart pounding in my ears.

"I do not," Max says, and his defiance isn't hidden. "She has flouted our rules as well as yours. She has practiced magic, which is not her right. Wizards remove our protection from her."

The silence is gone. A hundred voices speak at once. I don't like the looks on many of their faces. I don't like the hard, hollow expression on Max's. He doesn't look at me.

"She is a cheater," my father's voice says. "From the blood of cheaters. And she has refused her punishment."

Refused my punishment?

Oh. Got rid of the vampiric spirit. Out of the frying pan, into the angry fire that sent the frying pan, and is now annoyed that I jumped out of it.

"This must be mended," my father's body says.

I sigh dramatically, emboldened by the shitshow of the last couple of days and just *too fucking tired* to deal with any more of this garbage.

"Okay, Mr. Nameless Horror, I get it: moral relativism is a tough one to get used to. But"—I slide my amulet out from underneath my dirty shirt and hold it up, shining in the dim light I still can't source—"I am just not up for that today."

Again, the quiet. All eyes on my father's face. And a

twisted, sunken, broken version of my father's laugh fills the space around me.

It hurts. It physically hurts to hear it. I don't think that's magic, it's just… he never laughed in the hospital. He laughed all the time before. He laughed every time I made a joke. He laughed even when it wasn't funny.

"That is no concern. We will leave you here and remove the entrance. We will visit you in three days. If you are sufficiently contrite, we will close the earth tighter around you, so that your death may be hastened."

For a man into rules, he sure likes loopholes. Actually, that probably tracks.

My heart is beating in my ears again. I'd have a long time to regret my decisions. I'd have a long time to regret my pride.

They'd have a long time to make me try.

I look up at the gathered faces. Gigi, the people from the casino, the staggeringly alike men in brown suits with their various styles of thick-rimmed glasses.

And Aloysius, the chance demon.

His face is still unreadable. In a sea of expressive monsters, he's giving me… nothing. Absolutely nothing.

An assortment of unconnected facts come together in my head at once. I raise my gaze to the place where my father's eyes should be.

"I demand trial by combat," I say. "That seems like the kind of thing you people would be into, no?"

THIRTY-ONE

A Gamble

I think I like the kind of noises that erupt from the crowd now. There's some laughter. There's some approval. There are some obvious signs of violent blood rage.

Okay, I like some of them, but not all of them.

"What are you doing, Lizzie?" Max's voice comes to me, too low to be heard by the people here. Probably? I don't know what kind of hearing these things have. Me and Wilhelm are due for some quality time after this.

"Unless you have a better plan to help me, shut the fuck up."

Very unfortunately, he shuts the fuck up.

I check my math—my shoddy, speculative math.

The flower Aloysius gave me at the casino had felt like a reward for merit. For placing my life on the line in front of hundreds of creatures I didn't understand. When he'd given it to me, it felt meaningful—valuable. But when I stepped out of the casino, it had turned into something dry. Brittle. Easy to destroy.

That makes no sense unless that's the point of it. The flower he gave me was made to be destroyed. But why?

Magic likes destruction. The destruction of the medium in my fire spell. The destruction of my father's eyes in Max's spell. The other spells that I'd read about in my father's handwriting on the sticky notes in the trove— so many of them required something to be destroyed in order to work.

But if Aloysius gave me the component of a powerful spell, I should see that in his face. He should be indicating to me to think things through, to use what he gave me. He's looking at me now with none of that. He's looking at me with an expression so blank it astounds me.

Which must be the point. It must be that I *can't* know. The casino. The gambling. His joy in the gambling. The wink he gave me when he told Gigi he doesn't mess with probability. *Of course* he does.

Destroy the flower. Go out on a limb and put the highest stakes on the smallest odds. Walk into a casino with your life's savings and put everything not on black, but on one specific black number.

The highest stakes. The lowest odds. The greatest payout. This is the demon's gift—his reward. If I have the gambler's nerve to claim it.

"We will allow it," my father's voice says. It sounds almost uncertain, and it stings because that makes it sound more like my father. "But not with that amulet around your neck."

I nod. Of course. If the flower does what I think it does, then I need to take the amulet off anyway.

"On one condition: The wizard has to leave," I say.

My father's head tilts again, and I realize why it bothers me so much. It looks like someone without a body interpreting what a lack of comprehension should look like. It feels like someone has deciphered the symbols and is acting them out, but they don't land right.

"You want to save the wizard? He does not save you."

I let out a sharp, harsh laugh. "I want to get the wizard the hell away from my brain while it's not protected. He's been trying to get in there."

My father's head nods, and one of the gravelings steps forward. He walks to Max and guides him stiffly away toward some hidden exit. I make note of what direction it's in.

"It was nice knowing you, Beth," Max says over his shoulder.

"Go home, you're drunk," I say. Considering the vodka he'd chugged when I was in the box, maybe I'm not completely wrong. I *probably* should not have let him mess around in Henry's head when he wasn't one-hundred percent sober. Here's hoping that's the biggest mistake I make today.

When Max is gone, another of the gravelings comes up to me and opens his hand. I fiddle with the clasps, my fingers fighting me. But at last I get the thing off and put it into the graveling's palm. It carries my amulet to my father's body, laying the device in the hand that originally made it. Does the hand remember it? Would the hand remember me?

Okay. I check my math again. Pretty sure trial by combat means my life is on the line. I can't fight. I know nothing about it. I have no weapons. They're gonna pick a twelve-foot-high monster champion. High stakes, short odds. I look at Aloysius, and I study the blank look he still has on his face.

And I remember more of his words.

A true gambler doesn't stop when they've run out of their own stake. A true gambler bets more than they have a claim to.

The highest stakes. The greatest thing I can offer that isn't mine. *Cheater's blood*, the thing in my father said.

My chest feels empty as I hear myself speak. I don't want to own the words as mine. "And I want to do magic after this, *without* you coming after me and saying I'm breaking the rules and punishing me."

Some more scattered laughter. I'm guessing they don't think it's worth quibbling over what I'll do after this.

I don't think the thing in my father's body is going to go for it. That's fine—I didn't plan for him to. I need him to make me sweeten the pot.

"I'm not my father's only child. I'm not the only cheater's blood left. I will tell you the names of my sister and her children. If I lose, when I am gone, you can kill them."

I tell myself they'd do that anyway. I tell myself I'm not giving them anything they couldn't find out. But my permission *feels* like something they need. Or want. Permission. Allowances. Following rules. Maybe they wouldn't have killed her. Maybe that's not allowed.

But the thing in my father's body and the gravelings around him seem pleased. They needed it. They wanted it.

"I accept," my father's voice says. His lips curl back in a broken, decaying smile.

I feel sick.

The highest stakes. The lowest odds. That's it. It has to be.

As if following the orders of some unseen voice, the gravelings gather around me in a circle maybe twenty feet wide. Behind them, the rest of the crowd falls in. The gravelings look below average height, but I know they're not. Can the people behind them see?

But who knows how tall the people behind them are.

My father's body remains on its throne.

When the circle is complete, one of the gravelings steps forward. Now or never.

I pull the delicate flower out of my pocket. It feels so easy to destroy, but the movement in my pocket hasn't harmed it. That's got to mean something, right?

I can guess at the Right Mind for this spell, and I get into it with unnerving ease just before I crush the flower.

I bet I'm right.

THIRTY-TWO

A Dedication

The fight doesn't last long. I keep my glasses off. Maybe it won't affect anything if I leave them on, but why risk it? I'm risking enough.

Like at the fight in the casino, there's no ceremony. No one rings a bell or yells "start" or whatever a human would do. The graveling just pulls a spear out from his side and comes at me, impossibly fast.

Back in the warehouse, it had felt at the time like my bullets had done nothing. But I must have wounded the graveling I fought in the warehouse, because it didn't have the kind of fearsome, terrifying speed and grace that this one does.

Or, you know, maybe they just picked their best fighter to put down the insolent human. Gravelings might not like to fight much as a rule, but this one doesn't seem to mind.

Just before the graveling rushes me, I find myself wanting to step to the side. Just… *coincidentally,* I want to get a closer look at a graveling's enameled pin off to my left.

And then I *coincidentally* want to crouch down and look

at something glinting on the ground just before the graveling swings his spear, which goes whistling over my head.

I rise and examine the graveling's face. It's twisted in confusion and anger. My lips curl up into a smile, and a gambler's rush flows through my body.

"Nice try!" I say. My words aren't loud, but they have an outsized effect. Suspicious, confused looks fly through the crowd.

Then, just *coincidentally*, I want to stamp down that raised patch of soft earth a few paces to my left. A fraction of a second after I move to do so, the graveling lunges into the space I previously occupied.

"You almost got me that time," I hear my own hard, gleeful voice say. "Don't give up!"

His face is red now, full of rage. Blind panic flows through me as the graveling rushes toward me, and it hits me that I haven't felt compelled to move away from him this time.

But then he falls, his foot catching on something in the soft, disturbed earth of the circle. The graveling is laid out before me, flat on his stomach, arms and legs splayed out like a starfish.

His spear lands mere inches from my feet. Before the graveling can move, and with a grace I did not know I possessed, I reach down and scoop it up in my right hand.

I had thought I had been dealing with solid objects all my life, but I realize now I haven't. When I hold the spear in my hand, I feel a rightness, a steadiness. I feel the steadfast joy of humility.

I plunge the spear a few feet above what I see as the graveling's head. It connects. The graveling jerks once before lying still. Roots from farther down in the earth below pull the body away.

Ten or twenty seconds of stunned silence in the cavern follow.

And then one person's slow applause breaks it, and all eyes in the room turn to Aloysius. His stony countenance is gone. Instead, he wears a sharp, wide smile.

"Very good," he says as he strides toward me, breaking through the circle of gravelings. He reaches me and offers me his arm. "Elizabeth, I believe we're done here."

I take his arm, and he brings me back through the circle of gravelings, this time heading for my father's body. None of the other supernatural creatures I'd seen before are here anymore. The only figures around the ring and in the cavern carry the cold, fierce, unyielding look of the shadows of death.

That's better than "gravelings." Just saying.

The smile on the chance demon's face fades into an incongruent expression of warm civility as we go up to my father's body, sitting still on its throne. Too still. I wonder if it's just his body now, with nothing foreign inside it.

I don't ask. I won't rebury him. They'll do that. I'm more certain of it than I probably should be, but it tracks. Bodies belong in graves. They will return him to his.

I take my amulet from my father's hand. It offers no resistance. I try not to feel like this is him giving it to me, directly this time. I try not to let that feeling warm me, and I almost succeed.

It's a good thing the chance demon knows the way out. Even with the indication of direction I got from watching Max leave, I wouldn't have found it on my own. It's a long, low tunnel separated from the main area of the newly created cavern, and we don't reach the full moon's light shining at the end of it until we've walked silently for several minutes.

I'm roiling with questions, but I have to start somewhere, so I speak. "Why did you help me?"

The light is still low, but I can just make out his passive grin shifting back to a more active one.

"I told you… demon is a poor translation. Better to think of me more as a god of gamblers. And, my Elizabeth, I am delighted and optimistic about your capacity for worship."

Startled, I withdraw my hand from his arm. It doesn't seem to faze him.

What I risked rolls into me like a runaway train.

Oh, god. What if I had lost? What if I had been wrong? My sister, my nieces… It's one thing to bet my own life, but what I'd staked… I had no right. No fucking right.

I keep moving forward, feeling like I'm running but probably keeping the same pace. I feel sick. I want to throw up. The stench of decay that I've been fighting to block out surrounds me, holds me down. It's the stench of my father's decay.

I don't reach a hand out to steady myself. Just keep going. Just keep walking.

"I won't do that again. I'll never…" I say when I've had a chance to even out a little, my voice still harsh and breathy.

The answering voice beside me is gently pleased with itself. "I bet you will."

I look at him, straightening automatically. There's more and more light as we make our way, and I marvel at the striking hale and heartiness of his features. It's the kind of face you expect to see in period dramas about English lords out hunting.

A realization strikes me. "The casino doesn't take a cut, does it?"

The light from the mouth of the tunnel falls on him. He beams at me, like the moon borrowing the sun's glow.

"Why would it?" he asks.

His features are laced through with sharp pride, and the adrenaline must be wearing off, because the familiar weight of grief settles back into me. He regards me for a few more steps with a gentle, inquisitive concern that feels genuine before reaching into a little pocket sewn into his vest that I would have assumed was for decorative purposes only. He pulls out a small, brittle, faded blue flower.

"Would you like another one?"

I shake my head. "It wouldn't work now. I know what it does, so it wouldn't be a gamble. Why taunt me? I'm tired." My exasperation isn't really aimed at him.

His bolt of fierce pride is back. "Just so. However..."

He spins the flower by the stem in his fingertips, and when it stops moving, it's silver, jeweled, and enamel like the vase of flowers at the casino. It finds just enough light to glitter. In one unbroken movement, Aloysius touches the flower to the lapel of my jacket, and it stays put when he removes his hand.

"It's never bad to have a lucky charm on hand."

I don't think I could refuse the gift, even if I had the energy to try. We climb silently toward the entrance for a while. The growing light sheds something off me as we do, like the material that flakes off red-hot metal as it's forged. We're not far off from the entrance when a more mundane question occurs to me.

"Why did everyone down there go to the crossroads instead of walking out like we are? I mean, I'm sure for *some* of them it's closer, but I wouldn't think it would be for everyone. Wouldn't it be easier for some of them to get home from here?"

The god of gamblers fills every tiny, hidden space of

the tunnel with a laugh that sings of full tables and warm fires.

"Oh, my Elizabeth," he says with a sigh. "Did you think humans were the only social creatures in the world?"

He hits me with a mischievous wink, and with his next step, he's gone. I walk the last few yards alone to the mouth of the tunnel—and to the hunched, disheveled figure who waits for me there.

THIRTY-THREE

An Uneasy Peace

Max looks almost as tired as I feel. Actually, he looks *more* tired, but I don't think he has a right to.

"Where's the bus?"

He jerks up, surprised by my voice. His face wrinkles in confusion for a long moment until he gets the joke I'm trying—badly—to make and ruins it.

"I don't think not giving my life for you counts as throwing you under the bus."

I shrug and shiver in the night chill. "Whatever happened to chivalry?"

He laughs, and the gesture breaks enough of the tension that I can't help but join him.

While we do, the ground behind me fills itself back in, like the tunnel was never there. We're just two random humans—sort of—covered in dirt, in the middle of….

Nowhere, apparently.

"So, you met Aloysius," I hear Max say, drawing my attention back to him.

I shrug. "A few days ago. Why are we *here*?"

I pull out my phone, dismiss the notifications of missed calls and texts, and load up a map.

"We're close to a crossroads," Max says.

I look at him, confused as to why he'd know where the crossroads are if he can't use them. It's been a day.

"I saw a map once, in passing," he provides.

"I hate you." I smile at him. "Want to share an Uber?"

"I've got a Lyft coming. You can owe me a favor."

It's my turn to laugh. We're doing a lot of laughing. It feels easier than the alternative.

"I'll Venmo you. Owing a wizard a favor feels like a *really* bad idea."

"Not half as bad of an idea as accepting a gift from a demon."

I crane my neck to examine the flower on my lapel. It's pretty—no getting around that. It also seems to have attached itself to my jacket with a loop of metal through the leather. No apparent pin or clasp.

Huh. Magic.

"Now who's judgy?" I ask.

He opens his mouth to respond, but we hear our ride approaching, and it plunges us into silence.

The Lyft driver is high. I guess that's what we get for calling one out to the middle of nowhere at a weird time.

"Are you Max?" he asks Max, slow and confused. I want to shoot back that, no, he's some *other* person standing in the middle of a field in the middle of nowhere. But I've run out of energy even to snark. I let it ride.

I wouldn't put it past Max to talk about blatantly supernatural stuff in front of the college kid just trying to make ends meet by risking others' lives with his unsafe driving, but luckily, he doesn't. Quite. When we're in the car, he does say, "You shouldn't accept gifts from these people. All I'm saying."

I'm furious at him for saying that, but that's probably more from being tired than anything, so I don't indulge it.

"I have a feeling you have a bit more latitude in refusing gifts than I do," I say.

A long moment of silence concedes the point.

"Just something to keep in mind," he says at last. "Aloysius is not your friend. Neither is the troll. Or the statue, if you run into her."

Again, anger thrashes in me. Again, I try to tamp it down. He's not wrong. Gigi put out my lantern, and she was there at the trial. She didn't seem bothered. She could have warned me. She might not have known exactly what I was facing, but there were missing pieces about the *rules* of the treaty that she should have told me. And Wilbur seemed like he was going to help, but then he disappeared. Which I should have expected. Helping isn't his thing. Connections are. He'd done that.

"Thanks, Muppet. I know they're not," I say.

There are other things I want to get into, but the driver's poorly chosen pop music doesn't drown us out enough that I feel confident Max wouldn't go digging around in the kid's head as soon as we get out of the car.

"Don't call me Muppet," Max says, without a trace of joviality. For the first time, his exhaustion reaches his voice.

We sit the rest of the ride in silence. It's longer than I would have thought. It takes us almost forty minutes to get back to Max's house. That ride underground certainly *felt* like a long time, but I had no idea it actually *was* such a long time. Or maybe it wasn't. Maybe there was more magic. Who fucking knows.

My feet hurt as we get out of the car and I head toward my own, still parked right where I left it. The painkillers must be wearing off.

"Come inside for a second," Max says as the Lyft

drives away. He gestures at my torso. I hadn't noticed with everything going on, but blood has seeped through the fabric of my T-shirt. "I'll fix that for you."

Fuck it. Amulet. It's probably fine. And I really don't want to be stuck trying to explain to the good people at the hospital how I ripped out my stitches and also contaminated it so thoroughly. Plus, if he actually has any kind of healing magic, I want to know about it. I want to see it. As far as things the wizards know that would be useful to humans as a whole, healing magic seems pretty far up there.

Dread fills me as I walk into the living room. Too much horror happened here. Too much horror almost happened here. I shove it down.

"Probably easiest if you lie on the table," he says.

I sit down on the couch and start taking off my shoes. "Nah, feet first. Call it a trial run."

I can't tell if he's more confused by me saying this, or if he's just in a state of constant confusion at this point, but he doesn't fight me on it.

"When did you hurt your feet?" he asks, kneeling down. I don't answer, and he doesn't press. Instead, he starts peeling off the bandages I put on there earlier. It reminds me that Henry sat right here when Max wiped his memory. I miss him already.

"No one's seen these, right? I can just fix them all the way, and no one's going to get suspicious? I don't like cleanup."

I shake my head. "No one you haven't already *cleaned up*."

The words sound bitter, but I can't help that. He doesn't seem to let it bother him. For once, I think he gets it. Instead, he closes his eyes and centers himself, getting into Right Mind. Then he starts whispering at my right foot, and I jerk it back.

He looks up at me with a look of exasperation I'm getting used to seeing on his face.

"Sorry," I say. "That just… it tickles."

His exasperation melts into laughter, which I'm also getting used to seeing.

We reset, and he starts again, and I do my best this time to fight the reflex. It helps when I pull my glasses out so I can see the magic happening in real time. He's too far away and speaking too quietly for me to hear the words he's saying, but I can at least see what it looks like.

It's surprisingly subtle for how well it's working, knitting my cells back together the way they belong, good as new. What I see are sort of like ripples in the air from his lips to my feet, the kind you see if you look right above something very hot.

He finishes, and I pull my feet up to look at them closely.

"Do I pass?" he asks. He says it kind of joking, but it doesn't succeed in pushing space between us the way I think it was meant to.

My feet are perfect. Not just how they were before I punished them for having the misfortune to belong to me, but more like how they look when I walk out of sharing a pedicure with Olivia.

"Seems good," I say.

Max shoots me a plaintive look.

I sigh dramatically and smile. "It's amazing. You work miracles. Your skill is unsurpassed in the known world." I lay it on as thick as possible while maintaining the necessary smirk.

He stands and matches the smirk with his own. "Was that so hard?"

He's already moving toward the dining room. I follow him. My heart beats a little faster, but this feels like a straightforward situation the amulet should protect me from, even as exposed as I'm about to feel.

I climb up onto the kitchen table and lay down on my back. I pull up my shirt. Unfortunately, I have to pull it up higher than I'd like because the wound reaches under my bra, but there's no getting around that.

He pulls off the remnants of the bandages, and I ask, "What about cleaning it?"

"Not an issue," he says. "Part of the spell is sanitization. A lot of people say a lot of things about wizards, but we're not idiots."

He settles and sets himself and starts speaking the words again. The ripples in the air form from his lips to my torso. The wound is uglier than I would have guessed, and the stitches have definitely torn.

He's a lot closer to my ears now, so I can make out the syllables of the words he's speaking. I listen as intently as possible, while trying to keep it from being obvious.

It's hard to remember words in a foreign language you've never heard before, and there's zero chance I'll get away with recording him on my phone the way I did at the graveyard. But chances are, he'll keep close to me to try and steal my trove and find an opportunity to take my mind. And I'll keep close to him to try to learn what I can to add to the trove. I'll get to see him do this again. Eventually, I'll get a recording.

I've just got to plan ahead.

It's entrancing, watching him speak my wound clean and closed. I try to parse out his expression. It's easy enough to tell what Right Mind is for the mental magic I've seen him use, but this doesn't seem the same.

"What are you thinking about when you do that?" I ask.

I shouldn't have said it. But I'm tired, and I guess I didn't realize how quickly he would recognize why I was asking. Anger clenches his jaw and tenses his muscles. He pulls back, snapping the intimacy between us like an errant thread.

"Probably should stop there," he says. "Need to leave something for them to see when you go in to get the stitches removed."

He steps back, and the words I managed to hold back in the cab come spilling out as I sit up on the table and pull my shirt back down.

"What would you have done eight years ago?" I ask.

Anger lingers in his eyes as he looks at me. "What?"

"If you'd noticed what was happening with the vampiric spirit. All of it. What would you have done?"

His words strike me as cold—calculated. "I'd have killed the neighbor, like any sane wizard would have."

I knew it.

"You would have killed—"

He speaks over me. "And saved eight lives, yes, you're fucking right I would have killed him."

Amulet or no, the danger in his gaze seeps into my bones. I speak anyway. "You should have found another way." The words are strong, but my voice is thin.

He sighs. "Even if there were another way, chances are that it would have started a war. One life is worth a war? Really?"

"I did it. You could have done it."

He steps closer to me again, but it's a different kind of closeness. "You luck out with a *demon* helping you, and suddenly you know everything, don't you?"

"I know that my dad is dead because you didn't do your job."

The anger that phrase taps into brings volume I didn't know I was capable of right now. I'm half yelling, and I expect him to reply at the same volume, but his voice drops down and hollows out. There's something hard and cold in it. "Saving his life wasn't my job."

I match his volume, but not his tone. "It should have been. It should *be*."

He steps back. He looks small and tired. "It's late. Get out of my house."

I oblige.

The night around me feels worn through as I drive home. I don't consciously think of much, and I don't remember most of the drive as I turn into my driveway. I pull my phone out to check the time, wondering if the neighbors will think anything weird of me coming home at this hour. I see a notification instead.

Maxwell Jones has added you as a friend on Facebook.

Goddamn fucking wizards.

THIRTY-FOUR

A Reason

My feet don't hurt, and my torso only aches a little as I walk into the house. I want to go straight to bed, but I force myself into the bathroom first, wiping the grime off and rebandaging my wound.

I should really take a shower and wash my hair, but I just can't bring myself to do it. Partially because my wound seems a lot better, but I don't think it's one hundred percent closed, and I don't want to ruin the sterilization Max supposedly did. Partially, I think if I stand up under running water for anything close to the amount of time it'll take to wash my hair, I'll pass out and give myself a new injury to worry about.

Instead, I strip down and use a hand towel to at least get my skin clean enough that I won't feel disgusting when I wake up, and I patch up my wound with the same basic medical kit that I used to wrap up my feet a thousand years ago. It's still in the bathroom where I left it.

I wander into the bedroom, slip into some pajamas, and just about jump out of my skin.

"Hey." Faisal's voice, husky with sleep, reaches out to me.

I'm moving toward the bed before I fully turn and see him there, phone clutched in his hand. I don't have the energy to dive under the covers, but I fumble my way beneath them and up close beside him with more enthusiasm than I thought I had left. I pull myself into him, burying my face in the clean T-shirt on his chest that feels like sleep. He smells like sandalwood. He smells like him.

He doesn't ask me where I've been or why I'm just getting back. He just wraps his arms around me and holds me with a tightness he only uses when he knows I need it.

"I thought you were going to Naples after Zurich?" I say eventually.

He pulls back just enough to look down at me, and I lift my face up so that he can see it. He looks puzzled.

"I'd barely heard from you in days, and then Olivia sent me an email that said you were fine, but you were in the hospital. I told them I had a family emergency and needed to go home. They understood."

You shouldn't have lied to them. The words are on my lips, but I don't say them. He didn't.

"Do you want to talk about it?" He says the words like he's unwinding a wire for an electric fence, and he's not sure if it's live or not.

"I can't right now," I say. Tears well up, but I fight them back. I'll cry, but not for a moment. I can hold out for the length of a conversation.

"Dad was involved with some people, and his death brought them out of the woodwork."

He pushes a strand of my hair behind my ear, concern written on his face. "Do we need to call the sheriff's office? Earlier they were convinced you were fine, but if there's something you can tell them…"

"No," I say. "I fixed it." The words hurt coming out, and he sees that hurt. A different shade of concern overtakes him.

"Do we need to call a lawyer?"

I remember the cold metal of Henry's gun and the uncompromising certainty of the graveling's spear.

"No," I say. "It's all fine. I can't talk about it right now, but it's all fine."

He accepts my silence, but I can tell he doesn't believe my answer. That's okay. He might be right.

I nestle back into him, and he plays with my hair with his fingertips the way he always does. Until he stops abruptly.

"There's dirt in your hair."

I wince inwardly. "I'll wash it in the morning. I just can't take a shower right now. I'd get my wound wet."

I think I sound as tired as I feel, but he's already moving.

"Come on, I'll wash it. You'll sleep better if you let me."

He's not wrong. He helps me into the bathroom and settles me down onto the floor with my head leaning on the side of the tub, my hair cascading down inside it.

He turns on the hand sprayer and starts washing the death out of my hair. And the great big lie that's been tying together all the events of the last few days begins to unravel.

I'd been looking at it all wrong—like I was starting to get a look at the real world after being kept in the dark for so long. But this, right here, is the real world. The rest is shadows.

Faisal puts on a surprisingly passable imitation of my overly talkative, very opinionated hairdresser. Tears of exhaustion and grief and relief roll down across my temples as I look up at him, trying to parse everything I see there.

He's exhausted, and worried about me, and joking.

I'm broken, and worried about him, and laughing.

And this is it. This is my Right Mind—the house I live in that's bigger than a mountain. I want more of this—just this, with this man. I would take decades if that were all that was on the table.

But I don't think it is. I think that if I am very smart, and very brave, and more than a little lucky, I can have centuries.

I bet I'm right.

Epilogue

The next morning, I call my mom. I don't expect that destroying the vampiric spirit that stole her sweetness, past and future, will have somehow set it right. But some part of me hopes, so I check anyway.

It didn't. She's still scattered. She still remembers so little. In the past, this frustrated me, but I understand it more now.

She complains. I listen. I think of all the conversations both Olivia and I have tried to have with her, playing up all the good parts of our lives. How misguided we were. The way she talks makes sense now, and I notice something I hadn't before.

Everything she says has a negative bent, but inside every complaint is a thread of joy. Inside her complaint that Dad forgot her anniversary one year is the joy of all the years he didn't. Inside a complaint that the patio she usually goes out to dine on was closed today is the thread of joy that she goes and eats by the ocean most days.

Tears roll down my cheeks as I listen, and understand, and reach out to her in the only way that will touch her. I tell her how maddening it is that Faisal's always leaving his socks beside the hamper when he's home, and how lucky he is that I love him enough to overlook this high crime. I tell her how annoying it is that some of the older librarians don't appreciate Olivia enough, considering how good she is at her job, and how frustrating it is that she loves working there too much to leave. I tell her how even though I know that Sharon appreciates my hard work and has every intention of mentoring me, she's not the most expressive person, so I doubt it sometimes. I tell her how, at Ivy's piano recital, I got stuck behind a tall guy, and I wasn't able to see how proud she was when she accepted the ribbon for best performance. I sprinkle bitterness through all the sweet, like pouring Tabasco sauce on top of a pizza to discourage a greedy roommate with no boundaries.

We talk for an hour. When we're done, she tells me to say hello to Faisal for her. And it's the first time in the six years I've been with him that she's ever said his name. My tears intensify, and I'm barely able to get off the phone before I bury my head in my hands, sobbing with a kind of mixed relief.

It's not okay. If there's a way to fix it, I'll find it. But if there's any silver lining, it's the fact that she doesn't have much of her daily life she can tell me about. So her moment-to-moment present—the time she lives in and that the vampiric spirit couldn't touch—must mostly be sweet.

I go back to work, and I'm better. Mostly. Max is still hanging around, finding special projects to keep anyone from asking why. I keep my amulet on at all times, and I bring my glasses to work with me every day in case I need them. But I don't.

I go back to grieving, but it's easier now. The unfairness of it all hits a little bit differently, now that I know what my dad did was his choice. It wasn't a random act of brain chemistry popping up out of nowhere. It was the result of a gamble. And gambles don't always pay off.

I can live with that.

I avoid seeing Mr. Thompson, which is mostly easy. But the couple of times in the next couple weeks that we happen to be checking the mail or working in the yard, he seems lighter—quicker to smile and bursting with the kind of jokes that I haven't heard him make since before his wife died. I wonder if Max took more grief than he was given permission to. I'm not sure how to feel about it. I know there's nothing I can do about it.

A few weeks later, when Faisal has gone off to a university in Nicaragua, I head to Skyway Park. It's pouring rain, and I feel confident that I'll be the only person in the park on an afternoon like this. The only person other than Wilbur—hopefully.

I wonder where I should stand on the bridge to call out to him, but I shouldn't have worried. I'm maybe ten feet out onto the bridge when Wilbur comes swinging up over one of the side rails, appearing out from under the bridge like he's stepping up to the door to greet a visitor.

Which I guess he is.

"Still alive," he says, smiling. I've got an umbrella, and he doesn't. The water drenches his unruly hair and clothing both. It runs in droplets off the tip of his nose. If he were human, I'd be concerned he was going to catch himself a nasty bout of hypothermia. The weather's getting warmer, but on a day like today you can still feel the last tendrils of winter holding on.

"Still alive," I confirm. *No thanks to you*, I could add, but I don't. I'm not upset about the way he disappeared when I needed help. That's not what he does.

"I have a question for you. It's not a connection, but it's something I think you know."

The troll nods, good-natured indulgence seeping out his pores.

"My dad. Did he find you eight years ago? With the lantern?"

I can't read the expression on Wilbur's face, and it strikes me how alien he is.

"He did. I connected him with some people who wanted to sell a worthless field in the middle of nowhere. He didn't pay me. But I don't think that was the worst thing that happened to him that week."

I'm not shocked. I'd kind of guessed. But it still feels weird to hear him say it with no sense of… what am I expecting? Remorse?

"You didn't tell me that."

He shrugs. "There are a lot of things I know that I don't tell you. You didn't ask. And I helped you find out for yourself, anyway."

"What other things don't you tell me?"

He shrugs again. "Tell me what bridges you want to cross when you know, and I'll build them for you."

It's not an answer, exactly, but it's clear that's all I'm going to get on the subject. He'll answer questions and make connections where he's asked. But that's not the same as volunteering. Except…

"I didn't ask for the folder."

Wilbur smiles, blinking rain out of his eyes. "Humans make a lot of choices. It's all they ever do. I liked the ones your father made."

Max was right—Wilbur isn't my friend. Yet. But maybe he could be.

Do you eat people? Not lately, I remember.

"That reminds me," he continues. And then he executes a weirdly exact quarter turn to face NNE and steps into nonexistence. I look around automatically to make sure no one saw that, but there's no one here.

I'm just wondering if that's Wilbur's way of exiting a conversation, when he reappears, flanked by two much shorter men. They wear tool belts and well-worn workmen's clothing, but they seem remarkably put together for all that.

"Extor, Charer, this is Elizabeth—the unprotected human."

And then, with no further explanation, Wilbur turns due north and steps away into the crossroads again.

"Finally," says the man Wilbur addressed as Extor. "We've been waiting for a week at the crossroads. When Wilbur said he would connect us to you, I thought he meant soon."

The man Wilbur addressed as Charer rolls his eyes. "Always impatient. That's you."

I open my mouth, not sure what question to ask first, but the men start trundling along toward one of the covered picnic tables. They care about rain more than Wilbur, I guess. I follow along behind them, and when they sit next to each other on one side of the picnic table and look at me expectantly, I sit down across from them.

"Unprotected human," Charer says. "We call upon you as is our right, by tradition, to offer arbitration in a matter of disagreement."

What the fuck?

He continues. "I agree to be held by the result of this arbitration."

He looks at Extor, who parrots his words in an annoyed tone. "I agree to be held by the result of this arbitration."

I look back and forth between them. My glasses are in my laptop bag, which is in the car. I wasn't expecting to run into anyone other than Wilbur, and I already know what he looks like. I make a mental note that I need to be more proactive about making sure my glasses are *always* with me.

I lace my fingers together and set my hands out on the table in front of me, hoping that telegraphs more confidence than I feel.

"What seems to be the issue?" I ask.

What follows is… a lot. A lot of talking, and a lot of content. Both men are passionate about what they are saying and furious at one another. They offer far too many details, and I'd be bored if the picture that emerges isn't so disturbing.

The net of the matter is this: Extor kidnapped a human child when it was eight weeks old. I'm given a lot of background about how this is really in the best interests of the child and a traditional practice among his people. But still—definitely kidnapping.

When the child was older, Extor apprenticed the child to Charer, for years at a time, to pay an ancient debt. There's some back and forth as to whether that debt has been fulfilled or not, but after a mere fifteen minutes arguing the finer points of that contract, they both agree that this is *not* the matter they have come to me to resolve, and it should be left out of the scope of this discussion for the time being.

Now the child will not talk to either of them, and each one blames the other for having turned the child against him. Ample evidence of perceived poisoning of the child's mind is offered.

"So… this child. How old is he now?"

Neither man seems sure, but eventually I get it out of Extor that he stole him in the eighties.

"All right, so," I say, "a bit of a terminology update. By human standards, this makes him an adult."

Both men object that he's only in his thirties, but I insist that for humans, thirties is grown. I'm not sure they believe me, but they stop fighting me on it.

"I understand that what you've done is traditional. But, for us, what you did is…" They look at me expectantly. "…difficult to accept."

Extor begins to launch again into how dreadful the child's life would have been if he'd been left there, but I forestall him with a hand.

"I know. I understand. But that's still not how humans do things. And the *man* has probably come to that conclusion himself."

Charer looks smug. I turn to him.

"As for you—the apprenticeship you described might be normal for your people, but for us, child labor laws have come a long way in the last few hundred years."

I don't think he buys it, but I guess he doesn't have to. As long as he goes by what I'm saying, which he said he would.

"He doesn't need either of you to turn him against the other. He's made his own choices about who he wants to keep in touch with, and by human standards, you've both done enough on your own to earn him cutting you out of his life."

I have not made friends out of them with this proclamation. I try a gentler tone, while still trying to keep it authoritative. I only have the authority they choose to give me, and I need to hold on to that for dear life. Literally. They might not be able to kill me right this moment, but if I play this wrong, they'll plan ahead and find a way.

"You are not each other's enemy. And he might come around. You say he knows what you are. It's possible eventually he'll see things differently."

I retrieve my wallet and a pen from my raincoat

pocket, sliding out a couple copies of my business card. I cross out my job title and work phone number, leaving only my name, email address, and cell. I offer each man a card.

"If you ever need help interpreting a text, or a call, or an email, or *anything* with him from a human perspective, I can assist you with that. In the meantime, the less you try to push him, the more likely it is he'll come around."

They both consider my card. They seem less actively angry, though this wasn't the outcome either of them was hoping for.

"And this is outside my purview, I know, but I do *suggest* you consider not abducting any more children."

The two men roll their eyes at each other and stand. Then they step in decidedly different directions, and I'm left sitting alone in Skyway Park with nothing but the steady sound of the rain to witness what just took place.

From there, I head immediately to the Emporium. Weather being as it is, the cozy bookstore café is doing what I imagine is a brisk trade for a weekday afternoon. But at least Gigi's here this time. I've got my glasses in my raincoat pocket now, though I don't put them on to look at her.

She smiles at me with easy familiarity when I come in and motions to the same table she had me wait at last time I came here. This time, however, she doesn't close down the shop early. Instead, she has one of her workers take over for her at the counter and sits across from me with an ice cream sundae in her hand.

Max's words about not accepting gifts come back to me, but they're unnecessary. I have no intention of accepting anything Gigi gives me.

"You know, I just had the oddest interaction," I say casually.

"Oh?"

"I was called on to settle a disagreement between two supernatural parties. They told me their problem, I told them my ruling, and they disappeared."

Gigi narrows her eyes. "What did you expect? Did you think they'd write their disagreements on an apple and throw it at you?"

I fix her with a blank stare and wait for her to answer me properly.

"The wizard didn't tell you? I don't know why I'm surprised."

"You're still not telling me either."

Gigi gathers herself up and goes into what I can only call storytelling mode. It reminds me of what I imagine bards must have been like back when the oral tradition of myths and legends was alive. And it's probably exactly that. I imagine Gigi's old enough.

"Long ago, before the treaty, it was the custom of the supernatural world to turn to human arbitration to avoid war. Human lifetimes are too short to become embroiled with supernatural politics. They're not involved enough to form grudges. And there's a certain belief in the whole 'from the mouths of babes' philosophy."

I hit her with a wave of skepticism. "Seems unlikely."

Her sharp smile peeks out even through the wizard's illusion. "We tend only to use the practice as a last-ditch effort to avoid conflict. It's a coin flip, essentially. And it relieves a lot of tension to flip a coin that's so… disposable."

That seems more likely. My blood runs a little colder. The ice cream melts in front of me.

"Of course, in the treaty, the wizards outlawed the practice." Gigi looks thoughtful for a moment. "That's a bit of a common thread with them, really. They always seem to be far more threatened by ordinary humans than makes any sense. I've always wondered why."

Yeah, I'm not digging into that right now.

"So… when Max announced to everyone that I was not under the wizard's protection, that makes me fair game to be called upon to arbitrate?" I ask.

Gigi's smile gleams. "Yes. But don't worry—we haven't had a human arbitrator in hundreds of years. That makes you a resource. I doubt anyone will kill you out of pique when they don't like your ruling, as long as you support it well enough with evidence."

"Why do I not find that reassuring?"

Gigi rolls her eyes, and then leans forward conspiratorially. "You're not seeing the bigger picture. You want wizards' power—their knowledge. As much of it as you can get. Of course you do. But they're not going to just hand it over. Making allies can only help you. And a fair few supernatural beings have a spell or two stashed away somewhere. We can't use them, of course, but before the treaty, they could be used as a sort of currency. Accept the payment of a spell from a wizard for a deed done. Use it as payment to another wizard to get out of a jam. The treaty put a stop to all that, but that doesn't matter much. We have long memories, and most of us keep *excellent* records."

The cherry on the top of my sundae slides down the round edge of the scoop. Gigi sits still, perfectly patient. I guess she would have to be.

"Speaking of long memories and record-keeping, remember a couple of weeks ago when you destroyed my lantern?"

She frowns. "*Extinguished.* Not destroyed. You'll enchant it again."

"Not the point. Why?"

She looks away for a long moment, surveying her

domain. When she looks back, her eyes sparkle like the diamonds they are. "It seemed obvious to me we were dealing with gravelings. I wanted you to find him. I didn't want you to get it out of me that you shouldn't kill him."

"Again, why?"

She rolls her eyes but continues. "Because what you called 'Mr. Nameless Horror' is a difficult being to get in touch with. Even Wilbur can't do it. But if you killed one of its servants, I thought it might show up."

"And you wanted to talk to it? Why?"

Gigi leans back, suddenly a thousand miles away. "I wanted to ask it a favor."

"What favor?"

She frowns. "One it wouldn't grant."

I don't know the ins and outs of how the wizard's illusion works. Presumably, I'll get better at decoding it over time. It strikes me as one of the few truly useful things we got in the treaty. But, for a moment, I swear I see crow's feet form in real time at the corners of her eyes. Her cheeks hollow out. She looks older. She looks tired. So, so tired.

And then she snaps back, and she's herself again.

"But still, it ended up being a very interesting show. I'm guessing Aloysius helped you in some way, or you remembered a spell or something. But it's got *everyone* talking. You're building a reputation."

I shiver at the thought of what that *show* could have cost if I'd been wrong. I've been trying not to think about that. It's gotten easier with practice.

"While we're on the topic, I looked you up. You moved to Springfield and started applying for business licenses to open this place about a month after my father was committed."

"Yes," Gigi says innocently.

I glare, refusing to say *why* one more time.

Gigi laughs, and I hate how musical the sound is. "Wilbur saw that magic was being done in town when the town's wizard was elsewhere. He knew I would be interested, so he connected me to it. To you, essentially." I must look disturbed, because she waves her hand. "Oh, don't look so worried. I paid him, of course."

That's not really what I was concerned about.

"Why?" Okay, that was the last time. She wants something from me. I need to know what it is.

She leans forward again and speaks a little softer. "Because I've watched the world move forward. I've watched it shrink as human technology grows. To me, the way the wizards do things and the way the world has changed looks more and more like a powder keg every year. And, to me, you look an awful lot like a spark."

I absorb this as the ice cream continues to melt.

"And it doesn't matter what happens to me along the way," I say. It's not a question or an accusation. Just a statement of newly accepted fact.

Gigi shrugs and leans back. She lets her voice expand back out in volume. "What happens to a spark in an explosion? Does it die, or does it grow? Are you your heartbeat, or are you your goals?"

That's way too much philosophy for a Tuesday afternoon.

"And you're interested because you think you'll find it entertaining?" I ask.

"No," she says, the sharpness of her supernatural smile slicing through the wizard's illusion like the knife it is. "I'm interested because I think it's going to be *fun*."

I shake my head. "Bullshit. What's the rest of the reason?"

Her friendly nature is wearing thin. I don't care.

"When the world is falling apart, sometimes it just takes the right lever to make it fall your way."

I lean back in my chair. "You're mixing your metaphors. Am I a spark or a lever?"

Gigi watches me for an interminable moment. "Which would you rather be?"

The End

Thank you for reading book one of The Trove Arbitrations. To learn more about me and sign up for my newsletter, visit my website at author.amandacreiglow.com.